Naive Diamond

Naive Diamond

Des Thompson

Copyright © 2011 by Des Thompson.

Library of Congress Control Number   2011914915
ISBN: Hardcover   978-1-4653-5529-4
            Softcover   978-1-4653-4594-3
            Ebook   978-1-4653-5532-4

All rights reserved. No part of this book may be reproduced or transmitted in any form or by any means, electronic or mechanical, including photocopying, recording, or by any information storage and retrieval system, without permission in writing from the copyright owner.

This is a work of fiction. Names, characters, places and incidents either are the product of the author's imagination or are used fictitiously, and any resemblance to any actual persons, living or dead, events, or locales is entirely coincidental.

This book was printed in the United States of America.

To order additional copies of this book, contact:
Xlibris Corporation
1-888-795-4274
www.Xlibris.com
Orders@Xlibris.com
103548

PROLOGUE

The period was the beginning of the seventeeth century when James the First ruled England, a mock trial in period costume had been held in the Farmers Arms.

An aristocratic gentleman named Guy Fawkes, whose family lived in the local Manor House, had been caught trying to burn down the local courthouse.Bringing great shame on the wealthy family.

Serving wenches plied their trade serving Ale as the trial lasting two hours amid cat calls and petty arguments finally ended by finding him guilty and sentencing him to death by fire.

The ironclad wheels of the Tumbril drawn by two horses are rumbling along the streets again, the bedraggled prisoner in the steel cage was trying to shield himself from the tomatoe's and any old vegetables the massive jeering crowd lining the roads were throwing at him.

The'Olde Worlde'charm and calmness of the old Cotswold village, of Mochamton, is completely demolished as the tumbril wound its way to the Bonfire Pageant site where there was to be a giant bonfire followed by a firework display where the prisoner Guy Fawkes had been sentenced to be burnt at the stake.

The village peace and tranquility that Mochamton was reknown for, was not to return for a long time.

CHAPTER ONE

Mike Smith, Colonel Brown's farm manager, had returned to the bonfire site early to check the ashes of the fire, making sure there were no hot embers. Sergeant Hopper of the Warwickshire Constabulary also came down to the site with the same idea of making sure there were no hot spot's in the firebase. The local inhabitants always liked to collect the ash from bonfires. The wood ash made excellent fertilizer for their gardens; they dug it into the garden in the spring and it certainly seemed to make the plants grow.

Sergeant Hopper was expecting them to arrive at anytime with their wheelbarrows and buckets etcetera to collect the ashes for their gardens.

Mike still half asleep was leaning on his rake gazing at the large pile of cold grey and white ash that was lying dormant in the middle of his field.

"Rake over there in the centre, Mike, there's quite a pile of ash there" the Sergeant instructed, pointing towards the middle of the firebase.

Nonchalantly taking a step into the edge of the thick grey ash, Mike chucked his rake towards the mound of ash in the center landing with a thump the tongs sank into the mound. Thinking what a good throw he had made, Mike started to pull the rake back, but as he exherted the pressure to pull the rake the large mound of ash moved then a large piece of what looked like badly charred wood or cardboard came away from the mound.

"Bloody hell Mike! What's that? don't do anymore, until we have had a better look"

They walked round to the opposite side of the fire to have another look at the object.

Mike turned white then walked away and vomitted.

"Oh hell Mike! don't touch anything, I'll get on the radio for help"

Running over to his Police car to use the radio, the Sergeant contacted his headquarters in Stratford-on-Avon with the news of their find.

As the news spread, the serenity and charm of the village disappeared and the evil eye of suspicion descended onto all its inhabitants.

A feeling that was to test the solidarity and strength of the villagers and the local Police force.

The village Police force consisted of Sergeant Hopper and two constables; Constable Boyce and Constable Harris.

Their small Police Station was attached to the Sergeants Police house, the Cotswold stone sculptured plaque over the door read 1895 AD showing that the house and Police Station were built late in the nineteenth century.

Their 'headquarters' had two rooms that acted as general office and Sergeant Hopper's private office. The prison cell was attached to the back of the station, it was the same as any other cell in a Police station built in the nineteenth century, metal frame bed and a table both bolted to the floor, a toilet was in the opposite corner, with a wash basin that was fixed to the wall close by.

Sergeant Hopper was in his office writing his report when Chief Inspector Sullivan and his assistant Detective Sergeant Thomas from the West Midland Police Force arrived.

The Chief Inspector and his assistant were from Stratford-on-Avon that was six miles away, and had been assigned to the case and both were known in the Midlands as being very hard men to deal with.

Previous to their arrival, Sergeant Hopper had arranged for the forensic department and pathologist to come down to the site, and for extra help to assist his small force with the investigation.

After a quick mug of coffee, the local Sergeant took the two detectives down to the bonfire site.

On arrival at the site, Sergeant Thomas showing his authority suggested that they should not allow any of the fun-fare to leave without the Chief's permission and to put a policeman on each of the gates as soon as possible.

In reply Sergeant Hopper to show that he wasn't as thick as the Detective Sergeant thought replied, "That it had already been taken care of".

Taking care not to disturb anything the two detectives walked around the remains of the bonfire. Bending over as far as he could, first one way then the other, Chief Inspector Sullivan tried as hard as he could to get a good look at the object in the centre of the ashes. Still feeling some heat rising from the ashes Chief Inspector Sullivan stood looking at the centre of the fire as if in deep thought, then suddenly decided that there was not a lot more could be done until after the Pathologist visit, and, he had received his report.

Looking at his detective Sergeant then at Sergeant Hopper

"Well let's hope that the ashes have cooled down suffeciently for our Pathologist friend whose just come through the gate. I also hope they'll be cool enough for Forensic to sift through them. I think they'll have a nice warm job don't you Thomas?" the Chief Inspector said laughingly as the Pathologist walked upto him.

"Sorry to spoil your Sunday nap Doctor" he said "But I've got a warm job for you to look into, right in the centre Doc." pointing into the centre of the firebase.

Leaving the Pathologist standing at the edge of the ashes in his white paper overalls and his green wellington boots pondering on the next move to inspect the object. The two detectives and Sergeant Hopper returned to the small office in the local Police Station, instead of getting in the way of the rough and tumble, in the organisation of an incident room in the local village Hall.

Making himself comfortable Chief Inspector Sullivan asked Sergeant Hopper what he knew of the events leading upto the previous evening.

"I'm not quite sure where to begin because all the village was involved in one way or the other" Sergeant Hopper answered.

CHAPTER TWO

As usual, a suggestion was made, that the village should have a firework display for November the 5th.

Colonel Brown, who owned a large farm, offered the local Charities Committee the use of one of his fields for a firework display and bonfire pageant.

Bernard (Bernie) Watson the landlord of the 'Navigation Inn' and Joe Brompton the landlord of the 'Farmers Arms', both members of that committee, agreed that their two hostelry's would help to organise the event.

The rest of the committee consisting of parish councillor, Ted Broughton, Mrs. Joyce Simpson (WI), Mr. Tom Atkinson Treasurer, (accountant), Fred Perkins (retired butcher), and Bill Selby (Retired V.A.T., inspector); all enthusiastically supported the idea.

It was decided that 'Farmer's Arms' would organise the bonfire site, Funfair etc and 'The Navigation' would organise the Pageant.

'The Farmers Arms' accepted the offer of Colonel Brown's field and started to organise things accordingly.

'The Navigation' on the other hand had a much more difficult task on deciding the theme for their pageant.

Shortly after being given the task, two of the Navigation regular customer's Bob Shaw and Roy Woods, were chatting with the landlord Bernie Watson the subject of course being the Pageant.

After a few 'What ifs' had been put up and dropped.

Bernie scratched the back of his head.

"What about, doing something different, a torchlight procession.

For example, with someone dressed up as Guy Fawkes, starting from the church or from here at the Navigation the church and the pub date back to the pre. 1600 period. Then we could decorate the church and the village to be reminiscent of the night that the Earl of Suffolk caught Guy Fawkes in the cellars under the House of Lords; when he was going to light the fuse to the gunpowder that should have blown up the Houses of Parliament". He asked

Bob looked at his landlord.

"That's a damn good idea Bernie," he replied. "We could have a cart drawn by a horse, and a few blokes dressed up as jailer's, making a pageant procession through the village, finishing at the firework site".

"Ooh aye", exclaimed Bernie "Nobody has said anything about a bonfire, we'll have to have that".

They talked on for a few minutes, and then Roy rejoined them having thrown his darts in a darts match.

The landlord brought Roy upto date on their discussions then asked him what he thought?

He agreed with enthusiasm.

"Smashing" he said. "How's about putting Guy Fawkes on the bonfire then setting light to it immediately?"

"Cripes" said Bernie "How on earth are you going to do that?" "Easy". Said Roy. "During the afternoon, we put two ladders up the front of the bonfire, and one at the rear. When we arrive on site after the procession, two of us climb up the ladders with the prisoner. When we get to the top we have a dummy guy hidden, we then do a change over and tie the dummy to the stake. The original guy climbs down the ladder that's been put in place on the blind side away from the crowd".

"Eeh! That's brilliant, if it will work "exclaimed Bernie.

After a bit more talk, they broke up and Bob went home to try and catch his favorite TV program 'Boon', agreeing to talk about it later, when things were a bit more positive.

At the first meeting of what was to be known later as the 'Bonfire Committee'. Agreeing to go ahead with the firework display, the Committee decided it had to be on a smaller scale; also to have the bonfire and the torchlight procession making the night into a Gala evening.

The meeting broke up at 10 p.m. Bernie Watson went straight back to his pub, 'The Navigation', to inform his regular patrons, who were waiting with bated breath; as were the regulars at 'The Farmers Arms' for the arrival of Fred, Joyce and Joe. The decision to proceed with the event, by the Charity committee was welcomed with great enthusiasm at both alehouses.

Of course, Tony and Carol Lockwood were in 'The Navigation' when Bernie and Tom Atkinson arrived, naturally they were the first to offer their expertise to Bernie which he readily accepted, much to Bob and Roy's distaste, but at the sametime admitting, that their theatrical experience would be greatly appreciated. Bernie asked the four of them to stay on after closing time to formulate their plans.

Meanwhile over at 'The Farmers Arms', Joe Brompton the landlord, had already informed his social committee chairman Dave Wilson, who also had been waiting for his landlords return. After hearing what Joe had to say, he then informed his landlord that his committee was already building their barbecue?

"Already?" asked Joe "That's what you call forward planning".

The village was already starting to buzz with excitement.

Two days after the Committee meeting, Fred Perkins and Joyce Simpson were on their way to an appointment with Colonel Brown at Haydock Farm, which was on the Honeybourne Road, approximately two miles from Mochamton.

To get to the farm from the road you had to drive down a concrete road that the Colonel had put in, after taking the farm over from his father. The farm had been in the Colonels family for four generations, and the approach to it had never been changed from the day the farm had been built.

The house was a large five-bedroom Cotswold farmhouse with an old dairy built on the back of it. There was a large concrete yard to the side of the house extending to the rear, with stables and a cart shed and harness room on the opposite side of the yard. Dutch barns for storing hay and straw were across the bottom. A new cowshed and dairy had been built at the back of the cart shed; these were the Colonel's pride and joy.

Exercising his authority as a landowner, the Colonel was holding the meeting at the farm to discuss traffic and crowd control. Where better to hold the meeting, than here where he had all the plans and maps. He claimed, when he invited the local Police Sergeant George Hopper, known locally as 'Bouncer' because of the slight spring in his step as he walked. The Sergeant had arrived before Fred and Joyce, and, because he was not on duty, was enjoying a nice cool pint of beer, from the Colonel's cellar.

"Only the one", he said to Fred as they walked in.

Fred and Joyce declined a drink and had coffee instead. They found the meeting very enlightening for they had not realized that they had to get an entertainment license and would not get it without Police approval, and they would also require the Fire Service approval, whom the Colonel had forgotten to invite.

Station Officer Broome, the Fire prevention and safety Officer at the local Fire Station was contacted and asked to join them; being situated only four miles away in Broadway.

"Time for another beer" Sergeant Hopper suggested as he started to excel himself on his favoured subject of safety and vehicle parking.

"The pleasure's all mine Sergeant, help yourself", replied the Colonel helping himself to another brandy from a crystal decanter.

Mrs Brown showed Station Officer Broom into the room, and introduced him. The Colonel stood up and shook his hand,

"Good God man you got a jet?" he asked.

"Just a Ford Escort" replied the Station Officer as the Colonel handed him a beer.

Joyce and Fred excused themselves from the meeting shortly after the Fire Officer arrived.

"It was a good job we left when we did. We know what the Colonel is like when he gets reminiscing, don't we?" remarked Fred as they were leaving.

CHAPTER THREE

Two days before the first meeting of the Bonfire Committee, Ron Porter from 'The Farmers Arms' had made up his mind to obtain the price for the firework display, if what he had heard was correct, the thirteenth of November was the proposed date for the display. He had on a previous ocassion contacted Cobhams Fireworks in Birmingham, but he had not had much success, but he decided to contact them immediately. It was ten o'clock in the morning and the Sales Managers Secretary told Ron that he was engaged but she would ask him to ring Ron as soon as possible. The previous week Ron had been informed of a Company in Salisbury by Tom Atkinson he informed Ron that they did laser and firework displays. He had not received a call from Cobhams by two-o clock, he tried to contact them and was told that there was nobody available. Thinking that it was not unreasonable to assume that they were not interested in his small display. Ron called Fiesta Lighting in Salisbury and explained his position. There was a slight delay in the telephone conversation while Mr. Jones, the Managing Director consulted his diary reference the date being available. Mr. Jones confirmed that the date was available and that he would give him a quote for a half hour display the following morning.

The Managing Director of Fiesta Lighting kept his word and phoned the following morning with his quotation, he explained the type of display involved and gave an overall cost of 3,500.00.Pounds.

Ron could not believe this, and informed Mr. Jones to submit the quotation by the following day so he could submit it to the committee on Thursday evening.

Ron went to his meeting on Thursday full of confidence having received the quotation from Fiesta Lighting. As expected the meeting opened with the Colonel directing his question to Ron,

"Have you got the Price?"

Ron produced the envelope from his inside pocket and passed it to Ted, the chairman, who promptly read it out to the rest of the committee.

"What do you think about that?" asked Ron.

"Quite reasonable" replied the Colonel looking up, from his doodling and glancing across at Ron and then at Tom Atkinson, his accountant.

"I'll take care of that for you "he said, carrying on with his doodling.

"Will you Colonel? That's very generous of you "remarked Tom Atkinson the committee treasurer.

The quote having been accepted and other matters discussed the meeting closed at ten o'clock. They all went their separate ways except for Tom, Ted, Fred and the Colonel who talked on for a while about various things that were going on in the village and the surrounding area.

'The Farmers Arms' was a hive of activity when Joe Brompton arrived. Although he was the landlord and very active on the Social committee, he did not always know when they were going to hold a meeting and discovered they had held one this evening while he was absent. They had discussed the progress on the barbecue and the amount of food required and had agreed to speed things up a bit. They were quite pleased with themselves as they though they had everything well in hand and bought Joe a drink.

Over at 'The Navigation', Bernie Watson the landlord was feeling the same way with his committee. Although their effort was a little more complex than Joe's at 'The Farmers Arms', all the same he was very pleased and thought to himself that this Bonfire Pageant, as he called it. Was going to put Mochamton on the map and his committee was going to show everybody 'how it was done'.

The following week Ron Porter received the contract from Fiesta Lighting, two of his committee colleagues, Ted Atkinson and Joe Brompton signed it for him so he could return it.

During the week prior to the event, had you gone into 'The Navigation' in the evening for a drink or some food; you would have seen quite a lot of movement between the lounge bar and the back room.

Being an Outsider, if you had queried the movements, no way would you have received any information regarding was happening. Everyone was sworn to secrecy on the project in the back room.

Even the small local engineering company, 'Simpson's Engineering', was sworn to secrecy on their involvement.

By Friday lunchtime there was a very big pile of wooden box's and pallets on the spot where the fire was to be built, alongside the pallets was another big pile of tree branches and other rubbish including tyres and two barrels of oil from the local filling station.

At Bernies Watson's request, the committee had agreed to let 'The Navigation' social committee build the bonfire.

They started to build the fire around the box's and pallets that were already on the site, Friday afternoon making sure that nobody came to see what they were doing.

Sergeant Hopper visited the site once or twice just to see how they were progressing; after all 'The Navigation' was his 'local' and as he informed the crew building the fire, he had to make sure they were building it right.

Saturday the thirteenth dawned bright and sunny, which surprised everybody because it had been dull and dry all the week. It meant the fields that were going to be used would at least be dry for the large crowd expected at the display; at least that was the way that the villagers of Mochamton were thinking, (fingers crossed) etc.

Bernie Watson as usual was up and about early Tony and Carol Lockwood were at 'The Navigation' at six-o clock in the morning.

Everybody else in the village they hoped would still be in bed. Quite honestly, if anyone had seen the cohorts carrying the very long parcel between them, as they made their way to Tony's Range Rover, the Police would have been informed.

Sergeant Hopper was already at the bonfire site when the Range Rover arrived dressed in his overalls and working boots ready to help.

The Sergeant had obtained the two extra ladders required for the display; these had been put in position the previous day. He had also arranged for a patrol car to park in the gateway at the main road entrance to stop anyone coming on to the site without their knowing.

Tony took the Range Rover to the front of the bonfire where the ladders were laid in position.

Then they extracted the parcel out of the car and stripped it of its wrappings,

"Bloody Hell!" exclaimed the Sergeant "That's a bit of good work" standing back to get a better look.

It was a shop window dummy that some enterprising customer of Bernies had scrounged, and Tony and Carol's team had made and dressed it in a Guy Fawkes costume.

"Yes, it is rather good, isn't it" replied Bernie proud of his teams efforts "You had better thank Carols team for that. Let's get it up the fire and buried at the top so that Roy can do his changeover this evening".

Completing their task, they made arrangements for someone to be close by all day, to make sure that no one interfered with it.

By the time they were finished it was eight thirty and they all returned to 'The Navigation' for a good English breakfast.

By lunchtime the truck had arrived with the fireworks, and had been directed down to the boggy end of the field, the driver didn't like the site very much but finally gave in with a promise of free replenishment.

Mike Smith however did feel that because the ground at that end of the field was a little bit suspect. He had arranged for a tractor to be available in case of emergencies. He also knew that there were vehicles available from the fairground people, they had offered to help when they arrived on Thursday morning.

Back in the village things were beginning to happen, the old, type lamp standards with baskets on top (similar to the type, which lit the streets in London in the Seventeenth Century) were being erected on the route to the bonfire site.

During the afternoon Mike Smith arrived with two more trailer loads of branches; the fire was now growing to huge proportions.

Fred Perkins and Ron Porter had arrived on site with a tent and the barbecue from 'The Farmers Arms'. Seeing how the bonfire had grown, they were a little concerned, for they were responsible for the fire being out at the end of the evening. They were hoping that it would be out in time for them to be able to retire to the Farmers Arms for a drink after it was all over.

Jim Smethers and Charlie Higgins two more of their committee from 'The Farmers Arms' arrived to give them a hand to set up the equipment. They laid the framework of the tent out so that they could get an idea how to erect it. The tent had been specially made for this kind of event, with letter's painted on each joint that was supposed to make the building of the tent easy.

But, the more the four committee men tried to assemble the frame work, the more confused they got, no matter how they tried it never came out the size or shape it was supposed to be.

After about half an hour of struggling they all stood back totally confused.

"I think we had better leave this to Ted Atkinson, he can do it in about ten minutes" Ron suggested.

At three thirty Ted arrived and with all five of them working, had the tent up in less than ten minutes.

By half past four everything seemed to be coming on stream nicely, so Ron and Fred decided to leave their three associates and started to walk back to the village.

As they were strolling along the road, they noticed crowds of people were gathering along the roadside.

"Crumbs" said Fred "I hope we have enough collecting boxes".

"So do I" Ron replied, remembering how the committee had changed their minds. Now they were hoping to raise funds by donations from the public, instead of charging entrance fee's at the gate, realising that the spectators would be able to see the firework display from the road without going into the field.

The two friends were walking down the High Street, when the streetlights were switched on.

The streets were illuminated by all the beacons that had been put on the grass verges of the road between the light standards.

"That's fantastic, Fred, isn't it? "Ron exclaimed, stopping to look down the High Street, and across the green that was encircled with the old fashioned beacons. The baskets were glowing as if on fire, adorned with sticks and red paper, electric bulbs that flickered, were fixed in the centre of the baskets. Making the baskets look like live fire's illuminating the village green, their warm glow reflecting off the pond in the centre of the green. Then looking further over towards 'The Navigation' where the procession was forming, Ron saw some of the float attendants walking around in their Tudor costumes.

"Fred, look over there, look at the costumes, I'm pleased there's no judging to be done, how can you pick a winner out of that lot?"

"You can't can you? Look at those beacons, the whole effect is perfect isn't it?" Ron replied.

At that moment a Panda car stopped alongside them.

"Sight for sore eye's, isn't it?" Sergeant Hopper said, as he got out of his car and leant on the roof.

Hesitating he looked over at the two friends.

"It look's as if there's going to be a big turnout. I hope that you've arranged enough parking", the Sergeant remarked as if he had caught them doing something wrong.

He then got back into his car and started his engine.

"Mike Smith's in charge of that Sergeant". Ron replied as the Sergeant drove away.

"And goodbye to you too", Ron continued.

Unknown to Sergeant Hopper, Mike Smith was already on site in the car parking area and had already extended the car parking to three fields, one of them designated for coaches only, with three coaches from Solihull already parked in it.

As it gradually got darker the spectators were growing thicker as they formed along the route to the firework site.

Things were hotting up a little bit at 'The Navigation' where Roy Woods was changing into in his Guy Fawkes costume. The three serving wenches who would be following his float had already changed into their costumes complete with 'mop hats'.

The electricians working on the floats were trying out their lighting systems and being given the O.K. by the parade marshal.

Despite all the turmoil everyone was ready to start ten minutes before time. The procession was programmed to start at six thirty to give it an hour to reach the ground.

Winding its way through the village over the stream to the north side and back over the second bridge to the south again. The Pageant procession, gathering a carnival atmosphere slowly made its way out on to the Cheltenham road towards the firework display field.

The road was packed with people along both sides, poor Roy was pelted with old cabbages and tomatoes and to add to his misery he was chained hand and foot to the bars surrounding the open top cart, so that he could not defend himself.

When the procession arrived on the Bonfire site, the firework display commenced lasting for thirty minutes. As the last unit lit up wishing everybody goodnight, two spotlights came on lighting up the front of the bonfire showing Guy Fawkes, and his two jailer's struggling up the ladder's.

Reaching the top of the ladder's there was a terrific struggle as the two jailer's tied Guy Fawkes to the stake erected there. All of a sudden the prisoner went limp as one of the men hit him on the head, they then finished tying him to the stake and came down the ladder's, removing them when they reached the bottom.

The fire was lit and took hold very quickly.

Spectators screamed and children cried on seeing Guy Fawkes start to burn at the stake.

To pacify the public the Master of Ceremonies had to announce over the loudspeaker that it was only a dummy being burned.

As the fire died most of the committee retired to the 'Farmers Arms'.

A few, along with Sergeant Hopper remained to ensure the fire was safely out, were stood round the ashes discussing how many people they thought had been at the display.

Ron Porter said "about fifteen hundred" Fred Perkins said "two thousand" Jim Smethers said: "four thousand", "I reckon you can treble that" the Sergeant answered.

About midnight, feeling happy about the state of the fire and hoping that it would have burned out by the morning the four fire minders retired to 'The Arms' joining the rest of the committee who were still counting the money. It was three a.m. before Ted announced that the count was completed and the figure was 14,750.60 pounds.

CHAPTER FOUR

Chief Inspector Sullivan was a widower having lost his wife eighteen months previously in a car accident. Coming upto middle age, with grey streaks in his thick black hair. He was a little less than six feet tall, with an athlete's build that was turning slightly downhill because of his taste for beer served from the barrel. The Chief Inspector was an ardent rugby fan, having played for the West Midlands Police fifteen, and tried never to miss any of the Five Nations cup games.

His assistant Sergeant Thomas was in his thirties as tall as his Chief Inspector, with fair hair also played rugby for his local Solihull team. He's married with two children, a daughter Mary four years old, and a son Allen, one year old.

After Sergeant Hopper finished bringing the Chief and his Sergeant upto date with the Pageant, Chief Inspector Sullivan asked Sergeant Hopper if he had switched his tape on prior to giving the information.

"I most certainly did sir" replied the Sergeant.

"Good" replied the Chief Inspector "Give it to one of the W.P.C's for typing, I want that report on my desk first thing in the morning"

The Chief Inspector and his Sergeant walked out of the Police Station and over to the village hall that was being equipped as the incident room; extra constables were brought in to assist in the 'house to house' enquiries to establish if there was anyone missing.

The forensic personnel arrived on site to start their investigations, and on looking at the position of the body, stated.

"That in their opinion it must have been placed in a wooden box in the Centre of the fire, but they would take samples of the ash and what they thought was the box and see what they could come up with. With regards to the body, it would have to be handled with great care because it was thoroughly burned and whoever had put it there had known what they were doing".

"Bully for them", Sergeant Thomas remarked when his Chief Inspector informed him of the statement "Its just as if we're a bunch of amateur's sir, I mean we realized that, as soon as we saw it's condition, didn't we, sir?"

"I know Thomas, but it wasn't for our benefit was it? After all they do have to show their authority sometimes don't they?".

After the body had been removed the Police set to work and sifted through the remains of the fire, this took two days, finding nothing of interest, they gave the field back to Mike for him to spread the ashes as he wanted to.

The villagers usually helped themselves to the wood ash on these occasions, but were not interested in taking any for fertilizer for their gardens, "after this body business" as they called it.

The Colonel phoned Nigel Courtney, the owner of The Manor, with whom most of the village people had no association. But in fact the Colonel and his colleagues, Ted Broughton and Bill Selby knew him very well as a business associate.

He informed him of what had happened. Nigel listened to what the Colonel had to say about the incident, then remarked,

"That he didn't know what the world was coming to, when such a dreadful thing could happen in Mochamton".

The Colonel remarked,

"I do hope it was not the gentleman from the States who visited you last week".

"No" replied Nigel "But what made you say a thing like that? as a matter of fact, Colonel, he's gone down to London, he went last Wednesday he intends to call on some old friends of his", retorted an annoyed Nigel.

"Isn't that where those pallets came from?" asked the Colonel.

"No, they came from Birmingham. I told you the truck came from London, he was dropping the pallets off en route on his way back, as a favor to me". Replied Nigel still smarting from the earlier remark.

"Oh I see," said the Colonel "That's Okay then".

Shortly after the Colonel had finished his call to Nigel, Sergeant Hopper phoned to ask the Colonel to go down to the Village Hall to make a statement about his involvement in the festivities and his movements during the previous evenings events. He also informed the Colonel that he was asking the rest of the Committee to call into the office to clear them as well.

By the Thursday following the firework display all the people involved in the organization of the procession and the display had been to see Chief Inspector Sullivan and his assistant Sergeant Thomas.

They had certainly given the organizers a hard time, especially Joyce, she seemed to have been the only person in Mochamton who had seen a lorry off loading the pallets at the site on the Wednesday before the event took place. It was unfortunate that she could not remember the colour of the lorry or if it had the owners name on it. As she had stated, she was a passenger in a car and had only seen the vehicle through the gaps in the hedge.

The Chief Inspector and his Sergeant were very interested in this information and subsequently questioned all the organizers and volunteers on the matter all to no avail.

During their routine visits to isolated farmhouses and cottages, Sergeant Thomas and Constable Boyce visited the Manor House and found Nigel Courtney in his garage cleaning his Porsche.

The car doors were open and Nigel was knelt down vacuuming the interior, Sergeant Thomas walked round the back of the car and introduced himself.

When he finished cleaning the interior, Nigel carried on polishing the roof, but didn't say a word in reply.

This did not deter Sergeant Thomas he carried on pursuing his enquiries.

"You're making a nice job of that Mr. Courtney, I presume you are Mr. Courtney", the boot was open at the front of the Porsche, Sergeant Thomas continuing with his inspection of the car stopped and looked into the boot.

"Seems funny having the boot at the front of your car doesn't

It? "He asked, then continued "Small isn't it? Beautiful and clean though".

Nigel replied "Yes, I cleaned it out today as a matter of fact. As you can see I am cleaning the car now, I've just come home from the golf course. Would you like to have a look at the Range Rover, I haven't cleaned that yet?"

"I might as well" replied the Sergeant, accepting the invitation to inspect the Range Rover.

After the Sergeant had inspected vehicle, Nigel invited the Sergeant and Constable Boyce into the house, as they walked into the kitchen Nigel stopped to put the kettle on for a cup of tea. It was a typical farmhouse kitchen; it had been furnished accordingly with a large teak table in the middle of the room with six dining chairs. A large Welsh dresser went the full length of the back wall of the kitchen. At one end of the kitchen was a Rayburn cooker this was where Nigel had put the kettle to boil.

He asked his guests to be seated but requested them not to smoke. When the tea had been poured Sergeant Thomas explained that they were here to ask him where he had been on Saturday and the previous week. No doubt he had heard that a badly burned body had been found in the ashes of the bonfire and they were calling on everyone in the area to check if anyone was missing and had not been reported to the Police.

"Well" said Nigel "there's nobody missing from here. I live on my own. I do have a woman from the village comes in three times a week to see to things for me shopping, cleaning, etc."

"Has anybody been staying here lately?" asked Constable Boyce

"Oh, you've already seen Mrs. Woolford, she's my cleaner" replied Nigel.

"No" said the Constable "I'm stationed in the village. This is part of my patrol route and I saw a red Cavalier parked outside for a couple of days last week".

"God, you're a bit sharp, aren't you, to notice a car here last Tuesday and Wednesday" said Nigel, feeling a bit uncomfortable.

"That's what I'm paid to do, isn't it?" replied Constable Boyce.

"Okay" said the Sergeant "Can I ask who it was and where they were from?"

"By all means. He is a business associate of mine from the States. He arrived on Monday at Manchester Airport and he motored down here Monday evening and stayed until Wednesday afternoon has now gone down to London to see some friends and goes back home next Tuesday. I can't tell you any more than that".

"That's fine," said Sergeant Thomas "That's cleared your visitor, what were you doing for the rest of the week?"

"Sergeant" said Nigel getting impatient with the two policemen.

"Are you just making enquiry's or do you want a statement?"

"Well" said Sergeant Thomas "It all depends how you look at it, nobody seems to know much about your business activities and you do sort of keep yourself very much to yourself. Even Mrs. Woolford can't give us any information on what kind of business you are in".

"Good for Mrs. Woolford" said Nigel "At least it shows that not all the people round here are interfering busybodies. It does look Sergeant as if you want me to make a statement so I think I'll phone my lawyer to ask him to come here, or do you want me to come down to the station, as you people say?"

"I think you've been watching too much television, Mr. Courtney, but if you want him present while you give the statement, that's Okay by me. How long will it take him to get here, where will he be coming from?"

"He's Mr. Booth of Booth and Partners, Henley in Arden do you know him" said Nigel.

Mr. Booth arrived at about half past three and they all sat down at the kitchen table. Sergeant Thomas told Mr. Booth that at first they were only making a few routine enquiries and that Mr. Courtney had offered to make this statement of his own free will. Mr. Booth accepted that and said that he was sure his client wished to help the Police in any way he could.

Nigel gave his statement explaining his offer to the Colonel to supply some broken pallets and that he arranged through the Colonel and Mike Smith to have them delivered to the site on the Wednesday. He said he would let Mr. Booth have the name of the transport company, which he would forward to the Sergeant early the next morning (Friday).

After Nigel had signed the statement Sergeant Thomas seemed satisfied and got up to leave but as he was leaving he asked Nigel the name of his guest, he had only told them that he was from the States.

"It's Jose Cordova and he comes from Chicago. I'll give you his full address tomorrow when I give Mr. Booth the other information.

"I'll look forward to that" said Sergeant Thomas and promptly wished them both a very goodnight and a safe journey.

The following morning Chief Inspector Sullivan called his Sergeant into his office at the Village Hall.

"I've just had a call from the Path boy's they tell me that they have managed to get a denture print from the body, also they gave me an approximate height which was about five foot ten inches."

"Dead clever these Pathological boy's, sir. I expect they will be telling us the color of his hair next."

"Well, they did say that it was a male," said the Inspector.

"That's interesting," said the Sergeant "Constable Boyce and I called at the Manor yesterday and after questioning Mr. Courtney. Managed to get a statement from him with his lawyer present but the thing is, he had a visitor for two nights last week who left on Wednesday to visit some old friends."

"That is interesting. Do you know where in London he went? Can this Courtney chap give you his address?"

"No sir", said Sergeant Thomas "But Constable Boyce did see his car outside the Manor on Tuesday and Wednesday."

Inspector Sullivan scratched his head for a while in deep thought.

"I wonder if we can trace his car, he must have hired it from the airport. Get on to that and keep me informed."

"That will mean a trip to Manchester Airport. Can I take Constable Boyce with me?

"You might as well. He did see the car," said the Inspector.

At about six-o clock that evening the Inspector was tidying up his desk at the village hall when the phone rang. It was Sergeant Thomas reporting in from Manchester Airport to tell him that they had no success at all with any of the car hire firms on the Airport precinct. But they had asked the offices to check their head offices in Manchester to see if they had hired out the Cavalier. This again had not produced any results.

"Okay come on back. I'll see you in the morning. I've not had any luck today either."

As he was leaving the Village Hall the Chief Inspector met Sergeant Hopper, coming on duty.

"There's nothing exciting happening, keep sifting through those statements, we're missing something somewhere".

"Right, sir" said the Sergeant "I'll see what I can do for you" and carried on into the hall.

It was Tuesday, ten days after they had held the display before the organizing committee could hold their meeting to discuss the event in full detail, especially the police involvement.

The money had been taken into the bank in Stratford-on-Avon, which Ted Broughton had been able to arrange without much trouble. This was a great relief to the Farmers Arms Landlord.

Fred Perkins asked the landlord, Joe Brompton, if they could have the meeting at 'The Farmers Arms', which of course the Landlord agreed to. At the meeting Fred reported that all the takings from the Display, 14,750.60 pounds, had been banked.

This caused great excitement.

Tony Lockwood reported that he had been asked at work if this was to be repeated next year and apparently this was also being asked in the village and surrounding area.

Colonel Brown was in agreement with that but, remarked with a smile,

"I agree with everything you're saying, but, next year, don't have any police around, especially Chief Inspector Sullivan, the Chief and I don't agree on anything".

CHAPTER FIVE

Nigel Courtney arrived at his office in Solihull early on Wednesday morning. As he walked into his office, he told his secretary that he did not want to be disturbed for at least an hour.

He sat down at his desk and glanced through his mail, then telephoned his agent in Germany. Hans Gunther had worked as his agent on the Continent ever since Nigel had started running his heavy transport trucks over there, four years ago.

At that time he only ran three articulated vehicles. Neither Nigel or any of his drivers had any experience in obtaining permits and custom documents and after one of his drivers was held up at the Aachen border crossing on his first trip to Germany Nigel was recommended to Hans Gunther and had worked with him ever since.

His business had extended and the transport fleet had grown. He now had three lucrative contracts with three German vineyards that exported their wine to Britain. He also had some contracts which were far more lucrative but also far more risky.

They were precious stones that were brought into the country illegally on his trucks. He felt he did not want to lose this trade unless it got too risky for his drivers or himself.

After speaking to Gunther for approximately fifteen minutes on this matter, Nigel informed him of Jose's visit and his concern for his trucks being hijacked and to combat these problems he suggested a meeting in Antwerp. He informed Gunther that he could catch a flight from Birmingham Airport at 4:30 p.m. and could meet him at 6:00 p.m. This having been arranged Nigel spoke to the Colonel and asked him if he would like to join them in Antwerp. The Colonel agreed to this but advised Nigel to inform Mr. Jones in Salisbury just to put him on his guard and he would inform Ted and Bill of his departure.

Although Mr. Jones main business was Pyrotechnics it was only a cover for his other sidelines. Which as far as Nigel and his associates were concerned was an involvement with them on the illegal import of precious stones.

Having forewarned his colleagues of the possibility of some problems arising from their illicit trading.

Nigel sat back to relax for a while and reflected on how he had become involved in this business. He had a successful Civil Engineering Construction Company and an Engineering business, and, come to think of it. Despite the recession they were both keeping their heads above water, both were allied to the Oil industry, which was beneficial to his Transport Company in the U.K. for movement of oil field equipment. Nigel was thinking back to the time when he first met the Colonel and Bill in the Clubhouse at the local golf course. After introducing himself to the Colonel at the bar he had been invited to join them at their table and they had remained talking for the rest of the afternoon. It was been later that week when Bill had phoned him at his office to ask him if he would join him for a game of golf the following weekend. Bill had then suggested that he make an appointment with the Colonel to discuss a wine import contract from the Continent.

The Colonel and Nigel met in the lounge bar The Navigation to discuss the Colonel's proposal for Nigel to bring in wine from Germany once a week. As this would involve the need for permits, he suggested that they could put Nigel's vehicles in his company's colors and run their own account permits. Nigel pointed out that this would have to be arranged with the Ministry of Transport in Newcastle. At their next meeting Nigel discovered that Bill, Ted and the Colonel had formed a company and were selling wine to small off-licenses in the Birmingham area. This was how Nigel and his Company had become involved with the Continental business that had led him into the world of illegal importing of precious stones again through the Colonel and Bill. It was again during a game of golf with the Colonel that he had been asked if his next truck in Belgium could call at one of the Colonels friends in Lokeren; and pick up a small parcel for him that was a present for his wife and as it was a present there would be no need to declare it. That had been the beginning one movement had led to a second and it was soon three movements a week.

11 Nigel later learned that the favour for the Colonel was actually a favour for one of his ex-army colleagues who had a jewelers shop in Birmingham.

When Jose had visited last week he had disclosed that he knew about this business and made other suggestions. Nigel was very worried and decided that no way was he going to get involved with drug trafficking no matter what Jose said.

Nigel got a bit scared after Jose left and made arrangements to go to Belgium to discuss matters with his Continental Colleagues.

For similar reasons the Colonel, unknown to Nigel, made his arrangements to fly to Antwerp via London on the six-o clock flight. Nigel left Birmingham on the four thirty flight. Gunther had booked rooms for them at 'The Red Lion' Hotel in Lokeren that was just off the main square and well known to English drivers because it sold good old British beer.

Inspector Sullivan called Sergeant Thomas into his office to ask him how far he had progressed with his enquiries on the car and what was happening about the enquiryies in America. The Sergeant informed him that as far as the enquiries on the car were concerned they had reached a dead end. They had been up to Manchester again and checked all the hire car firms within a mile's radius of the airport without success.

"Right," said the Inspector "we will have to forget that for the time being and see what we can turn up from the States. I can't help but think that we are missing something".

"Yes" said Sergeant Thomas, "I have a feeling that one or two of the peasants know more than they are letting on".

"You'd better not let them hear you call them peasants Sergeant, you'll have them calling the Chief Super and we don't want him here, do we?"

"No, but they do get on my nerves a bit, Sir, they're very closed shop, are'nt they?"

"I know but you have to be a little bit patient with them, Thomas," replied the Chief Inspector smiling at his Sergeants remark.

At that moment a policewoman came into the office with a fax from the Manchester Police Missing Persons Department saying that they had not had anyone reported missing on the week ending thirteenth November which fitted the description they had been given and would like some further information.

"That's not much help," said Sergeant Thomas.

"No but a least we have someone else trying to help. That's more than our lot in Birmingham" said the Inspector "Anyway, let's face facts what have we got to go on at the moment? We've got a red Cavalier car, the name of someone from New York or Chicago, or wherever, plus a burnt body in a wooden box, which was brought to this village to be burned. Up to now all we have in our favor is that it must have been someone in the know who brought the body here. Now that tells me that the driver of the lorry must have known what he was carrying. What information have we got on him?"

"I think that is being handled by Sergeant Hopper, Sir".

"Well find out will you. We do not seem to be getting anywhere, as I said before".

Sergeant Hopper was not available until the afternoon and Sergeant Thomas, not feeling happy about the turn of events, started checking with the two constables who were helping Sergeant Hopper with his enquiries. He discovered that the Sergeant was still trying to run the village patrols as well as trying to run the office in the incident room. Of course, he felt this was wrong and reported the matter to the Chief Inspector.

"I know, Sergeant, I just wanted you to find out for yourself. Who told you that Sergeant Hopper was going to find out about the lorry driver?"

"Constable Wright, I think. He reported that he had been talking to his Sergeant about the lorry. Sergeant Hopper had instructed him to leave the matter to him. Because he was going to talk to Mike Smith who should be able give him more information. He was under the impression that Mike Smith had helped to off load the lorry".

"I see now," said the Chief Inspector "The Sergeant thinks that Mike Smith knows where the lorry came from and the name of the driver, does he?"

"Yes sir, but we already have them, haven't we? We got them from Nigel Courtney's solicitor the other day, so what are we doing about it? Who is supposed to have been given the job of finding the company who owns the lorry? For all we know it could be someone hired the lorry for the day".

"Get on it Sergeant and let me know will you? stop messing about chasing Sergeant Hopper you're supposed to be a detective not on the beat".

"Yes sir I'll get on it right away. Who shall I take to London with me Constable Boyce again? he seems to have a good head on his shoulders for this type of thing"

"Yes, Okay make arrangements to go down there tomorrow and go early so that you can be back tomorrow night. We don't want you both staying down there with those loose women, do we?"

"Have you got the addresses Sir?" asked the Sergeant.

"Yes. I've got the drivers address in Canning Town and the Transport Company on the East India Dock Road".

"Ah, here we are Sergeant." said the Chief Inspector looking through all the paperwork on his desk,

"I shall have to get one of the WPC's to sort this lot out for me while I'm out. I think I'll take a trip up to Birmingham and have a talk with our friend Nigel Courtney while you are down in London. I have a feeling that he knows more than he is letting on. What do you say sergeant?"

"I'm inclined to agree with you Sir" replied Sergeant Thomas "I think I'd better inform the Met that we are going on to their patch tomorrow to interview someone. If I don't do that they might cut up rough if we have to call for assistance".

"Okay, you do that Sergeant and I'll see if I can arrange this appointment with Nigel Courtney."

"I think you ought to take him by surprise, Sir."

"That's an idea," said the Inspector smiling, "A very good idea in fact."

"Thank you Sir" smiled Sergeant Thomas as he left the Inspector smiling to himself.

CHAPTER SIX

gAt the Red Lion in Lokeren, Nigel the Colonel and Hans Gunther were having breakfast and discussing how to sort out the problem that was being caused after Jose's visit.

Hans was saying that he thought Nigel was worrying over nothing, because Jose was only making suggestions at this stage.

"That is, what's worrying me", replied Nigel

"Do you think that he could become serious then?" asked the Colonel.

'Yes" replied Nigel "and he won't stop there. Jose can be very nasty if he wants to, I saw that when I was in the States once. He hit a bloke who had parked blocking him in a parking lot. He asked him once to move an when he did not move immediately, he walked up to him, hit him and got in the mans car, reversed it straight across the parking lot and rammed it into a big truck."

"Oh dear" said the Colonel.

"Yes, that's what I thought" agreed Nigel.

"Yes, but that's not to say that he will carry on like that with you" said Hans.

"No, but I don't want to be around if he does" said Nigel.

"So, what do you think we ought to do, Colonel?" said Hans.

"I don't know, at the moment, he seems to know what we are doing, doesn't he?" replied the Colonel "perhaps it would be a good idea to stop the operation for the time being, it's best not to take any chances, don't you think?"

Both Nigel and Hans agreed and were very relieved to hear it

"You inform your friend over here, Nigel and I'll inform my party. It's funny, isn't it, none of us know any names."

"No" said Hans "I think it is a good job we don't. I'm going to meet my friend later after you have both gone and will be flying back tomorrow, so I'll be in touch with you, Colonel, when I get back."

"Everything is all right otherwise isn't it Hans" asked the Colonel.

"The wine shipments are to go ahead just the same. Oh, I might be getting another contract, Hans, from another supermarket chain, apparently they were recommended to us by a close friend of mine in the City."

"That's good" said Hans "have you any details? Or am I a little previous on that?"

"No I have no details yet but I will let you know when I get them. I'll keep in touch. I think I had better get a move on, then I can catch an early flight to London I think there is one about three thirty".

The time was eleven thirty am so the Colonel had plenty of time to catch the Metro to Antwerp for his flight.

Nigel and Hans carried on discussing the viability of rerouting the trucks through different ports. It was as Nigel said up to the driver's own discretion as to which port they used.

"Well, Nigel, anyone wishing to hijack any of your trucks, would have to have inside knowledge as to where, and when your trucks would be if they wanted to take them, wouldn't they?" said @ans.

"I know," said Nigel "it just means we shall have to open some more accounts with agents in the other ports that we may use that's all."

"Yes, and you will have to open one with Sally Line at Ramsgate and Oulla Line at Sheerness."

They talked the matter through two or three times more before Nigel said that he would have to go and meet his friend from Antwerp although, as he said, his friend lived in Lokeren, he had never been to the Red Lion before,

"Well, it's a bit different from what we are use to, look at all the mahogany bar and all the glasses suspended from the top of it and the red velvet seating around the walls, not quite what we are use to, is it? Well, I'll soon find out what he thinks won't I?" He shook hands with Hans and wished him a safe journey back to Aachen.

Nigel went up to his room to have a shower and get changed ready to meet his friend Eddy at five o'clock. He had just finished his shower when the phone rang, it was his secretary in Birmingham, informing him that the Chief Inspector Sullivan had called at the office to see him, and, he was very angry that he had not been informed of Nigel's trip abroad. He had also told her to inform him that he had better get himself back home today. Also the Inspector wanted to see him, first thing tomorrow morning.

Nigel told his secretary to inform the Chief Inspector, that he could not leave today and, yes, he had forgotten to inform the Police of his intended travel plans, but would she please apologize to the Chief Inspector for him and make an appointment for tomorrow afternoon. Nigel then asked her if there was anything else, she informed him, there was not, he rang off and promptly poured himself a stiff whiskey. He then lay back on his bed to summarize what had been discussed earlier and what he was going to discuss with Eddy later.

He had an hour to wait before their meeting.

Nigel walked to the Square in the Centre of Lokeren arriving there as Eddy was parking his car. He crossed the Square quickly trying to stop Eddy locking his car so that they could drive to 'The Red Lion'. Asking how far it was to 'The Red Lion', he was informed that it was only a ten-minute walk Eddy suggested that it would be better for them to walk. As they walked around the sights of Lokeren, Nigel informed him of the change of plan in the movements of the goods. Also that the Colonel had suggested they temporarily cease operations until Nigel had more news of what was happening with the Murder enquiries in Mochamton.

Nigel then went into great detail of the happenings in Mochamton and Eddy agreed to the suspension of further operations because they did not know if there was any connection between their operation and the line of enquiry in the murder case.

Eddy then informed Nigel that he had a further shipment with him, being nervous of the operation as it stood at the moment Nigel refused to accept the package. After a lot of persuading from Eddy, he agreed as a favour to Eddy for the last time to take them back with him. He then asked Eddy if he had received any suspicious phone calls, Eddy shook his head asking what they would be about. Nigel refused to answer saying he was getting abit jittery about their operation.

CHAPTER SEVEN

When Colonel Brown arrived home from the airport, he immediately contacted his friend, Brigadier Smythe-White, the jeweller in Birmingham, to inform him of his visit to Belgium and the decision to suspend the delivery of stones. The Brigadier was dumbfounded and could not think that he was involved in any way with the goings on in Mochamton.

"No" replied the Colonel "neither did I, but we have to be prepared for anything these days, you should know that."

"Yes, but surely, I should have thought that at our age we should have finished with any nastiness, shouldn't we?"

"I know, I know, let's finish this conversation, you never know who's listening in on these things these days."

"Good Lord, you don't think they would, do you?"

"I don't know," said the Colonel putting the phone down. "He never improves" he muttered to himself picking up the papers that Mike, his manager, had left out for his attention.

Colonel Brown was settling himself down to go through his papers and starting to enjoy a cup of tea he had made. He did not like the Coffee that they drank on the Continent, he did not like it during the war when he sometimes had to drink it, and he sure as 'Hell' did not like it now.

Chief Inspector Sullivan and Constable Hopkins drove into the farmyard and the Colonel, not wanting to waste his cup of tea, he took two more cups and saucers from the sideboard then went to answer the door.

"Come in, Inspector, bring your colleague with you, want a cup of tea?" he said leading the way into his study.

"Sit down" he said pointing to the settee "milk and sugar?" he asked.

It seemed that no way was he going to let them spoil his cup of tea, the first he had made since his return from Belgium.

"To what do we owe the pleasure of the visit, Inspector?" he asked.

"Enjoy your holiday Colonel?" the Chief Inspector, asked, "You left in a bit of a hurry, didn't you? You never informed us that you were leaving as we had asked you if you were going anywhere for more than one night, in fact while this murder enquiry is on I should know the whereabouts of anyone in the village at all times. You and Nigel Courtney seem to think this is all a joke and that you can carry on, as you like. In fact, if it happens again I shall have no alternative but to lock you both up until you are both completely cleared of any suspicion. Is that clear, Colonel?"

"What the hell are you talking about, man? Do you know to whom you are talking to? I have never been spoken to like that in all my years in the Army and I certainly won't be spoken to by the likes of you. Do you hear?" replied the Colonel, sounding very annoyed.

"Look, Colonel, this case is turning out to be bigger than anything you, I or my superiors thought. It looks as if it may become International and I'm certainly not going to have my promotional prospects messed up by you or anyone else. Now, can you tell me where you have been for the last seventy two hours?"

"I certainly can. I have been to Belgium on business and as a matter of fact, I have just returned not two hours ago" he said looking at his watch "come to think of it, you were quick off the mark. Who told you I was back?"

"You were spotted turning off the main road by someone. News travels fast in these parts, you know. There's not much that happens in this village that we don't know about."

"Well Nigel and I apparently managed to slip away without you knowing, didn't I?"

The Colonel could see that the Inspector was getting a bit wound up, so he asked him if he would like another cup of tea, saying that, he was going to have one.

"Alright" said the Inspector, "but I am still waiting for an answer to my question where you have been. I don't mean just to Belgium. Where have you been and what was the business and whom did you see? I want some names and addresses, Colonel".

"I can't see that, that has anything to do with you, Inspector. That is strictly private between me and my colleague and has nothing to do with you or anybody else."

"It is when I am investigating a murder and especially when you could be involved."

"So. I'm one of the suspects am I? That's a laugh at my age. Don't tell them that in the village Chief Inspector. You'll have them falling about laughing."

"You may think that, Colonel but everybody in the village are suspects until cleared and at the moment you and Nigel Courtney top the list because both of you disappeared at the same time without informing us, and that, in my book, is very suspicious. I think both of you are involved in this somewhere along the line, Colonel and I want some answers quick as to where you have both been and what you have been doing."

"Well, Inspector, after that little outburst I suppose I had better tell you what I was doing over in Belgium. As a matter of fact, I was looking at some cattle over there. You see, I want to improve my stock and having read in the Farmers Weekly that some farmers in the South were going to import some cattle from Belgium, I decided to go to Lokeren, that's near Antwerp, you know, where it was reported that the farmers were going. As I had served in that area in World War 2,and know it well, I decided to go to the cattle auction there on Wednesday to have a look. No harm in that eh, Inspector? and if it happened to be the same day as Nigel went over there I can assure you that it was a coincidence."

"I hope you got all that, Constable," said the Chief Inspector.

"Yes, sir, it's a good job I know shorthand" replied the Constable.

"Good, good" said the Inspector as he started to walk towards the door. "Don't leave the country again without informing us will you, Colonel? We'll no doubt want to talk to you again sometime" The Colonel stepped in front of Chief Inspector Sullivan and opened the back door.

"What time do you expect Nigel to get back home, then?" Chief Inspector Sullivan asked the Colonel, as he was about to step through the open door.

"I don't know," said the Colonel being almost caught unaware as they all walked over to the police car.

"I really have no idea, Inspector" he said shaking hands with the Chief Inspector as they parted.

The telephone was ringing as the Colonel walked back into the house and as he picked up the phone he noticed that his hand was shaking,

"Oh, it's you, Bill" recognizing his friends Bill Selby's voice "Hang on a minute while I pour myself a stiff whiskey. I've just managed to get rid of the Chief Inspector and that Constable Hopkins that he always has with him."

"Well, first of all Ted and I would like to know if the trip was worth it and also Joyce is getting quite concerned because we don't seem to be doing anything about the food collection for Christmas".

"Well, may I say that the trip was enlightening for me, I found out that the Belgian cattle are not as expensive to buy as I thought they were. I stopped off in Antwerp and visited the cattle market on my way back to the airport. Good job I did too the Chief Inspector may do some checking there to make sure I was telling the truth. There was a market in progress and I stopped to make enquiries about the cost of shipping to the U.K. and found that it is not too complicated. In answer to your next question, I should think we could have a meeting next week sometime at 'The Farmers Arms', don't you?"

"O.K." said Bill "I'll see to it and I'll see you around."

"Right" said the Colonel "Bring the others down for a drink this weekend and we'll talk the food collection through first before the meeting next week. We'll have to invite Mike and his crowd from the Navigation to finalize everything as time is getting a bit short now, isn't it?"

"I agree" said Bill "I'll tell the others and call you back" and promptly rang off.

His farm manager Mike Smith had walked in while he was on the phone.

"My God, Mike. I don't want another day like this has been. Pour yourself a drink and sit down. Tell me some good news for goodness sake to cheer me up."

"I don't know about that Colonel. They've started combing through those ashes from the bonfire again. I've just left them. They are looking for any clues to the body's identity and they have circulated the prints of the dental X-rays throughout the country but they haven't had any replies yet. They've also sent some overseas but I don't know where."

"Ooh, let them get on with it" replied the Colonel "I've had enough for one day." He sat back in his chair and put his feet up on the coffee table in front of him. He then held his glass up to Mike to pour another drink.

Inspector Sullivan and P.C. Hopkins drove back to Mochamton the long way round and went up the drive to the Manor House to see if Nigel Courtney had arrived home. Knocking on the door and ringing the door bell did not bring any response. They had a look around the back of the premises but did not see anyone there or any signs that there had been any callers either. After having a further good look around the Manor House and satisfying themselves, that indeed there was no one in residence. They returned to their Crime Scene Incident Room at the village hall.

When the Chief Inspector reached his desk he picked up two faxes that had come from other stations giving a negative reply on any missing persons. He started to write a memo to his Chief Superintendent suggesting they should close down the Incident room and move everything back to the Station in Stratford on Avon. When a Woman Police Constable came in with a reply to their query to the Vehicle Registration Office in Swansea stating that a Mr. Jose Cordova of 421, Stockport Road, Knutsford, Cheshire owned a 1991 Vauxhall Cavalier and the color was red. The Inspector read the message through twice to make sure that he was not seeing things. Then called P.C. Hopkins to ask if he had heard anything from Sergeant Thomas in London. He replied that Sergeant Thomas was going to stay the night in London, something else had come up that they wanted to investigate.

"Thanks, Hopkins" said the Chief Inspector "Tomorrow, you and I are going to Knutsford to check this address and see what we can come up with."

"Yes Sir" replied P.C. Hopkins "What about this Nigel Courtney, when do you expect to sort him out?"

"After we return from Knutsford. I think I put the wind up his secretary when I called her the other day."

"You'd have thought he would have been back by now, wouldn't you?"

"Oh, he will be, Hopkins, he will be."

With that Inspector Sullivan looked at his watch, looked up at Hopkins and said,

"Right, it's your turn to buy me a pint."

He got up from his desk, grabbed his coat and walked out of his office saying, "Come on, Hopkins" and walked off at a fast pace towards 'The Farmers Arms' with P.C.Hopkins in full pursuit.

Later the same evening Fred Perkins went into the Farmers Arms to have a drink with Ron Porter thinking that they might have a quiet evening to discuss future events and also the happenings in the village lately. As things do happen when you don't want them to, some teenagers had decided to have a game of pool that had become a bit boisterous so they wished Joe, the landlord, goodnight and walked over the Navigation, which was a lot quieter. They had not been there very long when Tony and Carol Lockwood arrived and were pleased to join them, as they put it, they hoped that Fred could enlighten them as to what was happening in the village for the old folks.' Also enquiring if his wife knew if the Women's Institute was going to hold their Christmas Bazaar this year. Fred said he had not heard anything from his wife but would ask her. Then took the opportunity to ask them in return if they would help with the food collection this year as one or two of the Committee seemed to be tied up on other things at the moment. He explained there were leaflets to deliver and also two collection points to be arranged in local shops. They both agreed to help and the conversation became involved with details of the collection and the Christmas festivities for the village.

CHAPTER SEVEN

Sergeant Thomas and P.C. Boyce arrived at the East India Dock Road around mid-morning. They had no difficulty in finding
I.C.L. Containers, they were stacked high behind the wall which runs all the way along the east side of the road. As they drove up they found the turning on the right that led them to Garfield Transport as per instructions given to them earlier by the local police.

They had to go through a security check at the gate and were given directions to Mrs. Jenkins office. The guard informed P.C. Boyce that she was the person in charge of the whole operation that was quite substantial.

"You'll notice the size of the place as you drive round to her office, but if she is not expecting you, I had better call her first".

They followed the instructions to Mrs. Jenkins office, and found the reception office between two small office blocks that were actually bungalows. Which had been the living quarters for the Dock Policemen when the docks had been in use.

When Harry Garfield had started his Express Parcel Service, he had rented the area for his two 2-ton trucks to be parked and had built warehouses. He had lived in one of the bungalows and had consequently 'lived on the job'.

As the business expanded, onto the Continent and to the Middle East, he had started to work very closely with Jacques Giraud, a large French haulage company based in Rouen. Everytime he backloaded one of Jacques trucks he had received a French permit to allow him to send one of his trucks into France. French permits were very hard to obtain from the authorities in Newcastle and this he had discovered was one of the ways of getting round the allocation. He had eventually bought a house in Brentwood, Essex converting the bungalows into offices one for Accounts and one of himself and the other office as the Traffic office.

All this had taken place over ten years and had not been without its problems. Two years ago Jacques Giraud had come over from Rouen on a flying visit, which had extended to seven days and he went back to France as a partner in a holding company that had been formed over a late night bottle of wine. Giraud Holdings, registered in the Channel Islands now owned the two transport companies. This saved any embarrassment by the management on either side of the Channel.

In March 1992 Harry had a heart attack and died. Mrs. Jenkins took over the running of the company because she had worked with Harry since the beginning and had been to college to obtain the certificates that enabled her to run the fleet whilst he was away on business abroad. On Harry's death she was promoted to Managing Director. This had been a very wise decision as the business had improved literally overnight and continued to do so.

On meeting the police officers Mrs. Jenkins introduced herself.

"I'm Mrs. Jenkins, please call me JayJay, everybody around here does. What can I help you with?"

They explained the reason for their visit and she asked the Traffic Officer to bring the load manifests for any trucks which went to Birmingham on the ninth or tenth of November and also the Tachograph Charts of the trucks and the details from the drivers.

"I'm very strict on the paperwork here" she explained "We sometimes use casual drivers if we are really pushed to get a load out. I like to make sure that everything is correct. Just in case the Ministry or you people call round with an enquiry like this".

After having a cup of coffee and discussing business in general, JayJay went to collect the details she had requested returning almost immediately and giving Sergeant Thomas photocopies.

"Lets have a look and see if we can tie anything in. We've got the details on three movements to Birmingham two on the ninth and one on the eleventh. There was an emergency package came in for delivery to Witney on the ninth so we made a load up to Birmingham out of it and the driver stayed overnight in Birmingham. That's the truck that Nigel Courtney used to take some broken pallets down to the bonfire site. But looking at the manifest he did not take any boxes like you are describing from Birmingham to the bonfire site, but this delivery note shows that the driver did take a box on a pallet up to Ensign Storage, Smith's Industrial Estate, Witney, weight 100kg. He had to be there by seven o'clock that evening. It was delivered to our depot at six o'clock in the morning, according to the

Company dispatch notes it came from Capastrani Delicatessen Importers, Unit 2 River Road Barking Essex. There you are Sergeant, the drivers name is George Obayo, lives at Flat No. 245, Harbor Buildings, Dock Road Canning Town, that's just over the bridge, turn right and it is on the left off that road. He's a good driver, we shall be employing him, he's 'next in line'".

"Thank you, JayJay can you me copies of these delivery notes?,you have certainly made things easy for us. I think we will go and see friend, George, first and then we'll go, up to Barking. Do you think I should phone first to check he is in?"

"Certainly" said JayJay "There's the phone Sergeant. I'll get the number for you".

George informed Sergeant Thomas that he was not going out and it would be convenient to call on him straight away. He confirmed that he did take the load to Birmingham and that he did drop off a case on a pallet at Ensigns Warehouses in Witney. He also informed the Policemen that, there was a truck waiting to pick up the case. The driver was in a hurry; he had to be stopped at the security gate to sign the warehouse recieving notes. George said that he had to wait until the forktruck driver returned from the gatehouse, before he could get his delivery notes signed. But he admitted he did not think anything about it, new drivers did that all the time. He also confirmed what Courtney Transport had informed the police reference his movements the following day. After he had delivered the pallets to the bonfire site at Mochamton he had returned empty to Garfield Transport and had arrived at the yard at about three thirty. The notes that Sergeant Thomas had in his hand again confirmed this. After questioning George for an hour and a half, Sergeant Thomas left George thanking him for his co-operation.

On leaving they asked directions to Capastrani Delicatessen, at River Road, Barking. George said that he was not sure of the exact location but gave them instructions to get to the Trading Estate.

The two policemen arrived at Capastrani's at four thirty.

Sergeant Thomas went over to the gatehouse to request an appointment with whoever was in charge. He was politely informed that Mr. Henry Capastrani was out on business and would not be in his office before eleven thirty the next morning.

"Right" said the Sergeant "We will be back tomorrow at nine thirty".

"Suit yourselves" replied the security guard and closed the window.

Sergeant Thomas phoned JayJay to ask her for the name of a hotel where they could stay. She offered to arrange that for them and then asked

Sergeant Thomas if he would mind returning to the office because she had some information that may be of interest to them.

On arriving at Garfield Transport they found JayJay waiting for them in reception.

"Did you have much luck, Sergeant?" she asked, as they walked into the reception area.

"Well, as I told you on the phone, we have to stay overnight because we were too late to interview anybody at Capastrani's". replied Sergeant Thomas.

"I see" she replied "Actually that's what I wanted to talk to you about. I know this is Police business and it does not involve me, but I have heard one or two things about that company.

You know, if you want to know anything about other transport companies ask a truck driver.

The other day I overheard two drivers talking in the warehouse as I walked down the opposite side of a stack of pallets. One of them was saying that Capastrani's were involved in the illegal immigrant trade.

Then the other one replied that he also had heard that one of their drivers was sacked, when the old man had found out that he was involved in the immigrant trade.

This driver had evidently heard that something funny was going on and had decided to investigate.

So the next time a Capistrani truck was on the same ferry as him to Dover, he followed it to Lucy's Transport Cafe, on the A.2. just before it becomes the M.2. Motorway.

That's where all the drivers stop before they join the motorway. It was dark, and the driver had parked at the rear of the cafe close to a second vehicle.

The driver apparently got down from his cab and looked around, which made it look a bit suspicious, he then went to the rear of his truck and unlocked the box van doors, he must have cleared Customs in Dover, because it would have been Custom Sealed otherwise.

However, when he opened the door's, my driver saw ten little nigger boys jump out of the trailer and get into the back of another truck which he was parked next to, which was from the North.

The second driver must have been watching, because when the transfer was complete, he came out of the Cafe and locked the doors of his van and drove away.

I didn't see the drivers who were talking so I can't tell you any more".

"What you mean is, "said the Sergeant "That you're not going to tell us anymore, but it's interesting anyway. When did this happen? I'll have to inform the Governor, but I think he'll say it's an Immigration problem".

"I'm not sure when this took place. It sounded to me as though it may have taken place some time ago".

"I'll call the Governor and leave him the phone number of our hotel for him to call us, then I'll ask him if he wants any further information" said Sergeant Thomas.

"I've booked you into the Falcon, I always put people in there. Its clean, has good rooms and good grub and its reasonable, plus the fact that I can drop you there because I pass it on my way home. Your car will be safer in our yard under security. I'll call back in half an hour. The phone is yours to use as you want". Jay Jay informed the two Policemen.

Boyce looked at Sergeant Thomas "This sound's too good to be true. What is she trying to hide?"

"I don't know," said Sergeant Thomas "But I do agree it does look a bit suspicious, but we'll see won't we?" He then picked up the phone to start his search for his Chief Inspector.

CHAPTER EIGHT

It was half past nine in the morning when Chief Inspector Sullivan and P.C. Hopkins turned onto the Stockport Road at Knutsford. The Chief inspector saw a postman emptying the post box up the road.

"Pull over to the post box, Hopkins. I'll ask the postman the directions to '241' it might save time".

The postman had finished emptying the post box when they pulled up and was starting to walk to his van.

"Just a minute, Postie" called the Chief Inspector "Can you help us to find No 241, Stockport Road?"

"Certainly" said the postman. "You're on the Stockport Road and as you look up there to that road junction on the left, you will see a garage. Its called Ashwood Garage. Well that's No. 241. If you want to speak to Mr. Hodgkins you'll have to wait a couple of weeks, He's in hospital, went in on Monday night with a heart attack. He's doing all right though, anyway his daughter Margaret is there. She knows as much about the business as her old man. She's there now, I've just been talking to her".

"Thanks" said the Chief Inspector. As they drove away he said to P.C. Hopkins "Christ! I thought he was never going to stop".

"I know Sir. They're like that up here. He's only trying to be helpful. You forget, Sir, I come from Manchester, they're all the same".

"Well pull on to the forecourt and we'll go and see our Margaret. I hope she is going to be as helpful as the postman is. If she is I can see us being home for lunch", replied the Chief Inspector.

Adswood Garage was quite a reasonable sized garage with a Vauxhall agency. It comprised of a showroom; six petrol pumps, workshops and a small office on the side of the workshop advertising care hire. The two policemen walked into the salesroom and across to a desk situated in the corner. As they walked across, a tall slim blonde came out of a door marked 'Mr. Hodgkins'.

"Can I help you?' she asked.

The Chief Inspector flashed his warrant card and introduced them both. "I'd like to speak to Mr. Hodgkins, if I may".

"I'm sorry, he's not here, he is in hospital. Can I help?" asked the blonde lady.

"Oh dear, nothing serious I hope "responded Chief Inspector Sullivan

"I'm his daughter Margaret. I'm running things for him at the moment. What can I help you with?"

The Chief Inspector then explained that they were looking for a Mr. Jose Cordova whose address had been given by the Vehicle Licensing Centre at Swansea as 241 Stockport Road. Where he was registered as the owner of a red Cavalier. The police were only interested in tracing him to cross his name off their list of missing persons.

"Well, I think I can help you there. You see we have known Mr. Cordova for about six years. He first came to us when he wanted to hire a car. Every time he came to this country on business he did the same thing and one day my father said to him jokingly that it would be cheaper to buy a car than to keep hiring every time that he came over. He's over here on business about every two months for anything up to four weeks at a time. There are the odd times when he is only here for a couple of weeks but when you think of it, it is quite expensive for him. So now he owns the car and we look after it for him, keep it under cover, that sort of thing. We may sometimes use it as a courtesy car or hire it out if we are pushed, but only to people we know. For this, of course he is reimbursed and we renew the car for him every two years."

"I see," said the Inspector. "Where is he now then?"

"I suppose he is in bed in Boston at the moment he went home yesterday afternoon. He caught the five thirty flight. I drove him to the airport." Margaret replied.

"Where is his car, can I see it?" asked the Chief Inspector.

"Certainly" said Margaret "It's in the workshop waiting for a service. He did a lot of miles this time and he is due for a change of car anyway. I'll pass you over to the garage foreman Ted Morcroft and he'll show you where the car is then you can look it over to your hearts content. Call and see me on your way out, won't you?"

"I'll certainly do that small thing," said the Chief Inspector as he was introduced to the garage foreman. Ted led them across to where a red Cavalier was parked in the service bay.

"You're lucky" said Ted "The mechanic hasn't started on it yet".

"I see, so this is Cordova's car," the Chief Inspector said, checking the registration plate.

"Yes", agreed Ted "Here's the key's, look it over then give me a call on the way out".

Ted left them to have a look over the car, which they did very thoroughly.

After they had satisfied themselves they returned to Margaret's office.

Chief Inspector Sullivan knocked on the door and opened it when Margaret called them in. She was on the phone to a customer; she pointed to the coffee machine, then waved to some chairs for them to sit down.

As Margaret put the phone down, she asked them if they were satisfied with the inspection of the car and the Chief Inspector replied that all it seemed to need was for the ashtray to be emptied. She agreed that Jose was a heavy smoker.

After they had finished their coffee the two Policemen rose to leave and the Inspector asked her when Jose was likely to return to England. She replied that she was not sure but maybe in three or four weeks time, but he would fax her the day before he came over.

"Have you, by any chance, got a photograph of him?" asked the Chief Inspector" The one they faxed through from the States was pretty awful".

"Why did you get in touch with the States?" asked Margaret "Has he done something wrong?"

"No. We know he had visited the village where we are making some enquiries and we needed a means of identifying him and contacting him to cross his name off our list" replied the Chief Inspector, not wanting to reveal too much information at this stage.

"I see," she said "only if he has done something wrong we don't want to know him. We have too much to lose here. I'll have a look to see if we have one" she then opened a bottom drawer in the desk where she was sat, which was full of photographs of cars. After searching found a photograph of her father with another man standing beside a red Cavalier like the one in the garage.

"There you are. That was taken when he received the keys to the car from my father. I had just got back from buying my camera and was trying it out. You're lucky".

"I take it that's him on the right?" asked Chief Inspector Sullivan.

"Yes that's him, that was taken about eighteen months ago, and no, he hasn't changed at all Inspector", Margaret replied.

"Thanks for your help Miss Hodgkins, we'll be touch if we want anymore assistance", said the Chief Inspector as he prepared to leave the office.

"Only too pleased to be of any help" Margaret replied as the two policemen closed the office door behind them.

P.C. Hopkins pulled into the car park of a pub he knew just before they joined the M.6. Motorway.

"I'm pleased you did that," said the Chief Inspector "I wondered if you were going to wait until we were on the motorway before you stopped".

"No, Sir. "I know this Pub. The wife and I usually stop here, the food is good and you get a good pint here as well".

"That's good and I think it's your turn as well".

"O.K. I suppose I asked for that. I shouldn't have recommended it".

They entered the pub for lunch and a quiet pint and stayed there until about two o'clock discussing the events of the morning before continuing on their journey back to Mochamton.

On his return, the Inspector found the Pathologist's report he had been waiting for on his desk.

On reading the report he read that the corpse was male, also that it was approximately 32 years of age. Height approximately 5ft. 9ins. And it weighed approximately 14 stone. The report also stated that they had found a piece of badly charred suiting material where the body had been folded at the waist to fit into the crate. This material, when tested, was found to have originated on the Continent probably French, trapped in the material they found three small coins, one Spanish and two French.

Chief Inspector Sullivan passed the report to P.C. Hopkins for him to read.

"Blimey, Governor, we've been looking for the wrong person," he exclaimed.

"Well, not really, he had to be cleared from the list of possibilities" replied the Chief Inspector.

Hopkins passed him a fax saying, "You haven't seen this yet".

"That's all we need! Another, possible murder, when did this come in?"

"Just as we came through the door, Sir. George Obayo wasn't he the driver of the vehicle that brought the crate up to Ensigns?" "He was, Hopkins. Now you see what I mean. It could be a possible murder because it says that the car mounted the curb and hit him as he came out of the shop and then drove off. But we will have to wait until Sergeant Thomas gets back with his report".

Nigel Courtney was reversing his Porsche into the garage when the Inspector and Hopkins entered the drive. He closed the garage door and waited until their car stopped alongside him.

"Hello, Inspector. This is a nice surprise"

He welcomed the two Policemen as they got out of their car. "I was just closing everything down for the night. Do come in, it's too cold to stand out here talking".

He opened the front door and ushered them into the house.

Nigel took them into the lounge and asked them the reason for the visit. In answer to his remark, the Inspector nearly exploded.

"Where on earth have you been? When I visited your office, I told your secretary to contact you, and inform you that I wanted you back in this country straight away. You and the Colonel can't swan off like you both did.

When you are involved in a case like this, you should have informed us of your intentions; we wouldn't have stopped you. You are still a day later than you told your secretary you would be".

"Yes, I'm sorry about that Inspector, only I decided to visit one of my customers in London on my way back. I had intended visiting them next week actually but something else cropped up so I took the opportunity to call on them this week instead. I flew into the Inner City Airport and hired a car from there to drive to Tilbury and before you ask 'What kind of business' I might as well tell you that it concerns my engineering company. That manufacture's high-pressure valves for the oilfields in Kuwait and Saudi Arabia and we discussed the possibility of a joint venture on the development of a Slant Drilling Rig, which I don't expect you to be interested in.

"No. We came here to find out what you have been up to and to inform you that Jose Cordova is safely back in the States. So, where were you last night?" asked the Chief Inspector.

"As I told you, I was in Brussels and I stayed there last night so that I could catch the early plane this morning to London. I hired a car from Hertz and drove to Tilbury to see Alan Williams of Oilfield Mechanization Services at Dagenham Road. We had a breakfast appointment and I was there for two hours and then returned straight to my office. I don't think I was there any more than thirty minutes and I then came home because I am tired, Inspector. I've had a long day".

"Yes, Mr. Courtney but what was the purpose of your visit to Belgium?"

"I went over to see my agent in Lokeren and also to meet the agents I employ at Aachen who came to Lokeren".

"I see, did you by any chance meet the Colonel while you were there?"

"No, Why was he over there? you do mean Colonel Brown, don't you?"

"Yes, Mr Courtney. Colonel Brown of Haydock Dyke Farm."

"No, Inspector. I did not meet him over there and even if I had I did not have time to go socializing. Believe me, Inspector, when I'm away on business I don't have time for anything else".

"Thank you, Mr. Courtney, I think that is all for now but before you leave the country again, do let us know, won't you. It will save an awful lot of hassle".

"Yes, Inspector, I will do that for you now would you both like a cup of coffee?" asked Nigel, hoping that they would say no but he was wrong and they stayed for another hour talking about the village and the way of life there.

CHAPTER NINE

While Sergeant Thomas and Constable Boyce were having breakfast the telephone rang. It was Inspector Greaves calling from the local Police station informing them that George Obayo had been killed the previous evening by a hit and run driver the witnesses to the accident informed the Police that it was a red car. Being shocked at this news and of a suspicious nature Sergeant Thomas arranged to call at the Police Station to obtain any further details they might have.

Jay Jay picked them up at eight thirty as arranged she became very distraught when Sergeant Thomas informed her of the demise of George Obayo but, as she said 'life must go on'. She persuaded

Sergeant Thomas to ask the Inspector to keep her informed if any funeral arrangement's were made for she knew there were no members of Georges family in England.

The Sergeant and P.C. Boyce arrived at the security gate of Capastrani's warehouse a little later than intended. The security guard had been informed of their visit of the previous evening, and informed them that Mr. Capastrani had been in his office since five thirty, but because they were forty five minutes late he might not see them.
However Mr Capastrani did agree to see them but for five minutes only he had an appointment at eleven o'clock. On reaching his office they were kept waiting for ten minutes, his secretary informed them that he was on the telephone at the moment speaking with one of their French suppliers.
When they eventually entered his office he welcomed them and asked how he could help. Sergeant Thomas explained that they were here to enquire about a crate that had been shipped to Ensign Warehouses, Witney

on the ninth of September that weighed about two hundred kilos. Mr. Capastrani looked surprised at this and said that there must have been some mistake, he had his own transport and they delivered their own goods up as far as Birmingham, because they had several customers in that area. However he sent for the dispatch notes used for hired transport and was sure they would not find anything. The Sergeant then asked him if he had any problems with his drivers to which he appeared suspicious and scribbled a note on his pad but replied that he had never had any trouble with any of his drivers at all since he had started the company.

"You see," he said, "if you treat them right you always get good service for your money".

"Yes but don't they sometimes get up to some fiddle or other, like things 'falling off a lorry'?" asked the sergeant.

"Oh that old adage, I see what you are getting at. You know Sergeant we handle very saleable items and I always tell my staff that they can have what they want if they ask for it, but if they get caught taking it without asking they will be sacked on the spot. And I have only had to do that once. It hasn't happened since and we have been trading here for six years".

When his secretary brought the documents into the office, she laid them on the desk in front of Mr. Capistrani, then leant over and whispered in her employer's ear. He looked up at her very quickly and asked.

"Are you sure? How can they be missing?"

He then looked across to the policemen and said,

"I'm very sorry, Sergeant but there seems to be something wrong here. There seems to be some notes missing and we don't have anything for that date at all. Can I see your copy of the note?"

The Sergeant passed him the copy of the note that JayJay had given him.

"Well, Sergeant, this note is definitely genuine but it is one of those missing from this pad. Here take a look for yourself. It looks as if it was cut with a razor blade. Look!" as he displayed the pad.

"There is one thing that puzzles me though. It says on this note; 6 cartons German sausage, 6 cartons Pasta, 6 cartons Italian Tomatoes packed, non-returnable wooden crate, total weight 200 kilos. We did not make this note out. My staff would have written in the size and weight of each carton also they would have been put onto a pallet and it would have been shrink-wrapped. I think Sergeant that I ought to show you how we operate here".

Mr Capastrani stood up and offered his hand to show the way down to the administration office. He showed them how the orders were processed then transfered on to the office computer and passed to the warehouse staff and the orders were assembled ready for dispatch. He then explained that his operation was classed as medium sized and he had about two thousand customers on his books and of these half were regular deliveries. He explained that he operated a fleet of eight refrigerated vans also that they operated four vehicles on the Continent to bring in their goods.

The warehouse was a building 100 yards long, 60 ft. wide and 30 ft. high. It had loading bays at each end a small office just inside the sliding doors and storage racking from floor to roof down one side. This was stacked out with pallets of cartons containing dried food, pastas and the like, all imported from the Continent. Across the other side of the warehouse were two very large cold rooms with large sliding doors to enable the fork trucks to drive in and out. These were also racked out from floor to ceiling but only three pallets high. The front of the building had a loading bay to accommodate three trucks for goods outward, and the other end of the building had the similar facility for goods inward.

There were twenty people employed in the warehouse and half of these seemed to be driving fork trucks.

Mr.Capastrani explained that the orders were brought down each day at eleven o'clock and were then palletized and shrink-wrapped ready for delivery the next day.

They walked across the warehouse to the dispatch office and were introduced to the supervisor. He told them that he had not noticed that any notes were missing Mr.Jackson, the Transport Manager informed him.

When asked if it was possible for anyone to take anything in or out without being seen, he explained that each vehicle was checked as it was loaded and signed for by the driver and counter signed by the supervisor. It was then checked out of the gate and the driver's delivery sheet was stamped time and date. Nevertheless it appeared that someone had taken three dispatch notes. The Supervisor then suggested that the notes could have been taken before the pad came into his office for his use and that he only had one pad in use at a time that was meant to save any misuse of notes.

"I can see that a lot more investigating will have to take place on this problem but that will have to be done by the local C.I.D. they will take over from here" Sergeant Thomas replied.

He then thanked Mr Capastrani and his Supervisor for their assistance and left the office leaving them with a very worried look on their faces.

As Sergeant Thomas and P.C. Boyce were driving along the A13 towards Canning Town the Sergeant telephoned Inspector Greaves on his Mobile

Phone, informing him that he was not satisfied with the result of his visit to Capastrani's and asked him to take the investigation further.

The Inspector in return, informed him that he wished to see him immediately, something had happened in the last hour that might interest him.

On their arrival at Canning Town Police Station, Inspector Greaves informed them that a neighbor of George Obayo had reported that George's flat had been broken into. The officers sent to investigate the matter had found that there was no great mess, just some drawers that had been emptied onto the bed.

Sergeant Thomas remarked that it sounded to him as if the intruders knew what they were looking for or they had been disturbed.

While they were talking Inspector Greaves answered a telephone call; it was from his men at the crime scene.

Putting the phone back on its rest the Inspector looked across at Sergeant Thomas and Constable Boyce.

"The Officers at the Crime Scene may have found something interesting Sergeant, I think we should go over there now" he remarked

They proceeded down Silvertown Way turning on to Victoria Dock Road and pulling up outside Harbour Buildings. It did not seem to take them anytime at all as they emerged from the car P.C. Boyce was looking very white and shaken. The Inspector laughingly asked him if he didn't like his driving, Constable Boyce replied that he didn't enjoy travelling at such speed in that traffic.

"Oh, you get used to it down here" said the Inspector as they arrived at Flat 245 and opened the door.

"You're in for a surprise, Sergeant" he remarked leading the way.

On a table under the window were some porcelain figures that were being examined by two policemen in plain clothes.

"Oh, yes, Sergeant Millar, who do we have here?' asked the Inspector.

"Hello, Sir, this is Sergeant Taylor of the Antiques Squad. I thought I had better ask him for an opinion under the circumstances."

"I see, well I brought round some friends from the Midlands area I thought they might find it interesting. What's your opinion then, Sergeant Taylor? This is Sergeant Thomas and Constable Boyce from the Midlands. They're down here checking on Mr. Obayo and a company he did some casual driving for, they were just leaving to go back up North when you rang. Do you think the items are of interest Sergeant Taylor?'

"Well, Sir, my opinion, for what it is worth, is that our friend has got very expensive taste. These small figures are genuine Chelsea and these larger ones are French figurines and they, my friends are very pricey. I would say the ten Chelsea figures are worth, 500.00.pounds each and the six couples, because that's what they are, are worth about ,3,000.00 pounds a pair. Your Mr. Obayo knows his figurines".

"My God" said the Inspector "that's ,14,000.00 pounds hanging on the wall and these boys this morning didn't even look at them, so what did they do?" looking at Sergeant Miller.

"Well, Sir" replied the Sergeant "If you will follow me gentlemen, you will see that all they did was to empty some drawers full of clothes on to the bed. They were disturbed by Mrs. Wilson, the next door neighbour this morning when she came in to see if Mr. Obayo had any washing to be done, she does his washing and cleaning. She saw the door open and stupidly walked in, called his name and two thugs ran out of the bedroom, knocking her against the wall as they ran past.

"What's in the corner?" asked Sergeant Thomas as he walked over to what appeared to be an old fashioned tallboy made of modern wood but found that the two doors at the front were both locked. The key was found in a small porcelain dish on the dressing table.

Here we go, again" remarked Sgt. Taylor "look at them. Beautiful aren't they, Staffordshire pottery, worth about, 300.00 pounds the pair".

He gave the key to Sergeant Thomas who then opened the door to reveal what looked like a large bureau, the top flap being locked but was opened by the same key. Under this flap were three drawers. When the bureau was opened they found a computer and a fax machine. On inspecting the books that were in the desk they found that he seemed to be dealing in the commodity market.

As Sergeant Miller walked back into the lounge, P.C. Boyce shouted in surprise. He was standing on the far side of the room looking at a long narrow trapdoor that was open in the wall paneling.

It revealed an opening about twelve inches long, four inches wide, six inches in depth and lined with polystyrene. The opening was large enough to contain documents. Lying inside was a key and an envelope addressed to a firm of Solicitors in Lincoln's Inn Fields in the City.

"Well, look at this, Inspector I didn't expect this to happen when I leaned against the wall".

"No, but I'm pleased you did. Perhaps we had better check all the walls and we may find what the intruders were looking for".

They found two more secret hideaways, both had money and documents inside addressed to the same solicitors. The money when counted amounted to 2,000.00 pounds. The more the Detectives searched the more they realised the whole thing was becoming more involved and complicated than they originally thought.

After spending some time with the Metropolitan Detectives, Sergeant Thomas and P.C.Boyce made some notes for their reports before making their way back to their car, leaving Inspector Greaves to finalise his Investigation.

CHAPTER TEN

Colonel Brown and Nigel Courtney were having a luncheon meeting at the Falcon Hotel in Stratford on Avon. While they were waiting for the waiter to take their order, Nigel informed the Colonel that he had brought the last consignment of stones from Antwerp. Surprised, that he had risked bringing them through Customs on his own; the Colonel offered to deliver them to Birmingham, agreeing with Nigel that the least number of people who knew the better. Also they were not at all happy about the way they had been harassed by the Police since the bonfire.

"To be honest, I think my home has been broken into," said Nigel "I'm not too sure but I have found one or two things out of place in my study and also my bedroom. I haven't asked my housekeeper it may scare her, but I've just got that feeling. I have checked the burglar alarm and that's okay, I even asked the security firm who installed it to come out and check it again'.

"Ooh, that is a bit scary," said the Colonel "I've got to admit that since you told me about Jose Cordova being interested in the operation I have been a bit nervous. By the way, have you heard from him, lately?

"No, but I can tell you that he is back in the States, Chief Inspector Sullivan told me yesterday. That doesn't mean to say that he is not involved somewhere. I don't think we need to worry about our two friends Bill or Ted, they're nervous types anyway but if we stop completely old Smythe-White may play up a bit. I think he is in a bit deeper than we know, you see he has connections in South Africa and I think he gets all these stones through their organization. I know that when we refer to the jewelry business, whenever we meet, he mentions these connections. As you know, there are lots of stones coming in from Angola and South Africa and one would never be surprised at other commodities coming in. He always gives me the impression of being a little bit scared of them despite being proud of the connection.

"It would help me a lot, Colonel, if you would inform the Brigadier that this is the last consignment of stones we will be bringing and also that I am selling my Transport operation. Anyway, Colonel, you don't want to be involved in this kind of thing at your time of life. You should to be taking things easy, surely, you can find plenty of things you can do in the village, can't you?"

"I suppose so"; the Colonel replied reflectively "there's the Christmas food parcel collection to organize. I hope that Joyce has already started distributing the leaflets, yes Nigel, there's always something to do in Mochamton, I'll find something to keep me occupied".

On leaving the restaurant, Nigel told the Colonel he would contact him with details of where and when to pick up the stones and stressed that he make arrangements to get rid of them straight away.

On arrival at his office at Solihull, his secretary informed Nigel that there had been a call from the police and also one from Jose in Chicago.

Trying not to upset his friend the Inspector anymore. Nigel contacted Inspector Sullivan and made arrangements to see him that evening.

He then contacted Jose in Chicago and informed him on what had happened on November the fifth at the bonfire. He also told him that he was considering disposing of his Transport Company because his two other companies were starting to occupy his time. Jose then told Nigel that he was pleased that he had called, and that he was under pressure from his friends in London to discuss the feasibility of some sites in the Manchester and Newcastle areas. Nigel explained that although he was the owner of the civil engineering company he had no say in the contracts they entered. Furthermore the Managing Director ran that side of the business very efficiently, but if Jose would give him the number of his friends in London it would be passed on to the director concerned. Jose then said he would contact his friends and call Nigel back.

After Nigel had replaced the phone and had scanned his paperwork, he was trying to puzzle out the meaning of the call and felt it was a serious threat. These people in London could be involved with drugs and they could be trying to coerce him into being involved through his transport company with smuggling.

He considered this was the time to talk with his Inspector friend.

As Nigel was driving to Stratford Police Station for his appointment with Chief Inspector Sullivan, he swore to himself that no way would he get involved with anything illegal again. He started to think of Bill and Ted and the hassle he had caused them by persuading them to put up the money to cover the cost of the stones. Because the stones had to be paid for on collection and Brigadier Smythe-White would not pay for them until he received them. This made him realize more than ever that now was the time to dispose of the transport company.

On arrival at Stratford Police Station, Nigel could not find a parking place in the Police Station car park. He had to park in the market square, as he walked back to the police station, he had a nasty feeling that someone was watching him, the hairs on the back of his neck were starting to stand on end.

He stopped to tie his shoelace and bending down he looked back towards the market square. He could not see anyone but still had this feeling and wondered if he had been followed all the way from Solihull. On entering the police station he was greeted by the Chief Inspector.

"I am pleased you have found time to call in, Nigel. I know that you are a very busy man but I only have a couple of points to clear up, so we won't be long".

They entered the Chief Inspectors office and he offered a chair to Nigel and a cup of coffee from a coffee machine that was standing on top of a filing cabinet in the corner.

"All mod cons here" he said as he poured out two cups of coffee.

"Right, Chief Inspector" said Nigel. "What do you want to know?"

"Well, I won't beat about the bush, how well do you know that London driver that brought the case up from London?"

"What case from London?' asked Nigel.

"The one that had the body in it" replied the Chief Inspector.

"I don't know anything about a body. All I know is that a driver from London called George Obayo brought some machine parts up to our warehouse in Solihull, I asked him to take some broken pallets down to a bonfire site at Mochamton, that was after I had got clearance from his company in London.

Chief Inspector, I've told you once and I'll tell you again, I don't know anything about a body in a crate".

"Alright, alright. I asked you how well you knew George Obayo the driver from London".

"I don't know him at all, Inspector. All I know is that he drives for Garfield Transport in Canning Town, London."

"Well I can tell you that he is dead. He died from a hit and run accident in Canning Town. I just wondered if you knew anything that can help us".

"I'm sorry to hear that Inspector, but, how on earth can I help you? He lives in London. How can I know anything about him? Oh come on Inspector you must be clutching at straws".

"Not at all, not at all. We have to check all avenues and clear as many people as we can, as soon as we can in cases like this before we can get down to the serious work. I must say that we are not doing much good at the moment. However, we can disassociate you from having anything to do with George Obayo and the crate".

"Definitely". Agreed Nigel.

"Okay, I think that is all for now Nigel. I may want to speak with you again later so I'll say goodnight".

Nigel hesitated as he reached the door, as if he was going to say something else but he changed his mind and walked out of the office.

Looking both ways as he left the Police Station car park at the front of the building. Nigel walked quickly back to his car in the market square.

On arrival at his car, he walked round the vehicle twice, then got on his knees and looked underneath; there was nothing there.

Looking around once again, then getting his car keys out of his pocket and still not seeing any movement in the Market Square.

"So far, so good", Nigel said, talking to himself.

After unlocking the door he gently opened it, nothing happened. He slowly lowered himself into the driving seat and sat still for a minute or two.

He then put the key into the ignition lock and started the engine, still nothing happened.

Not believing this he started to laugh.

"You silly fool", he said again talking to himself "You wouldn't have been sitting here like this if there had been a bomb under the car".

Settling himself down into the driving seat, he reversed out of the parking slot and turned in the direction of Broadway.

As he headed out of town he kept looking in his driving mirror, convinced that someone was following him.

Happy that no one was following him, Nigel sank down further into his driving seat, looking forward, after a strenuous day, to his drive home.

Driving past a garden centre situated on the crest of a hill on Broadway Road, a car pulled out of the entrance to the garden centre and followed him down the hill and along the road, not making any attempt to pass him.

Nigel accelerated and then slowed down but the car stayed in the same position letting Nigel play his little games.

When he reached the turning for Welford, Nigel turned left and carried on towards Long Marston, taking the road just short of Long Marston to Pebworth the village where he lived. The car had not followed him and he started to relax as he made his way home along the back roads.

He swung the Porsche off the road into his drive with great gusto, relieved that he had made it home without any incidents.

As he approached the house his headlights lit up two cars parked near the front door. Not recognizing them immediately, he slammed on his brakes and jumped out of the car, leaving the engine running and lights full on. He ran towards the front door, as he reached out to put the key in the lock, three shadows emerged from the bushes at the side of the house.

CHAPTER ELEVEN

Nigel was scared to death as the shadows approached him, remembering his feelings of only a few minutes earlier in the evening.

"What the hell do you want?" Nigel shouted, "Indentify yourself or I'll call the Police".

"It's alright Nigel, it's only us".

It was then that Nigel recognized the Colonel followed by
Bill Selby and Ted Broughton.

"My word you're late aren't you? "remarked the Colonel.

"Yes, I had to call on Chief Inspector Sullivan on my way home". Nigel replied.

"I hope it was nothing serious" said the Colonel. "We felt we would like to see you tonight to discuss the closure of our little operation. I do hope that you don't mind us dropping in on you like this?"

"Actually, I'm very pleased that you have done. I have had a bit of a fright really. I had to park in the market square in Stratford and walk back to the Police Station, I got this awful feeling that I was being followed. When I came out of the Police Station I got the same feeling again, but no matter how hard I looked around I couldn't see anyone. But, that's not all, I think I was followed out of Stratford as far as the Welford turning, I think I lost him when I turned off into Welford and took the back roads to here.

Anyway, why are we standing here on the doorstep, let me go and turn my engine and lights off, then we'll go in and have a drink".

They all walked into the kitchen where Nigel filled the kettle and set it to boil on his Rayburn cooker then filled his coffee machine and set it to make the coffee.

Satisfied, he led his guests into the lounge and told them to make themselves comfortable while he finished off in the kitchen. On his way back into the kitchen he stopped at the door to his study, but hesitated and carried on into the kitchen. After checking the coffee machine and kettle, he set four cups and saucers on a tray with some biscuits, then returned to his study to check his fax machine and if there were any calls on his answer phone.

Nigel opened his study door and switched on the light, what he saw made step back against the wall for support, his hand flew to his mouth in shock. He looked round the room a second time, to make sure he was not seeing things.

What he saw made him speechless and he froze where he stood.

Everything was scattered all over the place, his desk was in pieces and papers were even stuck to the wall with blood. The body of a man whom he recognized as one of his warehousemen was laid over the remains of his desk, his throat cut from ear to ear; one of his ears appeared to be missing.

Pulling himself together, Nigel switched off the lights and slammed the study door shut, then ran back into the kitchen and vomited violently.

On hearing the commotion in the hallway, his three visitors' ran into the kitchen to see what was happening.

The Colonel leading the way as usual ran upto Nigel who was standing at the kitchen sink, his face as white as a sheet.

After checking that Nigel was all right he enquired what all the noise was about.

"For heavens sake don't go into my study", shouted Nigel.

"Ring the Police, there's been a murder while I've been out!"

The Colonel dialed 999 and asked for the Police, then reported what had happened.

He then poured every one a cup of coffee remarking.

"I can see we're in for a long night".

The Police arrived very quickly.

Two Constables were the first on the scene and were shown into the study, one of them came out of the study very quickly and vomited outside the front door. He was still recovering outside when Chief Inspector Sullivan and Sergeant Thomas arrived.

Sergeant Thomas having arrived home earlier in the evening.

"What's the matter Constable can't you take it". The Chief Inspector asked as he entered the house.

"My God, Nigel there's no rest for the wicked, is there?" asked Chief Inspector Sullivan when he met a very pale looking Nigel in the kitchen.

"What have you found this time?"

Nigel explained how he made the discovery when he entered the house with his friends, and had gone to the study to check if there were any messages on the fax machine.

The two detectives followed Nigel to the door of the study Chief Inspector Sullivan pushed the door open with his pen. Taking one step inside to look around the room.

"What a mess" remarked the Chief Inspector," Do you know him?"

"Yes, he's one of my employee's, or, used to be" replied Nigel,

"He worked in one of my warehouses; but don't ask me what he was doing here. I couldn't tell you".

The Chief Inspector asked his two constables to take statements from Nigels guests, instructing them to also inform each one of them that he would probably want to see them in the morning. He then explained to Nigel that they could do nothing more until the 'Path. Boys' had finished in the study, asking at the sametime if they could use another room to have a talk.

Nigel led the way to the dining room, which was along the passage towards the front door.

It was a fairly large room, long and narrow, furnished with a long refectory table and twelve chairs. Nigel only used the room when he entertained important business people at home.

They sat at the end of the table nearest to the door, with Nigel facing the two Policemen. Sergeant Thomas took out his notebook preparing to take notes. Chief Inspector Sullivan asked Nigel to describe in detail his movements of the evening.

"Well Inspector". Nigel began. "I suppose you are my alibi for the evening, I was with you from seven until eight o'clock, wasn't I? I then came straight home, and, as I said, I found the Colonel, Ted Atkinson and Bill Selby waiting for me.

The Colonel told me they had only been waiting a few minutes when I arrived".

"Were you expecting them?" asked the Chief Inspector.

"No", replied Nigel "But I did have lunch today with the Colonel at the Falcon in Stratford, and we had discussed various things concerning the village. I had mentioned that I would quite like to be more involved in the various activities that took place. He evidently had mentioned this to Bill and Ted and that is why they were here when I arrived home.

Obviously they're upto their necks in it again".

He then informed the Chief Inspector of his suspicions that his house had been broken into on Wednesday the previous week. Saying that he had noticed one or two things on his desk were not in their usual place, also when he had checked in the kitchen he had found that things had been moved in there. He knew it wasn't his daily help because she knew where he kept things, so she always put things back in their place when she cleaned.

Having noticed these things and checked with his daily help, he then checked the burglar alarm system and, had it rechecked by the installers, who also found nothing wrong with the system.

Sergeant Thomas asked Nigel

"Why he hadn't contacted the Police?"

"What Sergeant am I going to say to you, that I think that someone had broken into my house, then you would ask was anything stolen? When I replied 'no ',but I think something has been moved', what would be your reply Sergeant?".

Sergeant Thomas looked at his Chief and shrugged his shoulders.

"Yes Sergeant, exactly as I thought" Nigel continued "Now I'm like you I'm asking, how on earth did they both get in here?"

"Yes Nigel, that is what we're all asking, but we can't do any more tonight, we'll have to wait until morning".

Nigel explained to the two detectives that the house and farm buildings had a preservation order on them, so he had to get the best security system that he could find that would not cause any damage or alterations when installed.

As Nigel was explaining his security system to the Chief Inspector and his Sergeant, they were interrupted by the Pathologist who had called in to say that he had finished his examination for the time being and that he was going home to bed.

Nigel suggested that they had a cup of coffee before they left.

Giving him an opportunity to go to the kitchen to make arrangements to give the precious stones he had brought from Belgium to the Colonel the following day.

He needed to remove the parcel of stones as soon as possible from where they were hidden in his warehouse.

He felt that tonight's event might be related.

Having arranged the time and place for him to pass the stones over to the Colonel, Nigel returned to the dining room with a tray and four cups.

The Colonel had given his statement and was waiting for his friends, to take them home when the Police had finished taking their statements.

On entering the dining room and starting to pour the coffee, Nigel was asked by the Chief Inspector where he had been at five o'clock that afternoon.

Nigel looked at him and replied.

"Well you should know Inspector because I think, I was talking to you on the telephone at that time when we were making arrangements for me to see you at seven this evening".

"Yes, I thought it was about that time when we were talking to each other. Only, the doctor here says that it was about that time, when the victim got his throat cut".

"Really, Chief Inspector, do you have to put it like that? After all couldn't you show some respect for the poor soul?" The doctor remarked.

"I suppose so, but I am getting a bit fed up with this case. I've had more dead bodies in the last three weeks than I've had all year. If you've finished with your inspection of the crime scene and the body has bee removed, perhaps Doctor we can go home to bed, that's, if it is all right with you Nigel? "The Inspector asked looking across at Nigel. Then giving instructions he remarked.

"And I don't want you to touch anything. I'll leave a Constable here all night, just to keep an eye on things and we'll be back in the morning to wrap things up".

"You mean you are coming back in the morning to carry on with your investigations, that's alright by me, but I'll inform my housekeeper, she'll have to take care of you as I shall have to be at my office in the morning. I'll be back here about half past two. If that's alright with you?"

"That's okay," said the Chief Inspector as he got up to leave.

"See you tomorrow afternoon. I see what you mean about this front door. They aren't made like this anymore".

"No" said Nigel I should like to know how they got in. They must have had a key because they did not force an entry last time when I checked".

"We'll find out tomorrow. Get a good nights sleep," said the Chief Inspector as he and the Sergeant left.

CHAPTER TWELVE

The following day was Thursday and Nigel rose early.

His intention being to arrive at the warehouse in Solihull before any of the staff arrived. He could then remove the Diamonds from the place he had hidden them without being seen.

He was having a cup of coffee with the Police Constable left on duty from the previous evening. When he remembered that he had made an appointment with his Bank Manager at Henley in Arden.

He was annoyed that the events of the previous evening had spilled over into his working day, for this was going to upset his schedule for him.

He had an important appointment with his Bank Manager to arrange funding for a new drilling rig project and he had persuaded his Bank Manager to make all the morning available for this meeting.

Nigel thought, "There's only one thing for it, a quick dash into the office and pick up what I want"

He left the house at seven fifteen a.m. and drove like a madman all the way to his office. On arrival, as he switched Off his engine he looked at his watch and saw that it had taken him the usual time, one hour fifteen minutes, so that with all the risks he had taken it had not made much difference. He collected his briefcase from the rear seat, locked his door and instead of going straight upstairs to his office went into number three warehouse which was used for long term storage (anything over 180 days). Fortunately there was no one around in the warehouse although Bert Pearson, last night's victim, who used to be in charge of this warehouse had a man who assisted him with the paperwork and general cleaning. He was not in the office either so Nigel assumed that he was probably assisting in the Express Parcels section.

Nigel walked around the warehouse for a short while checking to make sure there was no one around. He walked over to the office and looked into a pallet that was outside the office door. It was full of Lucas car parts that had been there for about twelve months. He looked around again to make sure that no one was watching. Then put his hand down to the bottom of the pallet and pulled out a small package and put it into his briefcase. Covering his actions he went into the office to take a printout from the computer of the days storage movements. He then telephoned the Colonel, asking him to meet him at Henley instead of Birmingham as was first arranged. The Colonel readily agreed saying that it would make things easier for him. They agreed to meet at Nigel's bank at 10am. Nigel checked around the office for a second time then went upstairs to his own office to check his mail. Noticing that time was getting short he asked his secretary to ring the bank in Henley to inform them he may be a little late for his meeting. He left his office in a hurry running down the stairs and out to his car.

As he was getting into his car, he noticed a red Ferrari parked opposite the entrance to his premises. It had been there when he had arrived but he had not taken much notice of it, however he now noticed there were two men sitting in the car, one of them reading a paper and the other one watching him. Feeling a little uneasy he decided to leave by the rear entrance. As he was driving round to the back of the premises, he called the main gate and asked the Security Officer if the red Ferrari had gone. Security informed him the car was still there and that he had seen it there when he had arrived on duty at six o'clock. Nigel asked to be informed if it moved within the next half hour and if not they were to inform the police and request them to move the vehicle as it was impeding the entrance to the warehouse. The Security Officer followed proceedure and made a report in his notebook and also wrote down the registration number of the Ferrari.

It was quite a pleasant morning for the drive back to Henley-in—Arden although it was chilly, the sun was shining and settling himself down to his drive Nigel was thinking how pleasant it was to have sunshine instead of the usual fog in November. The traffic was quite heavy and he had just overtaken a heavily laden transport when his carphone rang. It was his secretary telling him that his bank manager was getting rather impatient as he was already ten minutes late and when could he expect him. Nigel instructed his secretary to inform the bank manager that he would be with him in another ten minutes. He then accelerated along the straight road before the run down the hill into Henley-in-Arden. As he was descending the hill passing through the railway bridge, his phone rang again. This time it was the security officer reporting that the Ferrari had left five minutes ago at great speed. As Nigel replaced the phone he glanced in his rear view mirror and noticed a white Mercedes 180S sports car behind him.

Driving through the railway bridge and down into the town center; he stopped before he turned right at Lloyds Bank where he had his appointment. His heart missed a beat when he saw that the white Mercedes was doing the same thing but he settled a little as it drove past him when he parked his Porsche at the back of the bank.

Seeing his colleague enter the parking lot, the Colonel ran across to Nigel as he got out of his car.

Nigel immediately pushed the small parcel of precious stones into the Colonel's hand,

"Thank God. They're your problem now", he remarked

The Colonel thanked him off handedly and informed him that he wanted to see him that evening. He had received a phone call from their associate, Mr. Jones in Salisbury, who had been very angry when told they were stopping the deliveries.

"Can't stop" Nigel said "I'm in a hurry, I'll call you later"

As he left the Colonel standing with his mouth open in amazement as he negotiated some parked cars as he ran into the Bank.

The Colonel did not realize what was happening until he saw the back of Nigel disappearing through the door of the Bank, shrugging his shoulder's, he got back into his Range rover and continued on his way to Birmingham to see the Brigadier.

The Brigadiers Jewelry Emporium was a large impressive building situated at the back of the Bullring in Fortnum Street. On entering ones feet sank into a luxurious carpet, as you walked through the store it seemed as if everyone was speaking in whispers.

As the Colonel approached his colleagues' office he was delayed for a short while by one of the department managers who wanted to talk to him about his son going to Cirencester Agricultural College. The Colonel assured him that he would help his son to find a good position after his spell at the College. As they were talking the Colonel noticed a striking blonde leaving the Brigadiers office and thought he recognized her but was not quite sure.

He usually visited the Brigadier after the office staff had left at around four thirty, but this being an unusual circumstance he was shown into the office immediately, by the Brigadiers secretary, Miss Watson.

The Brigadier greeted him with a firm handshake and a false hail and hearty smile.

"Hello, Colonel, this is an unexpected pleasure to what do we owe the pleasure of your company?"

"I was just passing and I thought I would call in for a coffee and make our last consignment to you a personal one".

The Brigadier coughed,

"I don't know what you are talking about, Colonel".

"I think you do sir" replied the Colonel "After all I did inform you of our intentions in our last telephone call and now it is time to say our good-byes. Shall we say 'cash on the nail?' and not as usual after all. We had to pay up front this time, because it was the last transaction. A banker's draft will do, Brigadier. We will have time before lunch to collect it if you advise them now and no tricks, Brigadier I have four chaps from the regiment watching every movement. So, be a good boy for once. I know you have been keeping bad company lately".

"My God, Colonel, what do you think I am? Of course you can have your damned bankers draft. I have a very honorable position in the jewelry business. What do you think they would say in Hatton Gardens if I was as untrustworthy, as you think I am?"

"Yes, sir, I trust you alright but only as far as I can see you and, by the way, who was the pretty blonde who came out of your office as I came in, a friend of yours? Nudge nudge wink, wink" said the Colonel tapping the side of his nose.

"I can see that you are not trying to be reasonable, Colonel. As a matter of fact her name is Miss Hodgkinson and a very valuable customer of ours. I hope that satisfies you and now lets conclude our business and get it over with".

The Brigadier went over to his safe that was built into a corner of his office and unlocked it. Taking out a briefcase he handed it to the Colonel.

"You can see Colonel that I was prepared for you as usual, I am always prepared for emergencies. That is the difference between you and me. Now Colonel, please check the money. It is all there and in used notes. Count it and get out! I have far more important things to deal with".

"Why cash? Why not a bankers draft?" asked a suprised Colonel

"You know we only deal in bankers draft it's safer".

"Not this time Colonel, I thought that this being the last trip, you might feel better with cash", answered the Brigadier with a smile on his face.

The Colonel quickly checked the notes in the briefcase just in case paper or forged notes had been used. Finding it full of fifty-pound notes and satisfied that everything was in order, they said their good-byes and the Colonel left the Brigadiers private office.

He walked very briskly through the workroom at the back of the shop and into the staff toilet. He locked himself in and quickly transferred the money into the shopping bag which he had used to carry the stones in counting the packs of notes and finding one hundred packs of fifty pound notes each containing one thousand pounds. He started to worry at the thought of carrying so much money. After he had packed the money into the shopping bag he took off his driving coat and turned it inside out thinking that this was the first time the coat had been used properly since he had bought it at a Gloucester cattle market six months previously. He then took an old Deer Storker hat out of his coat pocket, put it on his head and walked out through the workroom and into the shop. He ignored the floor manager to which he had spoken to earlier and walked out of the Jewelry store to his car, parked in the multistory car park nearby, feeling a lot happier. He hesitated as he approached the Range Rover looking round to make sure he was not being followed and quickly got into the vehicle and drove out of the car park.

Although the Colonel had not seen anybody he still did not trust the Brigadier to have handed over all that money and not try to get it back. He drove around the Bullring twice much to the annoyance of some drivers. Then drove to Longbridge past the Rover car factory and instead of heading for the Motorway took the back road to Redditch, thinking that it was quieter and he would be able to see if he was being followed. He stopped in the town centre and phoned Tom Atkinson telling him he was on the way over and the matter was important and would he wait for him. He did not inform the accountant how much money he was carrying.

He took his favorite route through the Vale of Evesham which, in Springtime always gave him such a pleasure seeing all the apple blossom like snow covering the trees showing different intermingled shades of pink, red and green. He could see all this in his mind as he drove along, being brought back to reality by the blasting of a klaxon sounded by the driver of a heavy transport behind him who was flashing his lights telling him to move over to allow him to pass. The Colonel read the sign correctly and pulled over, allowing a few other vehicles to pass at the sametime.

He realized that he had been dawdling along holding up the traffic and this was not really like him. He also realized the light was beginning to fade on this grey miserable November afternoon and decided to speed up particularly if he wanted to catch Tom Atkinson in his office at Stratford-on-Avon as arranged.

The Colonel arrived at Atkinson Associate's offices on Sheep Street by five o'clock. It was very dark which pleased him considerably as he wanted to be as inconspicuous as possible especially as he was carrying the shopping bag with all the money. The offices were in a renovated block of terrace houses of the Tudor period. With the old moss covered red clay pantile's and white stucco with oak timber trusses in the outside walls. The doors were made of Oak planks with latches to keep them closed. One would expect to see old-fashioned locks with keys weighing half a ton, but instead there was a sophisticated Chubb Security lock installed in such a manner that did not spoil the exterior of the door. The interior was kept in the same style as the exterior with low timber beamed ceilings white walls and large stone paving slabs on the floor.

At the rear the small back yards had been made into the office car park.

The Colonel managed to find an empty parking slot when he arrived and parked his car; he quietly opened the back door and walked up the small staircase and into Tom Atkinson's office.

He dropped the shopping bag on the desk saying.

"I'd like you to put this in your safe overnight then transfer it to your safety deposit box at the bank, until a decision is made on which way we have to dispose of it".

He then explained to Tom what Nigel and he had done reference the last consignment of precious stones and that he was meeting Nigel later to discuss the winding up of the operation. Tom offered his help, if it was needed and they left the offices after first storing the money in the office safe.

CHAPTER THIRTEEN

Chief Inspector Sullivan arrived at the Police Station at six a.m. He walked through to his office doing his customary thing picking up a cup of tea and toast from thpe canteen. He then walked over to the fax machine to see if there was anything of interest for him. This morning as he glanced through the messages he grabbed at one in particular and quickly returned to his office.

He sat down and read the fax through again.

"Bloody Hell! I'd never of thought of that" he exclaimed.

Sitting back in his chair and starting to eat his toast, he was deep in thought when Sergeant Thomas walked into the office.

"Good morning. Sir. Anything wrong, you look a little bit disturbed?"

"Look at that" snorted the Inspector flicking the fax across the desk to the Sergeant.

"Grief, sir. How did they get involved? I mean, who got in touch with Interpol?"

"I did. I had a talk with the Super last week and I mentioned that the lab boys had come up with a report on the clothing of the body from the bonfire remains. He agreed that it was worth a fax to their missing person's section "pointing at the fax, the Chief continued.

"That reply seems to answer a few questions doesn't it?"

"Well, Sir, this bloke what's his name, Jean-Claude Fischer lives at, or did live at 145, Rue de la Vente, Antwerp, Belgium. You've written, height 5ft. 1ins. weight 87 kilo, then, 'same', what do you mean? It's the same as our bloke.

"Look at the lab report, Thomas. Come on, wake up, we can't say anything about the colour of his hair or the colour of his eyes but the height and weight are near enough to be going on with aren't they?"

"I suppose so, but what about this other one? George Obayo. Do you think they are in this together, Sir?"

"Could be, try a telephone call, to find out Thomas. Let's see what we can turn up. This could be our big break through".

"What I can't understand, Sir is that this Jean-Claude is an Investigator Diamant. I suppose that means that he is a Diamond Investigator. But what is he doing here?"

"That's what we will have to find out and who reported them missing, because it looks as if the two of them could have been working together, I'll give Interpol, London a call and find out as much as I can from them. If I can't find out whom they were working for I'll have to ring Paris. Let's try to keep it all to ourselves without bringing in the Yard, for the time being shall we? by the way, I managed to get the Super to arrange for an office here at Stratford, instead of Solihull, purely to stop him interfering with us. So now lets see if we can keep the Yard out".

"Good idea, sir" replied Sergeant Thomas as he stood up "I'll go and phone Inspector Greaves at Silvertown nick, let him know about George Obayo and see if he has come up with anymore info on the case. You know sir our Mr. Obayo seems to be a very mysterious character doesn't he? I mean, when I met him in London, he was an out of work lorry driver. Then we went to his flat and he turns out to be an antique expert, also a property investor. He also thought a lot of JayJay the manager of that big transport outfit in Canning Town Way. Now there's the possibility that he might be tied up with a Diamond Investigator from Belgium or France. He gets about a bit, doesn't he?"

"I know Sergeant, don't let it worry you. Give your friend a call and see if anything fresh has come to light. I'll see what I can come up with and then we'll get our heads together".

Leaving his Chief Inspector, Sergeant Thomas went to his office next door, which he shared with one of the local Sergeants. Although an extra desk had been put in the office for him, there was only one telephone that his office partner was using. He returned to the Inspector's office but found he was also using the telephone so he went down to the front desk and used the duty Sergeant's. This did not please the Duty Sergeant at all and complained bitterly to Sergeant Thomas when he finished using the phone half an hour later.

The Duty Officer called him into his office to ask him the reason for using the Duty Sergeant's phone.

"Well, sir, it's a good job I did use that phone. Nobody was on duty on the front desk at the time and I happened to glance through the report book and found two messages had been left for the Chief Inspector and myself and not passed on to us. One was last week and the other one yesterday, both calls had been left, asking us to call these people back and we were not told. Now, sir, how many more are going astray?"

"I'll look into it Sergeant" the Duty Officer replied, taken aback at the duties of his staff being questioned by a person of lower rank than himself.

"I'll have to report this to the Chief Inspector Sullivan. Lets hope that they weren't two important calls, shall we?"

Sergeant Thomas returned to his own office, which was now empty and made the two calls that he had found. One was to JayJay.

"Ah Sergeant, I'm pleased that you called. I was getting worried and thinking you weren't interested in the information I have for you regarding George Obayo".

"What have you got on him for us then?"

"First of all let me tell you that I am now a free woman so next time you are around don't forget to give me a call".

"What happened? What have you been up to?"

"Not me. It was my husband. About two weeks ago I was supposed to have gone over to France on a business trip. It was only an overnight trip to see Jacques Giraud, but it was cancelled at the last minute. When I returned home unexpectedly at seven o'clock that night I found my husband in bed with one of the girls from his office so I kicked him out and have filed for a divorce.

The other information I have for you is that George Obayo's solicitors have contacted me and apparently he made me the sole benefactor in his will. He told them I was the only friend he had in England. He made this will three months ago and the assets are worth around half a million. There is property in Birmingham and in London but in Dover there is a boarding house and a fast food shop just outside the ferry gates. The boarding house is more like a hotel, it has twelve rooms, and some are bedsits. I'll soon change that! But, Sergeant what I wanted to discuss with you is that there is an offshore account in Jersey which holds about two hundred thousand pounds. There have been regular payments for the last eighteen months from a Banque de Pari Bar, in Paris at twenty six thousand francs every month. What do you think he's been up to, Sergeant? Do you think there has been anything funny going on?"

"I don't know about anything funny JayJay, but I'm very pleased that I have spoken to you today" replied Sergeant Thomas getting a bit agitated about the information that he had been given.

"I'll call you back this evening if I may. There is a possibility that I may be coming down that way soon but I'll let you know tonight" he continued; trying to put the reciever down.

"Okay", said JayJay "I'll look forward to your call tonight".

The next call he made was to Ensigns Warehouse and he was put through to the warehouse manager immediately. The manager seemed to be agitated about something and asked the Sergeant to call and see him straight away. He said he would rather not talk over the phone as it was a very private matter.

The Sergeant and Chief Inspector Sullivan arrived at Ensign Warehouses, Witney, early afternoon, having discussed the telephone conversation Sergeant Thomas had with JayJay on the way.

The Chief Inspector remarked that George Obayo appeared to be 'the flavor of the month', especially down in London.

Sergeant Thomas agreed adding that he wondered what this little trip was going to add to it.

Mr. O'Reilly was waiting for them in the reception office when they arrived; he asked them if they would like a cup of coffee and if they had eaten. When they said yes to the coffee and no they had not eaten, he took them to the restaurant on the Industrial Estate for lunch. This was part of the old Smiths canteen, situated in the centre of the Estate with a big lawn at the front, which was often used in the summer for barbecues and parties by some of the small companies. After the three of them had sat down at their table for lunch, the Chief Inspector asked what the problem was. Mr. O'Reilly looked round the room before he spoke,

"Well, last night our office was broken into and the only thing that was taken was the file relating to the packing case that your Sergeant was investigating when he called on us three weeks ago. Since his visit, I have been keeping a close watch on this account. As you know, with express parcel accounts the company who dispatch the parcel either pay the freight charge with the parcel, we call that 'payment up front' or charge the company monthly if it is a regular customer. In this case, Garfield Transport has contacted Capastrani Delicatessen who was supposed to have dispatched the goods and they deny all knowledge. I have tried to trace the customer at this end who collected the case from us, the address on the notes being Valley Farm Engineers, Station Yard, Shipton under Wychwood. I have visited the address and find there is a Station Yard but no farm engineers there. Obviously, Inspector, we have to put this down to experience but as there was no storage time involved we would have only charged the minimum handling charge".

"How much would that have been?" asked the inspector.

"Only about twenty five pounds".

"I expect that the local police have been informed of the break-in. As we are only interested in the case movements and the people who picked it up we will have to speak with them. If I were you Mr. O'Reilly I would check everything again to make sure that nothing else was taken. Have you any records of the account?"

"Yes, we have them on the computer. The ones we had in the file were the ones that were sent to London, when they were returned I took them with me to Shipton under Wychwood. You don't think anybody brought them up on the computer while I was over there?"

"We don't know do we? But what I am suggesting is, that one of your employees has seen one of the culprits. So you had better take great care of your staff".

"Oh, crumbs! That was my foreman. He stayed back specially for them they said it was urgent and we could charge extra for that but we haven't been paid anyway, have we?"

"Well, take extra care and don't let any of your men work on their own, especially your foreman and don't tell anybody of this conversation. We will explain things to the local police. They may want someone up here to keep an eye on things but we'll speak with you before they do anything".

"What do you think I should do about the account? Should I take another copy from the computer?"

"I think you ought to take duplicates of all your records on the computer just in case then come back and do some serious damage to your office".

"I see, inspector, its a serious as that, is it?"

"Safety first Mr. O'Reilly. Its no use moaning about lost records, if that should happen. I would like to use your phone to call the local police, if I may".

They returned to the Ensign Warehouse office, where Inspector Sullivan rang the Witney Police Station, making arrangements to see a Detective Sergeant James straight away, instead of his Inspector who was out of his office for a while, and was given directions to the Station.

Inspector Wilson of the Witney Police managed to arrive back at the Station just ten minutes before Chief Inspector Sullivan arrived with Sergeant Thomas. His Sergeant had only just informed him of their impending arrival. He was not too pleased for he had been investigating a break-in at a paint warehouse at Carterton and had a lot of writing to do for his report, before he went off duty at six o'clock.

When all the officers had been introduced and the Chief Inspector had explained the reason for his visit, Sergeant James came into the office and gave his report of the incident at Ensign Warehouses. He remarked that he thought the fact of only one file being taken from Mr. O'Reilly's desk was rather strange as usually when an office was broken into some damage is caused and in this case there was none. Inspector Wilson remarked that the case from which he had just returned was practically the same no damage other than the door being forced and twenty gallons of paint thinners and thirty gallons of white paint being taken.

"Oh no," said Chief Inspector Sullivan "Just the stuff for setting off a good fire. It looks as if it could be the same people".

"Well" remarked Inspector Wilson "it looks as if we've got something here and my overtime costs are going to go by the board".

"Can I make a suggestion?" asked Sergeant Thomas "only put three men up there tonight, One in the gatehouse with their security and two with the security patrols. I should think that the Security Company operate similar to the police using their vehicles as decoys and the officer patrols part of the site where he has parked his car but tonight put officers in the car so that they patrol in pairs. These people are dangerous, we know that they have killed two people possibly three so we must be doubly careful".

"Point taken, Sergeant. I'll have a word with my boss on this one. Perhaps you would like to speak to him Chief Inspector Sullivan".

While the Inspectors were in with the Super the two sergeants were having a cup of tea in the canteen when Sergeant Thomas was called to the telephone.

It was the Duty Sergeant from Stratford-on-Avon.

"I was not able to speak to your Chief Inspector but I think you should know, we have another murder. Mike Smith, Colonel Brown's manager. He copped it sometime this afternoon. Inspector Carter and Detective Hopkins are over there at the moment"

"We'll be right there," said Sergeant Thomas "I'll soon stop this bloody meeting". With that he slammed the phone down and ran out of the canteen. He only had a short distance to go to get to the Super's office.

The Chief Inspector came out of the Super's office as Sergeant Thomas was reaching for the door handle.

He quickly informed his Chief of the message he had just taken.

"Come on sergeant, we have to get back to Stratford. We must find out what happened at the Colonels place".

They drove all the way back to Stratford with the blue light flashing; as they walked into the Station they met their own boss, Divisional Chief Superintendent Hathaway.

"Well, Sullivan, you seem to have got yourself another corpse, what is the count now?" the Divisional Chief Superintendent remarked as the three Policemen went into Chief Inspectors Sullivan's office. Ignoring the remark the Chief Inspector instructed Sergeant Thomas to be on his way to Haydock Farm to see what was happening there and that most likely the he, along with the Divisional Chief Superintendent would be out later.

Sergeant Thomas made his way to his car knowing that the Chief Inspector was going to enjoy himself with his Superintendent. The Super always worked to the book but, Sullivan was quite different and got his results other ways.

When Sergeant Thomas drove out of the Police Station car park it was seven o'clock in the evening and a very dirty night. There was still some fog around and he drove steadily along the A439 towards Bidford where he turned left off the main road towards Honeybourne and Haydock Farm.

As he approached the turning to the farm he noticed that the entrance to the lane was floodlit and two Constables were on duty. He pulled into the entrance and stopped showing his warrant card as he got out of the car and informed them that the Divisional Chief Inspector may be coming to have a look around. He then continued to the farm and found floodlights and orange tape around the Dutch barn at the bottom of the yard, and that the barn was half full of bales of straw. D.C. Hopkins, who greeted him with another surprise, met him half way down the yard.

"By the way, Sergeant, I've been given temporary promotion to the C.I.D. while this is on so I shall be working with you a lot on this case", he greeted his Sergeant smiling.

"I suppose congratulations are in order then Detective Constable", the Sergeant said emphasizing the new rank, then continued, "O.K. lets go and have a look, shall we? I suppose Carter has had the body removed, has he?"

"Yes, he allowed them to remove it after the doctor had been. He said that Mike had died at approximately two o'clock this afternoon but I got the idea that he was not satisfied with the situation and he had the photographer take a lot of pictures. Inspector Carter thinks it is suicide but I think they suspect murder".

By this time they had arrived at the spot marked where the body had been lying, but the gun had been left where it had fallen.

"You can see, the gun is lying close to the body and pointing to where the head was. What do you think?"

"I don't know. I'd like to have seen it earlier but as you say it doesn't seem quite right. The other victim that I have seen that had blown his brains out, the gun was lying on the floor pointing away from the body. We'll have to wait for the pictures.

Chief Inspector Sullivan and his Super arrived and Inspector Carter explained that the body had been removed when the Doctor had given the all clear, but Hopkins had insisted they leave the gun in the position it had been found.

"The Doctor said he would have everything ready for us by lunch tomorrow. I accept that it appears to be suicide and the Doctor didn't say otherwise".

"Did you ask him Inspector?"

"No but it looked quite obvious to me".

"What do you think Hopkins?" asked the Chief Inspector.

"Well sir, I don't like to disagree with my Inspector but I think it's murder, sir. I was explaining to Sergeant Thomas about the position of the gun, it didn't look right to me. I think that he was killed somewhere else and brought here, and, they used the gun on him to make it look like suicide. The hole on the back of his head was too far up for him to have shot himself".

"Now Inspector, what do you think, do you still think it was suicide?"

"Sir, I was taking notice of what the Doctor said, and he didn't say that it was murder or that he wasn't sure that it was suicide".

"I see, so you took the easy way out did you? We can't do any more here tonight, and Carter I want you to get hold of the Pathologist and tell him that I want to see him down at the morgue at eight o'clock in the morning, and, I want you and Hopkins there as well".

Making certain that Carter had made the necessary arrangements for a guard to be kept on the premises all night.

The Chief Inspector walked over to his Sergeants car and opened the passenger door.

"Right Thomas", he said as he got into the passenger seat, "Drop me off at home and I'll see you at 7.30 in the morning. I want to see that body before the Pathologist starts mucking about with it. It certainly seems a bit fishy to me. I'm going to close my eyes for a few minutes. Wake me up when we get to my place" the Inspector said reclining the car seat and snuggling down into it.

The following morning Chief Inspector Sullivan and Sergeant Thomas walked into the mortuary at Stratford General Hospital just after eight o'clock and were greeted with a cheery "Good morning" from the office.

They looked over and saw Dr. Walker the Pathologist, rising from his chair in his office to greet them.

"I was told you would be calling early so let me show you what I have found".

"Blimey Thomas can't we do anything without the Town knowing what we are doing?" Whispered the Chief Inspector out of the corner of his mouth.

The Pathologist went over to the body on the table and lifted the sheet to show the head and shoulders.

"There, see that bruise on the right hand side of the neck, I think he was struck by a Karate chop from behind" the Doctor demonstrated a chopping movement with his hand "I wanted to show you that bruise before I investigated further"

"Good" Said the Chief Inspector looking over to his Sergeant "I'll point this out to Inspector Carter and D.C.Hopkins when they arrive and prove to them, that you don't accept everything at face value when you arrive at a situation like this".

Dr. Walker covered the body again and they walked back into the office and were halfway through a cup of coffee when the other two detectives arrived.

"Coo, good, coffee" said Inspector Carter as they entered the office.

"I think I can squeeze one out for each of you", answered Dr. Walker.

"While he does that come and have a look at this", said Chief Inspector Sullivan leading them to the table and showing them the body while explaining the findings of the Doctor.

"Are you happy now, Chief Inspector?" asked Dr. Walker "If you are I can get on with the job when you are gone. Quite honestly, gentlemen, I think you're looking for a professional killer. We know the neck is broken and the gun was used to make it look like suicide. I know the neck can be broken with a powerful Karate chop but you have to know what you are doing".

"Thanks Doc., that's all we need, this gets worse and worse".

"I'll let you have my report this afternoon Chief Inspector, but I don't think I'll find anything further".

Chief Inspector Sullivan and his three assistants had adjourned to office at the Stratford Police Headquarters, to discuss the death of Mike Smith, whom they all knew personally.

After a lengthy discussion and exchange of ideas the Chief Inspector gave his instructions for the day.

As they were about to leave the office D.C.Hopkins asked

"By the way have any of you heard anything about Mike's wife having an affair with one of the chap's at the place where she works?"

Inspector Carter was the first to speak.

"I don't believe this, when W.P.C Millar visited her at work yesterday to break the news to her of Mikes death. She seemed to take it very well, but bad news affect's people in different ways doesn't it?. I mean, she was shook up a bit, but then that's expected, isn't it?"

As if to justify the question DC Hopkins continued.

"I just thought that I'd ask, I overheard two chaps talking in the pub last night, when I called in for a drink on the way home. I met Sergeant Hopper in there, he was as surprised as we all are".

The Chief Inspector informed his team to bear this in mind during their enquiries, but also instructed D.C. Hopkins to make a few more discreet enquiries, just to make sure that there was no 'jiggery pokery', as he put it.

As they were leaving, the pathologist Dr. Watson telephoned the Chief Inspector. Reporting that his first thoughts on the cause of death were correct and a blow had definitely caused death with a blunt instrument. The blow had been struck with great force from behind, as I had previously suggested by someones hand, or a wooden stake seeing as the murder was committed on a farm. The amount of damage to the neck would have been sufficient to kill an ox. He said that all the details would be in his report that he would send in later.

"Well Sergeant, it looks as though we now have three murder's with a possibility of another one down in London".

Chief Inspector Sullivan remarked as the two Detectives drove out of Stratford-on-Avon on their way out to the recent Crime Scene at Hoylake Farm.

"All we have to show after three weeks on this case is a lot of mileage on our cars and piles of Computer paper. We also seem to be making a habit of collecting murder victims. What do you think about it all Thomas?". The Chief Inspector asked.

Before his Sergeant could reply, the Chief Inspector continued as if thinking out loud.

"I'm certain that our friends the Colonel and Nigel are involved in this case somewhere, I know they didn't commit the murders but, they may know something, I'm not happy with those two, Thomas".

"You could be right sir, do you think they could be illegally importing something? they were both on the Continent at the same time. Perhaps they brought it back then, but we had a body before that didn't we".

"Brought what back Thomas? What are you talking about man?", asked the Chief Inspector exasperatedly.

"I don't know sir, I was just thinking out loud like you were sir,"

"Well Thomas when you think out loud again, try and think with some sense in it will you?" replied his Chief Inspector sounding a little annoyed.

"By the way sir, have we had a reply from Interpol reference Jean Claude and George Obayo? There could be something there".

"As a matter of fact Thomas, we had a fax in this morning. It now seems that, they were both employed by a private investigating company".

The Chief Inspector replied reaching into the inside pocket of his jacket and pulling out the fax.

"Apparently, they were both employed by an organization called Francoise de Mere Securite Services", he continued reading from the fax, "Now there's a thing Thomas, they both worked out of the organization's Paris office, but the headquarters' are in Antwerp, and what do you think Thomas? they were investigating illicit diamond smuggling. You could be right about our two friends; we'll have to watch them a bit more closely.

I also think we'll have to contact this office in Paris to see what Jean-Claude and George Obayo had found out.

But in the mean time when we return to our office, you can get in touch with your friends in London and see what you can find out about Obayo's movements over the last month or so".

CHAPTER FOURTEEN

It was the first Tuesday of December and the night for the Charities Committee meeting.

The members all met in 'The Farmers Arms' for a drink and a chat while they waited for their committee room to warm up, the wall heater's were never turned on until approximately an hour before their meeting or for whatever the purpose the room was being used for.

Fred always collected the key from the caretaker on his way down to the meeting and called in at the hall to check that everything was all right, especially on this occasion as the Police had been using it for three weeks as their crime scene office. He found everything in order and checked that the heaters were working before proceeding down to the Farmers Arms to meet the rest of the Committee.

Joyce and Ron were the first to arrive followed shortly afterwards by the rest of the Committee Member's, including

Nigel Courtney who had been invited to the meeting by the Colonel.

While the Committee Member's were gathering and enjoying their pre meeting drink, the Colonel gave his reason for inviting Nigel along.

After finishing their drinks they all proceeded to the village hall to commence their meeting at eight o'clock.

The meeting got underway without any reference to what had happened at the Bonfire and Firework display, much to the Colonels and Nigel's relief. The Committee discussed the carol singing event where the local church choir and the choral society walked round the village carrying lanterns and collecting money, it was agreed that this year the money should go to the church.

They then discussed the Old Folks Christmas party, then went to arrange the food parcel collection for the under privileged families, this food parcel collection was very popular in the village. The villagers gave generously and on an average two hundred Christmas Hampers was distributed each year to the under privileged families.

Sergeant Hopper, who had arrived late, listened to the discussions then suggested.

"In the light of recent events, they should make their collection's over a shorter period of time, and to concentrate in one area at a time". Pausing he added "The carol singing and collecting should start at about six o'clock finishing at about eight thirty, so that people could get home earlier".

After a short pause for any response to his suggestions, Sergeant Hopper continued, "If that was possible, I might be able to arrange for one or two off duty Constables to accompany them".

"That's an idea", Nigel interupted "I might be able to help there, I'll see if I can arrange for some of my Security men to help".

Sergeant Hopper looked at Nigel.

"Do you think that you can arrange that? I mean they will have to travel down from Solihull won't they?"

"Not everyone of my employees live there, you know. I have one or two who live out this way, I'll see what I can do".

"Right, it would be a help Mr. Courtney if you could do that". Sergeant Hopper said, rising from the table "I've got to go now, duty calls, thanks for letting me interrupt your meeting, but I thought that it was worth mentioning".

"I didn't think there was any danger here now", said Joyce.

"You can't be too careful", said the Sergeant picking up his hat and leaving the hall.

"What do you make of all that?" asked Bill after the Sergeant had left.

"I think he maybe taking it too far" the Colonel replied "But, mind you he made a good suggestion regarding not spreading our efforts in small parties all over the village. It might be quicker to concentrate in one area at a time, and also we may not need so many people out at the same time."

"Yes" agreed Joyce "all the handbills have been distributed by the Guides and Scouts and they have agreed to help us provided that we can arrange for, adults to be with them at all times. The respective group leaders are a bit concerned over their safety and I agree with that. Can you arrange for any of your security boys to come along, Nigel?"

"I think I can. When does it begin?"

"Next week, beginning Monday evening then every evening until we finish. It usually takes four or five nights depending how many people we get to help."

"Okay" said Nigel "I'll see how many I can muster and I'll see if I can scrounge any donations from our food distributors."

They discussed the collection for another ten minutes and then went on with other business.

"Are we going to have a Christmas tree on the village green?" Ron asked.

"I think that in spite of everything that has happened in the village. We should have the light's around the green again with carol singing around the tree and the hot chestnuts the same as we did last year" the Colonel repleid

"I agree" responded Nigel enthusiastically, warming to the idea of the coming event, "You tell me where you want the tree collected and I'll arrange for that, it's the least I can do. I am only just realizing what I have been missing in village life."

"Well" said Joyce "I'm afraid this is the way of village life. Town people say it is interfering and being nosy but it's our way of helping each other."

"It is really nice to be accepted by the village," said Nigel.

The meeting closed at ten-o clock so that they could have a nightcap as usual at the Farmers Arms.

Colonel Brown was the first member of the committee to reach the bar. After ordering the first round of drinks, he turned to the rest of the members saying.

"That's the best meeting we have had for ages."

"It's not very often I agree with you, Colonel but this time I do and to prove it, the next round is on me" said Joe, the landlord returning to his side of the bar.

"Crumbs" exclaimed Joyce, looking at her watch "My Bert will wonder what has happened to me. I'd better go, anybody else coming my way?"

"I think I had better be off as well" remarked Fred Perkins "Coming, Ron?" he asked his old colleague.

All three left the Farmers Arms and the remaining four started to discuss the problems the recent spate of deaths were causing them.

"Careful" said the Colonel "Walls have ears."

Bill Selby suggested they ought to discuss what action they were going to take to avoid getting any further involved.

Nigel informed them of his intention to have a meeting with Inspector Sullivan. Because of information he had received from Jos'e of pressure being brought to bear on him by a London Company wishing to do business with his Civil Engineering Company. Also he thought they were interested in taking over his transport company and according to Jose they were unscrupulous individuals.

"Oh, good heavens" said Bill "not more people getting involved. This could mean more people getting hurt and I was under the impression that there was no risk at all."

"Stop whining, Bill, you know there is always risk when you are making money that's what life's all about. Nigel didn't say that anyone was going to get hurt, he said he did not like the type of pressure that was being brought on him by the London Company. It has nothing to do with you, Tom or me. Am I correct, Nigel? Asked the Colonel.

"You're quite right, Colonel. I should not have mentioned it; it is none of your business. I'm sorry that I did."

"That's alright," said Tom "It's just that Bill and I are not used to this sort of operation, we thought that all we were doing was to have money available for insurance. We did not realize how big the thing was until the Colonel brought the money to me for safekeeping. I know you have other things on your mind, Colonel but when are you coming to put it in safe deposit?"

"I'll come round on Thursday," suggested the Colonel.

Nigel arrived home at eleven thirty to be met at the front door of his Manor House by his Chief of Security, David Simpkins.

The Security Chief and Nora his wife, at his suggestion, had moved into the Manor House with Nigel two days after Bert Pearson's murder so that Nigel would not be on his own at night. Mrs. Woolford still did the housework for Nigel, leaving Nora clear to keep her position as a teacher at a school in Solihull.

Since his arrival at the Manor, David had been modifying and updating the security system. He had installed a laser beam at the front gate that sounded a bell in the kitchen and bedroom when you broke the beam as you passed through it. He had also installed three video cameras that recorded all movements around the house day and night. After dark, infrared beams when broken switched on floodlights and started the cameras, which was similar to the system at Courtney Holdings Companies.

David joined Courtney Holdings when he had finished his twenty years of service in the investigation division of the Royal Military Police ending his career with the rank of Captain.

He organized and maintained his Security Department at Courtney Holdings with military precision.

As they went into the study to check the video cameras, Nigel mentioned that he was considering reporting his conversation with Jose' Cordova to Chief Inspector Sullivan. David suggested he should consult some private investigators first because the police did not seem to be making any headway. He then advised Nigel of some of his ex-colleagues who had formed a company and would be available if he wished to use their services. Nigel said he would like to think about this and would let David know his decision the next morning.

The following morning, when David arrived in his office on the top floor of the three-story office block, his secretary informed him that Nigel would like to see him in his office.

As he entered he saw Nigel standing by the window looking down into the yard at the front of the warehouse entrance.

"You know, David, there isn't much that goes on in this office and warehouse complex that you don't know about is there".

"Quite right, Sir" he replied pompously "I think I can safely say that I have the confidence of the staff, they have consulted me on some of their domestic problems at times. I had complete confidence in Bert Pearson when he was killed, despite, the gossip that Bert was involved in a burglary at the house, and there must have been an argument."

"You have to admit, it does look a bit like that but we know different, don't we?" said Nigel. "Mrs. Woolford, poor soul, feels that she is responsible for what happened, it was her who asked him to go up to the house to check the fuel tank in the first place. She has been my housekeeper since I moved in four years ago and it was the arrangement that whenever I was away she would visit the house during the afternoon to check the burglar alarm and that the floodlights were working. When he collected the keys for the house she had told him the lights also appeared to be faulty. His murderer must have caught him completely by surprise when he came up from the basement after he had reset the trip on the junction box because the lights were on when I got home. The Police agree that must have been what happened."

After Nigel had finished, David looked across at him and asked

"Now, Sir, would you mind taking me into your confidence, like all the rest of the staff, and let me know everything?. I have the same feeling as Inspector Sullivan and his Sergeant that you are not telling them everything. You see, sir, if you don't confide in me, I can't help you. Everything you tell me will be confidential and I will not break that confidence at any time, it would be against my code of ethics."

"If you are quite sure" said Nigel guardedly and looking his Security Chief straight in the eye. "There is something that hasn't been mentioned to the Police but there are more than me involved and if I do give you this information it will have to be in the strictest confidence."

Nigel then started to tell David all that he knew of the case including how he had become involved with a Brigadier through the Colonel and his two associates the Bill Selby and Ted Broughton". Pausing Nigel then continued, "I feel completely knackered. That was worse than talking to the police."

He walked over to the drink's cabinet and poured them both a stiff whiskey.

"Here's good health and let's hope we have a quick conclusion to all this. What do you think our chances are?"

"Well" replied David thoughtfully "I would say that the four of you are the most 'Naive Diamond' smugglers that I have come across. I have caught one or two when I was stationed in Germany and I don't know how you have lasted so long, but having said that, you should thank those two drivers you had on the smuggling runs for keeping you out of trouble. I only hope that you're not into anything else, are you?" he asked, then continuing," I'll take these notes back to my office and give you my thoughts on how to solve the problem tonight."

Nigel suggested he should invite the Colonel over to dinner this evening, he thought the Colonel was the only one of the three who he could rely on, and he could also give him more information on the Brigadier.

David went back to his office, on his way through his secretary's office he said.

"No callers or calls for the rest of the day except Mr.Courtney".

"Understood Mr. Simpkins" replied Vera without looking up and carrying on typing.

He sat down at his desk and started to read all the notes he taken whilst he had been talking to Nigel.

After reading them a second time he went over to a typewriter on a table by the wall and started to type out all his notes making alterations where he thought necessary. When he had finished he sat in deep though for a few minutes and then said to himself "where's the motive?" and grabbing a note pad on the table beside the typewriter wrote:

MOTIVE

1. Cash - No.   No.
2. Diamonds etc.   Could be.
   Brigadier.   Doubtful buys them anyway.
   Who else interested
   Police   Doubtful, big shout if first body was one of theirs.
3. Drugs Doubtful.   Police As above. Drivers Two.

Driver One.

Brian Buckley (Gentleman Brian). Always smart, wife works, new Honda Civic, good timekeeper, trustworthy quiet nature.

Driver Two.

Tom O'Keefe. Clean and tidy, good worker, wife works, buying his own Council house, very good timekeeper, trustworthy, new Rover Montego. 'TOUGHNUT'.

Traffic Manager cannot fault their work very good reports from Customers.

When he had finished the list, David remembered the report on the red Ferrari, parked at the front of the warehouse. He checked back through his files and when he found it, added the details of the report to his motive list. He then put everything in a folder and placed them in his briefcase for reference later. It wasn't until Vera put her head round the door and wished him goodnight that he realized the time.

"Good days work and a nice piece of window dressing", he said smiling to himself.

Nigel arrived home early to ask David's wife Nora, if she would be kind enough to prepare a meal for four people, informing her that the Colonel would be coming to dinner. He was too late her husband had already informed her and asked her to cook Nigel's favorite Scotch Angus Beef steak's.

After a hearty meal, the three men retired to the library for further Brandies and for David to question the Colonel. When he finished, he felt satisfied that what the Colonel had told him tallied with what Nigel had already informed him.

"So, that's okay, now Colonel, what can you tell me about Brigadier Smythe-White, can you give me chapter and verse on him or shall I have to get it from the army files?"

"I can't tell you much about him, David. I served in the desert with him. We were First Lieutenants in the Blues and Royals and we were posted to Palestine, after that we came back to Aldershot then we split up and he went to Germany and I went to Karachi, India. I didn't meet him again until '72 or '73. That was at Tidworth on Salisbury Plain where he was my Brigadier, but he was stationed at Aldershot and I was a Colonel, my command was at Tidworth. We served together for our last five years and we each completed thirty years service. It was when he was serving in Germany that he started dealing in jewelry. He used to go to Amsterdam for it and he would sell it in the mess or downtown in Nuremberg where we were stationed. I know that when he went on leave he would always travel by road, stay overnight at Amsterdam and then caught the Ferry from the Hook of Holland to Felixstowe. I only traveled with him once, he was too devious for me."

"Thank you" said David "I'll check with army records and see what else I can come up with. They might have had an eye on him. I know that I didn't come across him when I was in the service."

"By the way" said the Colonel "the police think that they may have found the knife that was used on Bert Pearson. They found it this morning in my old cart shed it was tucked up in the rafters with a pair of rubber gloves that were covered in blood and they were in a Safeway carrier bag. It seems the police think that Mike may have been sat in his office and that he spotted someone down the yard, got his gun from the gun rack and went down there to investigate. You see the cart shed is close by the Dutch barn where he was found. Police think he was attacked from behind with a blunt instrument such as a pipe or piece of wood."

"Why did he pick up the shotgun?" David asked "Surely he didn't reach for his gun every time a stranger entered the yard?"

"No but we don't know the circumstances at the time, do we? The wife and I were out, Tom and Harry his two hands, were doing hedge cutting and laying down the hedge on the twenty acre on that day and they wouldn't have been expected back until about half fourish but they would have been bringing the cows back in for milking with them anyway. So, if he saw anyone acting suspicious, especially being on his own. I think there may be a possibility he may have picked up the gun as a safety measure, don't you?". The Colonel asked.

"Maybe, but thank you, Colonel" said David "that has helped me a lot. Now I think that the same person has killed three, or four, people. We have two broken necks, they're the first and the fourth, the second was a hit and run, the third could have been another broken neck but the killer couldn't use that method so he had to use his backup that was the knife. Now I think my initial plan of action will be to hire in one of the two people I mentioned to you this morning Nigel. I'm going to keep a low profile on this investigation because I think I'm too well known in the underworld to start with. I helped to put too many behind bars when I was in the Special Investigation Branch. I'll arrange for my friends to come over to my office in the morning for a briefing then we'll start our fight back. I think we'll start from the farthest point, Antwerp, seeing as the first victim came from that area and that the second one was associated with him. I received this information from a colleague down at the local nick just before dinner; he also informed me that he heard on the grapevine that one of their Inspectors was going over to the Continent on this case. Apparently he's on an early shift tomorrow so he will be able to check the files for me to see if there's any further development's, and will contact me if he needs to".

"Great" said the Colonel "we seem to be starting to do something at last. I hate this waiting game. If you want any errands run at any time give me a call, David."

"What about money to finance this project?" asked Nigel. "I suggest we use the money that is in Tom's safe at the moment, Colonel."

"Good idea" agreed the Colonel.

"Can I ask you what you are going to do with this money?" asked David. "Can I suggest that it is brought to your office Nigel for easy access? It would also be safer in your office than at Tom's with your security system."

"Right" said Nigel "You arrange for your two friends to pick it up when they come to your office tomorrow. I'll phone Tom in the morning and tell him to expect them and give him their details for identification. I'll tell him they are going to take it to the bank for us. By the way, David, the money to pay for the Diamonds came out of my offshore account in the first place, so you needn't worry about it being traced through the works or my personal account."

"How much is there?" asked David.

"Ooh, I should think about a quarter of a mil. wouldn't you agree Nigel?" replied the Colonel.

"I would think about that," replied Nigel nodding his head.

"Jesus! As much as that?" answered David surprised at the nonchalance way that his two colleagues answered, "No wonder you suggested my friends pick it up for you, even I wouldn't feel safe with that much on me."

"Okay" said Nigel "I think that is everything. It's getting late and I think we ought to join Nora for a nightcap before you leave, Colonel nothing more is there David?"

"No that's all for now" replied David, still feeling shaken after the revelation of the amount of money involved.

"What's happening down on the farm, Colonel?" asked Nigel as they proceeded down the passage to the lounge to join Nora.

"The wife and I are still sleeping at her friends place. We have done that since the night that it happened. The police have been swarming all over the place but I'm certain they have now finished. There was only one policeman patrolling out there the other afternoon when I went out to the farm. Oh! By the way, I've asked Harold Johnson if his lad wants a job. He's left school and can't find a work anywhere and he's a pretty bright lad too. I've told Harold that if his son does start on the farm, and he likes it I will pay for him to go to the Agricultural College at Cirencester. That should give him an incentive, shouldn't it?"

Nora couldn't help overhearing the conversation as Nigel and his colleagues entered the lounge.

She looked up at the Colonel.

"If he doesn't want the job, let me know because my sister's son, he's seventeen, got two 'A' levels, but can't find a job in Walsall so he's trying for a position in the Parks Department. I'm certain that he would jump at it," she asked.

"Okay" said the Colonel "Ask him to come and see me, you can tell him that if he accepts the job, he can sleep in with us. I've got plenty of rooms to spare and between you and me if they both accept and they are both good workers. I'll put them both through college. There's not enough youngster's coming into the farming industry today."

They settled into general conversation for the remainder of the evening, also having a nightcap before the Colonel left.

CHAPTER FIFTEEN

The Chief Inspector was reading the forensic report on the knife and rubber gloves that had been found in the cart shed at Haydock Dyke Farm and found the blood group was the same as Bert Pearson's. At the sametime he was muttering.

"I'm sure someone is playing silly buggers here, and got caught by Mike as they were hiding these in the cart shed where they would easily be found; hoping it would throw suspicion onto the Colonel or Mike. Now, who is that someone?"

He started to walk towards the door of his office, stopped, changed his mind, walked back to his desk and sat down, deep in thought.

He gazed out of the office window.

The sun was starting to break through the clouds on this dull Friday morning of the first week of December. He watched a car drive past the police station with its luggage boot lid up and a Christmas tree hanging out.

"Crumbs! It's nearly Christmas and I'll be working if I don't get this case sorted"

He continued to sit there for a sjort while longer, then picking up the case file, which by now was quite thick, he opened it and picked out the last reports that he had received and started to read through them again.

When he had finished them he got up from his chair and went through to Sergeant Thomas's office. Who, looking up from his typing asked, "I was just going to ask you if you wanted a cup of coffee".

"Good idea" replied the Inspector "let's go down to the canteen for one".

After they had finished their coffee and toast, the Inspector pushed the plates to one side and pulled two sheets of blank paper out of his pocket and looked over to his Sergeant.

"Do you know, Thomas, it is only seventeen days to Christmas and if we don't get this case sewn up, we'll be working over Christmas. Now, as I see it "continued the Chief Inspector, taking a pen from his pocket "I think that we can close the investigation down on the farm, there isn't anything more there for us. Its nearly a week since Mike Smith was murdered and I think we have found all we were intended to find, but not probably exactly the way it was intended. What do you think?"

"I'm inclined to agree with you "the Sergeant agreed nodding his head "I've just written out my reports and they don't tell me anything. I was going to suggest that I pay Mrs. Smith's boy friend a visit but that's about all I can think of, for the moment, there was another idea I was going to suggest, sir and that was that we go back to the beginning and start again".

"What makes you say that, Thomas?"

"Well, sir, we have four victims and, as I see it, two were intended and two weren't. The last two stumbled on to something that they shouldn't have done; they were in the wrong place at the wrong time. I think that the root of our problem is in this area, Stratford-on-Avon, but I don't think we are going to find it digging around here. I think we are going to have to go to London and work our way back here".

"You're thinking along the same lines as me, Thomas." The Chief Inspector was writing as he was talking.

"You can tell the Colonel that we are closing investigations at the farm this afternoon. That should please him, I'm sending Carter and Hopkins over to Antwerp and you, Sergeant, can go down to London with PC. Boyce. You can also call at Interpol's office, ask to see Mr. Fraser, he's in charge of drugs and precious stone offenses or so he says. I'll have to clear this first with the Super but I think it will be Okay; he's having his backside kicked by the watch committee. I think I'll check out this boyfriend while you're away. Where does Mrs. Smith work?"

"It's a transport company over at the airfield at Honeybourne, sir. It's called I.T. Transport Ltd. "said the Sergeant referring to his notes "The Company's at Unit 22 The Old Airfield, Honeybourne. Do you want the Managers Name? or will you ask for Mrs. Smith? The manager is Mr. Terrence Baxter. He has been with the company the whole time it has been out there". Carried on the Sergeant reading from his notebook "They started up in West Bromwich eight years ago and have been at their present site for five years. That was when they started warehousing and groupage deliveries to the Continent, and have been expanding their fleet over the last three years. They have twenty vehicles operating at the moment, both here and abroad and are one of the few companies who run four Multi-lateral permits."

"My word, Sergeant, You have been doing your homework"

"Not really, sir I have a friend in the local Chamber of Commerce and he found most of this for me."

"Those are the right kind of friends to have, Thomas. I'll nip over and get the O.K. for these trips from the Super and you get off to the farm" Looking at his watch, the Chief Inspector said "I tell you what we'll do, Thomas. It's nearly half past twelve. We'll go out to the farm together and you can buy me lunch."

"Blimey. I'm being caught again, aren't I? We could call in at 'The Coat of Arms' at Welford. I'm told they serve a good pint there as well as good food and the interesting thing is that a few people from the airfield get in there at lunchtime. If we miss them, the landlord may still be able to tell us something."

The Chief Inspector and Sergeant Thomas arrived at Haydock Farm just after one o'clock.

The Colonels wife was just coming out of the back door of the house as they drove into the yard.

She walked over to the policemen's car.

As the Chief Inspector got out of the car she informed them that the Colonel was down in the fields with the men fixing some electrical fencing.

"That's alright, Mrs. Brown we just called to tell the Colonel that we are closing down the investigations here this afternoon. I hope that we have not disturbed you too much. I understand you have been sleeping at your friends."

"Yes, Chief Inspector, we've been staying at a friend of mine, you may know her or her husband. He's a solicitor. Hilda and Ron Fletcher, they live at the Poplars, it's a nice house, stands off the road on the way to Bidford, on the other side of the village. Very nice people, wouldn't take anything for our keep, she says 'that's what friends are for in time of need'".

"Yes, quite Mrs. Brown. If you wouldn't mind telling your husband when he comes in that we won't be bothering you anymore".

The Chief Inspector got back into his car and Mrs. Brown walked slowly back into the farmhouse; quite forgetting what she had intended to do before she saw the policemen come into the yard.

Sergeant Thomas, in the meantime, had found Inspector Carter and P.C. Hopkins in Mike Smith's office, which was established in the old harness room on the opposite side of the yard. The room had been built on the side of the feed store and had been converted into a large office with a cloakroom. It was furnished with a large desk positioned near the window enabling anyone to see down the yard. Along the inside wall was a long worktable and on it were a computer and several plans of the farm.

Hanging on the long outside wall were two, two-foot square photographs of the farm. They had both been taken from the air at different altitudes.

On the same wall was the shotgun cabinet that had a high-quality combination lock on the door. The Colonel and Mike were the only one's that knew the number's that opened the lock.

The two aerial photographs had intrigued Sergeant Thomas when he first saw them on the night that Mike Smith had been murdered. Now he seemed to be more interested, so much so, that after he had told Carter and Hopkins to close down their enquiries at the farm. He walked out to his Chief who was sitting in the car awaiting his return, and asked him to come over to the office to have further look at the photographs.

Sergeant Thomas pointed out to the Chief Inspector that the photographs were taken from different altitudes and that the one taken from the higher altitude showed two lanes, one each side of the farm.

"That lane, on the north side is quite open, but this one, on the south side has high hedges along it and it stretches right across the picture. As if it could have been a disused railway track and, as you can see, that hedge there runs across from the farm up to the track. So whoever committed this murder could have parked their car there, where the old track crossed the road. It would have been hidden from anyone on the road also from the farm and they could have run along this hedge into the farm without being seen.

"I agree, Sergeant. Have you checked this out, Carter" asked the Chief Inspector.

"Yes, sir we've checked both lanes thoroughly. That one on the north side showed plenty of tractor tire marks but the other one is all stones left there from the old rail lines and its well and truly overgrown with weeds."

"I think we'll give it the once over before we leave, Sergeant. Come on, all four of us can go, we'll take the car's over, then we can call at the pub afterwards".

The two cars with the four Policemen drove round to where the old railway used to cross over the road. As they drew up Sergeant Thomas looked across at his superior officer and said,

"It looks as though we have about an hour and a half maybe two hours of daylight left, sir, although as it's been a bit sunnier today we may have a bit longer".

"Yes, Thomas, I have noticed. So let's get on with it. How many men did you have to check this over?" Chief Inspector Sullivan asked as they all walked on to the old permanent way.

"I had four constables, sir from the local Nick," replied Inspector Carter.

They carried on walking down the old track to the farmhouse.

"How long did they spend checking it?" the Chief Inspector asked again.

"About four hours, sir. It was raining very heavily and blowing half a gale on the day but they did say that they had been very thorough, sir".

"They all say that, Carter. Didn't you or Hopkins keep an eye on them? Really Carter, when are you going to learn? You book types are all the same you believe everything you are told. It seems to me that there are a lot of tire marks about. I suppose this place gets used a lot".

"Yes, sir" said Carter "Old Harry Bartlett, one of the Colonel's hands told me that both of the lanes are used frequently by courting couples in cars, especially in the summer months and after the pubs close, he say's some evenings you've a job to put a pin between the car's".

"How does he know that? is he a pimp or something ?".

"He occasionally patrols the farm, you know, turkey patrol near Christmas, like now and also at lambing time, sheep rustling etc." They reached the gate, which gave access to the farm and as usual it was open.

"The Colonel, as you see sir, has adopted the track on both sides of the road, and put gates into all his fields on both sides to give access from the track, so that it saves him having to cross any of his fields after they're seeded", said Carter.

"So I can see, Carter. I think you had better get those men back tomorrow and give this place a good going over, again, and do it better than last time and take it both sides of the road as well".

"Yes, sir" replied a rather subdued Carter.

"Sir" called Hopkins as the other three policemen were walking back down the track. "I think I may have found something, sir. It looks as if somebody has parked their car as close to the hedge as they could. There is about four or five foot of tyre marks along the side of the stones, finishing here almost at the hedge and, look sir, there's some broken branches as well". Chief Inspector Sullivan was squat down on the track looking closely at some tread marks,

"It looks as if the other back wheel was here, Hopkins, when they stopped".

"Yes, sir, they must have got some very bad scratches on their car. Look at the size of these branches that are broken".

"You'd better get the forensic boys out here as well, Carter and you'd better hang on to the office until you have finished here.

So, clear it with the Colonel, wont you?"

Chief Inspector Sullivan and Sergeant Thomas left the other two detectives closely examining the tire marks and walked back to their car.

As they approached the car, the radio was calling the Chief Inspector. He answered the call and found it was an urgent message asking him to telephone Jose Cordova at the Midland Hotel in Birmingham. He returned to the incident room at the farm and telephoned Jose', who answered the call at the first ring,

"Hi, Inspector, I've been waiting for your call. I've got to talk with you. Where can we meet?", Jose said in desperation.

"What's the rush, Jose? Can't it wait until tonight?"

"No, Inspector, I've got to see you as soon as possible."

"If it is that urgent, do you know a place on the outskirts of Birmingham called Shirley?"

"Yes, Inspector. I do".

"Right. On the Henley in Arden road out of Shirley there's a pub called 'The Chestnut Tree'. Its quite a big place and has a restaurant on the side of it, I'll phone and book a table for three for half past five, I'll ask for a quiet table where we can talk without being disturbed. If you are there first ask for Mr. Sullivan's table. By the way, have you still got the Cavalier?"

"No I have not, why do you ask?"

It is just that I would have known if you had arrived before us"

"I see," said Jose hesitantly "You said three. Who is the other one?"

"The other one is my Sergeant. I have to go now if we are to meet you at the Chestnut Tree at half past five, I'll have to go back to my office to pick something up and then I'll be on my way. See you later". With that he put down the phone.

As he walked out of the door he looked at his watch.

"Come on, Thomas," he said "we'll have to get a move on if we are to meet Cordova as planned. While we are at the office I want you to arrange for the forensic boys to be there as well".

"We can't do that, sir. It's not our patch" protested the Sergeant.

"Don't tell me what I can and can't do, Thomas just do as I say".

"What do you want them out there for?"

"I thought they could take a plaster mould of his tires and anything else they can think of. I don't think you have anything to worry about Thomas because, if I'm right in my thinking he will park his car out the back, out of sight and I want you to get out there as soon as you have made these arrangements. I want you there before he arrives, cos. I can't remember if he said he had changed his car or not when I asked".

"Well, sir, you didn't give him much time to. You put the phone down on him too quick".

It was a dry chilly evening when Jose arrived at the Chestnut Tree public house, all the floodlights were on and only two cars were in the car park. He drove very slowly onto the car park as if he were looking for someone, still driving slowly he carried on round to the back of the public house to the restaurant. He drove into a parking slot and stopped then looked around again. It was as light as day with all the floodlights on and he switched off the engine and relaxed as if he were safe here. He glanced at his watch and noted that it was only three minutes past five.

He did not see the car that had arrived after him and parked on the public house forecourt.

Jose sat awhile then decided to wait inside the restaurant for the two policemen. He was about to get out of the car when there was a tap on the window. The door was partly opened and a voice said.

"Are you Jose Cordova," The stranger asked in a gruff voice.

"Who are you?" asked Jose nervously.

"I'm Sergeant Thomas, Chief Inspector Sullivan's assistant. Here's my I.D. The man took a step back, pulled his hat down further over his eyes and reached into his inside pocket. Jose, thinking that the man was who he said he was, didn't move at all and realized too late that the man had pulled out a revolver with a silencer on it. He fired two shots into Jose's head. Jose slumped forward over the steering wheel; his killer grabbed him and pulled him back against the driving seat. He then placed him into a position to look as though he was sleeping in the car. The killer walked back to the front of the public house and got into his car. As he started the engine, he leaned back, took off his hat and shook out his long hair.

Sergeant Thomas drove onto the car park followed by Tom Davies from the Stratford-on-Avon Police forensic team.

He knew they were fifteen minute's early, having noticed the time on a clock hanging outside a jeweler's shop as they drove through Henley in Arden.

They both drove slowly round to the rear car park by the restaurant. As they stopped Sergeant Thomas noticed a dark blue Vauxhall Carlton parked on its own. As he undid his seatbelt, he looked across at the car, noticing the driver was slumped backward in the front seat with his head against the doorpost as if he were asleep.

He got out of the car picking up his torch from under the seat. It was a long metal torch that showed signs of long service by the dents on it. He walked across to the Carlton and knocked on the window, the driver did not move. He tried to open the door but found it locked. He shone his torch into the car and still got no response. It was only when he shone his torch through the windscreen onto the driver that he recognized Jose Cordova and saw that he had been shot in the head.

Tom, who had been sat in his car, keeping a low profile until the coast was clear for him to take a plaster cast of the tires on Jose's car, got out of his car when he saw Sergeant Thomas lean over the windscreen. He ran over to the edge of the car park and picked up a brick. As he ran back to the Sergeant he shouted,

"Stand back, Sergeant, we'll have to break the window",

With that he gave two hefty blows to the drivers window, which broke on the second blow. He dropped the brick and leaning into the car placed two fingers on the driver's neck, no pulse beat, he turned to Sergeant Thomas.

"He's dead, Sarge".

"That's the bloke we have come here to meet", replied the stunned Sergeant Thomas. "Oh hell, Tom! What next! That's five that have been chopped. I wouldn't be surprised if the Yard is called in now".

"Between you and me, Sarge, I've heard that they are already in and there's a Commander Benfield and his sidekick already on their way here" replied Tom Davis.

"Thank heaven for that" replied Sergeant Thomas "I think that old Duffy Sullivan is a bit out of his depth with this one. He's all right on burglaries and single murders but when you get something like this, you don't know if you have a serial killer or gang warfare. I think this is something that's too big for him anyway, I'd better call him on the cellular and tell him what's happened. He can't be too far away".

Whilst the Sergeant was on the phone to his Chief Inspector, Tom brought his car over and parked it on the opposite side of the Carlton. He took a blanket from the boot of the car and covered Jose. He then stood with his back leaning against the car covering the broken window so that anyone coming into the restaurant area could not see anything.

The Chief Inspector arrived on the scene quicker than the Sergeant expected. He took a quick look at Jose and asked if they had done anything. Tom replied that nothing had been touched and if he did anything it would only be what he was here to do because he was on somebody else's patch and it was no concern of his.

The Sergeant looked up quickly at his Chief.

"I think I will go into the pub and see if they saw or heard anything".

"Right, Thomas. I'll get on to the local nick and inform them. I'll wait for you in the restaurant, so I'll be in there if either of you want me".

They both left Tom to get on with, 'what he had come over to do'.

Sergeant Thomas reported to the Chief Inspector in the restaurant that only one of the bar staff in the public house had seen anything. That was one of the barmen when he was closing the curtains in the bar, saw a man get into a Citroen that was parked facing the road and drove off turning left as if it was going to Henley in Arden.

"I have all the details, sir. He said that the car drove off about an hour ago, so I didn't think there was any need for us to panic".

"No, you're quite right, Thomas". I'll wait here for the local police. You go on back and take Davis with you. I'll see to everything here. I'll see you in the morning".

CHAPTER SIXTEEN

David Simpkins and his two associates were sitting in his office having a well-earned cup of coffee.

The collection of the money from Atkinson & Associates office had gone off very smoothly. David thought he saw a look of relief on Tom Atkinson's face as he said goodbye to them and watched them drive off the office car park.

They had now returned to his office and were discussing the case and deliberating what steps he and his two colleagues Brian Tomlinson and George Oaksey of Tower Investigations would take in the case. After a lot of talking and heated discussion it was decided to put their proposed plan of campaign in writing and get the approval from Nigel Courtney. In the meantime Brian and George were to return to their own office in Birmingham to get things organized and be ready to start on the case the following morning.

It was agreed to bring in someone not so well known around the underworld in Birmingham and London as they were. That someone they hoped would be their new partner who should be joining them in two weeks time but whom they hoped would start working with them immediately.

On arrival at the office of Tower Investigations, Brian asked his receptionist to contact their new partner, Brenda Armstrong.

When Brian answered the phone he apologized for making his call two or three days earlier than agreed, afterwards explaining his reasons for the call, he then gave the thumbs up sign to George. Brenda accepted his apology and agreed to meet them in the morning. She said she was getting bored with her holiday it was six weeks since she had left the Army.

Brenda lived at Bromsgrove, so it was arranged that she meet George at Courtney Transport in Solihull.

The following morning David Simpkins and George Oaksey were standing at the window in David's office looking across at the main gate into Courtney Transport when a black Ford Escort XR3 drove into the parking area in front of the office block. The drivers door opened and a very smart, well dressed young lady in a camel driving coat and black skirt got out of the car. Her hair was dark shoulder length and well brushed she carried a brown leather brief case.

She locked the car door and walked over to the office.

"That's the lady we've been waiting for," said George turning away from the window.

After being introduced to David, he asked Brenda,

"If she could handle cases of a very complex and confidential nature"

"I would not have contacted George and Brian if I hadn't thought I could. I think that my rank held in the army and my CV. should be sufficient to clarify that point, Mr. Simpkins" Brenda replied sharply "It was because of men like you that I didn't try for the police force. After twenty-five years in the service; I joined when I was seventeen. Working my way through the ranks in the Royal Military Police. I think I can handle men like you Mr. Simpkins" continued Brenda still smarting from the remark "Incidentally I'm a woman, not a dyke. I like men but business always come's first. I retired from the service with the rank of Major. Do I qualify?"

"I'm sorry, Brenda" David replied sheepishly "Such questions have to be asked".

He then left George and Brenda in his office.

Returning a short while later with a pink manila wallet. As he sat down he took a blue plastic binder and a sheaf of papers from the wallet.

Giving the binder to Brenda he said,

"That's my full report of the case I suggest you read it here and we will meet later to discuss it. I have arranged for you to use the boardroom, you will not be disturbed there".

The meeting reconvened in David's office at two o'clock when he asked Brenda for her opinion on the case.

"I think it's a very complex situation and, by rights, the people involved should be locked up for smuggling, but seeing that they have stopped they should be warned that if they started again it would be reported to the police," said Brenda.

"Oh, I don't think they will try again, Brenda. I think they have been well and truly scared off by the events that have taken place".

"I hope so, I really hope so. If it's what I think it is, we're playing a dangerous game and I will only play it if the police are informed that the Colonel and his associates are employing us. Our mandate being to try and solve the case but it looks to me as if we are being employed mainly to keep them out of trouble, am I right?"

"Yes and no. We keep them out of trouble if we can but if we have to sacrifice, we will do. Understand?"

"Mr. Simpkins, lets get one thing very clear," said Brenda getting up from her chair and walking round the office "If, and I repeat, if, I take on this case, I play it my way and my way only".

"Okay, Brenda we'll play it your way. By the way, I've just been informed that there is a Commander Benfield and his side kick Inspector White coming up to help Inspector Sullivan. I don't think he will like that, do you George7"

Before George could answer Brenda said,

"Oh crumbs! Benny Benfield and Snowy White the Terrible Twins. We worked on an arms smuggling case together. Bennie thought he was a ladies man until I slapped him down once or twice then we got on well together. He's very good, very clever I look forward to meeting him again. When are they due here?"

"Either today or tomorrow, my informant tells me".

There was a slight lull in the conversation as Brenda referred to her notebook.

"I think I'll make an appointment with Chief Inspector Sullivan tomorrow to inform him of our intentions. I hope he will then introduce me to Bennie. I'm firmly of the opinion that nobody is supposed to know anything of this latest move on your part, are they?". Brenda asked looking questioningly first at David then at George for confirmation.

Ignoring the question George asked

"Do you need a partner on this one or do you still like to work alone" asked George.

"As you know, George, I'm a loner preferring to put everything on tape" said Brenda pulling a small tape recorder from her handbag and showing both men that it was working.

"I'll ask for assistance if I require it later".

David was just closing the meeting when Nigel Courtney walked in. "I'm sorry I'm late. I promised my local village I'd supply a Christmas tree for the village green and I've just got back from Shrewsbury where I had to collect it.

Brenda was introduced to Nigel who welcomed her 'on board' and holding her hand a little bit longer than necessary. He looked into her intelligent green eyes and delicately made up face with his big brown eyes, he immediately offered her an office next to his on the top floor saying that it would be far more convenient for her to work from here than from the centre of Birmingham. Brenda accepted the offer saying,

"On the few occasions I will need an office away from base it will be handy."

"Good, when shall I expect you, tomorrow?" with that Nigel picked up her brief case and escorted her to her car, "I sincerely hope you get things sorted out pretty quickly, Brenda. I'm really getting scared and I know the other three involved are worried in fact the Colonel told me the other day that Bill Selby and Tom Atkinson are going to Tom's villa in Spain for January and they're scared to death".

Brenda looked up into Nigel's eyes, smiled and said,

"Yes, I know how you feel, Nigel. I'll do my best for you. I'll see you tomorrow after I've been to the police in Stratford".

She started up the engine of her car and drove out of the car park turning right towards Bromsgrove.

CHAPTER SEVENTEEN

Brenda had been discussing the case with Chief Inspector Sullivan for over an hour.

At the beginning of the meeting, the Inspector was not at all overjoyed at the thought of discussing the case with a third party, especially an outsider. Even if she was a private investigator engaged by one or two of his prime suspects. The mere thought of discussing his case with a female appalled him.

Commander Benfield walked into his Chief Inspector's office without knocking he always said that it was one of the privileges that went with his rank.

The Commander was approximately five feet eight inches tall, and approximately twelve stone in weight, he looked very fit for his 42 years. His brown wavy hair was brushed back he wore a navy blue very fine pin stripe suit, with a white shirt and a navy blue Metropolitan police tie. The white handkerchief in his top left-hand pocket was protruding the correct three-quarters of an inch, and his shirt cuffs were also protruding the correct half-inch disclosing the Metropolitan police cuff links.

When Brenda saw him she smiled,

"Good old Benny", she said to herself, "Nothing like creating the right image on your first day."

"Sorry to interrupt, Chief Inspector", he said, noticing that his Chief was not alone as he walked into the office.

As he put the documents he had in his hand onto the desk, he looked across at the Chief Inspectors visitor a look of surprise came over his face when he recognized who it was.

"Major Armstrong", he cried, walking round the desk, and picked up Brenda's left hand and kissed it "What a surprise, what are you doing here?"

"I'm not Major Armstrong now Commander" Brenda replied "I left the Army six weeks ago, I'm working for a company of Private Investigator's, which is the reason for my visit".

"I see, I see", said the Commander. "Can we help her Chief Inspector?"

"I don't know sir, you know we don't like private investigators interfering with case's that we are working on, and the one that Miss Armstrong has come about is the one that we are working on now. I have explained this Commander, Miss Armstrong suggests that we could possibly help each other by passing information to each other at the moment. But that isn't the way we do things in the Police force, is it Commander", the Chief Inspector replied, putting the ball entirely into his Commander's court. Commander Benfield moved a chair to the end of the desk, so that he sat at an angle facing Brenda. He noticed how smartly she was dressed, in a fawn cavalry twill costume, the collar of her dark brown blouse was standing up at the back of her neck with the points laid flat over the lapels of her jacket. The hem of her skirt just above her knee's as she sat with her legs crossed; she was resting her notebook on her thigh.

The Commander had always fancied his chances with Brenda, since he first met her, irrespective of Brenda rebuffing his advances, "Perhaps" he thought, "She's just playing hard to get."

"I'm afraid that I have to agree with the Chief Inspector, Brenda, however, what can you tell me, or, can I ask you? How well did Mr. Courtney and his friends know Jose Cordova?

"Did! Did you say 'did', Commander? Am I right in thinking that something has happened to him?"

"I'm afraid so, he was shot at approximately 5 p.m. last night, at the 'Chestnut Tree' restaurant at Shirley."

"I know 'The Chestnut' Commander, It's a very popular place. But I can give you an alibi for Mr. Courtney, Commander, because he was in his Chief Security Officer's office at 5 p.m. With Mr. Simpkins his Chief Security officer, Mr. Oaksey and myself; I left them at about 5:30 p.m."

"That clears them, Chief Inspector, you still haven't told us how well Mr. Courtney knew him."

"As far as I know he was a business acquaintance. I think that they were discussing the possibility of a business partnership. Something to do with oilfields, I don't know a lot about it, but if you're interested I will find out more for you. Better me than you Commander, charging about like a bull in a china shop."

"Right see what you can do, then, we'll see what we can do together."

The Commander stood up, walked over to Brenda, picked up her hand, kissed the back of it,

"Aurevoir, Mademoiselle Brenda", he said, then turned and walked smartly over to the door.

"You never change, Commander", Brenda remarked, as he turned and looked at Brenda, opening the door he smiled

"Till the next time Brenda", he said quietly, and left the room.

She smiled and shook her head.

"Follow that Chief Inspector, I hope you're not like him."

"No, I hope they broke the mould after he was born", he laughed, "I couldn't stand two of him in the station, anyway Miss Armstrong, I hope you can help us obtain more evidence on this case, because we don't seem to be getting anywhere at the moment, I'm sorry to say."

The phone rang and the Chief Inspector picked it up, he looked across at Brenda, "I'll be right there", he said and put the phone down.

"Please excuse me", he said dashing to the door "Forensic say they have found something that they think I ought to take a look at".

Brenda followed him out of the room.

The telephone call had come from Sergeant Thomas, who was with his friend from forensic, Tom Davis. They were at Haydock Dyke farms; he had called his Chief, after Tom had found particles of red paint on a hawthorn bush, on the old railway track. The bush was close by the spot where D.C. Hopkins had found the tire prints the previous day. It was while he was taking the plaster cast of the prints, he found some small footprints showing where the person 'possibly a female' had got out of the car and walked in the direction of the farm, also the return, which Tom had told the Sergeant showed that the person was in a hurry,

"These" said the laboratory technician "Should be reported to the Chief Inspector immediately before they get anymore rain damage."

Chief Inspector Sullivan arrived at Haydock Dyke Farm in a very short space of time accompanied by his by now, very favorite Commander Benfield. As the Chief Inspector got out of the car, the Commander asked him to get his 'Greenies' out of the car boot for him.

"I don't want to dirty my trousers before I meet the 'press' this afternoon, do I?" he said.

"What press? This afternoon" replied the Chief Inspector.

"Oh, I thought, I ought to speak with the press and let them know that I'm in charge of the case now and also tell them what progress we're making."

"Look sir, you run thing's your way, but, don't drag me into these press releases, the local paper's know that I will call them in when I have got something to report, now let's go and see what Davis and Thomas have for us."

"Alrighty Chiefy, it's the way we do thing's at the yard, we like to keep the press happy, right I'm ready, what do you think?" the Commander said settling a deer stalker hat on his head.

Chief Inspector Sullivan had started to walk towards Sergeant Thomas whom he had seen standing at the window of the Incident room watching their arrival, he stopped and turned around, when he heard his Commander ask him what he thought? He looked at Commander Benfield in his 'Greenies', black military style raincoat and a deerstalker on his head.

"My God" he said "Bloody Sherlock Holmes, that's all I need", shaking his head as he turned and continued walking toward his Sergeant.

Sergeant Thomas watched his Chief Inspector approach the incident room muttering to hisself shaking his head. Then switched his eyes over to Commander Benfield who was now standing in the middle of the yard, looking across at the farmhouse, as Chief Inspector Sullivan came through the door.

"Why do the yard have to send me a "Dandy" like that, Thomas? He doesn't want to get his feet dirty, and look what he's got on his head, he only wants a cape and Dr. Watson then we can all go home."

"Oh he's here already sir, he's over on the old track with Tom Davis."

"Is he now? Thomas, what's he like? I hope he's a lot different to him out there."

"Yes sir, he has his Greenies the same as his boss, I suppose these people from the smoke, think it's the in thing to wear green wellie's when they are in the country. Anyway he hasn't got a deerstalker, he has the conventional yard trilby hat, not like us sir", said Sergeant Thomas putting on his tweed cap.

They both continued to watch their new Commander now doing his gyrations in the yard, looking at all the buildings, as if he had never been on a farm before.

To bring things back to normal, it started to rain.

"I don't know Sergeant people seem to be scared of getting their head and their feet wet. They're all wearing their "Oilies' with a hood on, and "Greenies' to protect themselves. Where as us, we're still wearing our force issue raincoats and "Dunlop Blackie's", come on Thomas, we mustn't keep Sherlock Holmes waiting".

The Chief Inspector took a plastic packet out of his raincoat pocket, when he opened it, he pulled out a yellow plastic 'Sou, wester' rain hat, he put it on his head, looked over at his Sergeant.

"It's the latest type of head gear, Thomas", he said smiling and patting the top of his head.

He then walked out into the yard to join his temporary senior officer, closely followed by Sergeant Thomas.

DI White walked over to join his Commander, when he arrived at the investigation site. Because of the dull wet weather, the Police photographer had set up his floodlights to illuminate the Crime scene.

"Now, what have you got for me DI, you seem to have thing's well in hand, tell them to put the light's on, I want to have a closer look at thing's".

"Yes sir, but these light's are only running off batteries sir, and they don't last long," replied D.I White.

"I know that, White, why didn't these people bring their generators, instead of fiddle faddling about like a bunch of amateur's, get them over here for me man, if they run out of power, they'll have to get some more batteries, won't they?"

"Yes sir", DI White replied sheepishly, leaving his Commander to find the photographer and instruct him to put his floodlight's on as his master instructed.

Chief Inspector Sullivan and his Sergeant witnessed the humiliation of the DI.

They both looked at each other shrugged their shoulders and went over to Tom Davis, who was squat down checking the plaster cast of the tire prints.

"They all right Tom?" asked the Chief Inspector.

"Yep, they're okay Chief, it's these I want to show you" Tom replied. Pointing at the shoe prints in the mud and taking a couple of side steps to his left.

"They look like a woman's footprint to me."

The Chief Inspector squatted down to get a closer look.

"You could be right there" he said, "Are there any more?"

"Well I think so sir, over there by the gate, but it looks as if they've been trod on, but, look here" again pointing at some more prints close by.

"It looks as if these were made when she returned, see", again pointing with a pencil, "The toe is deeper as if she was in a hurry and those two prints there were made as she got into the car."

"Right get some photos Tom", said the Chief "Get Sherlock Holmes, Thomas, before he starts taking cuttings, for his window box, off that bush he's inspecting. Show him these, but don't let him touch them Tom, by the way do you think you could get any cast's of these prints? I'm going to have a look for some more prints over in the paddock next to the yard, join me there, Sergeant".

"I'll try" replied the technician, "but they're old prints, we'll see how they come out."

"Good, do your best, right you two, get on with it and get it wrapped up quickly, we don't want to be out here all day in this weather."

The Chief Inspector walked slowly back towards the farm checking the ground as he went. Trying to find more footprints that had been missed on previous investigations.

He didn't find any until he reached a five barred gate into an orchard, which was at the side of the farmhouse. A four feet high beech hedge separated the house from the orchard, which had eight or nine fruit trees in it.

The Colonel used the orchard as a nursery in the spring.

His Shepherd made shelters out of bales of straw, and kept the lambs that had lost their mothers in them. These poor little orphans had to be bottle-fed this had to be done until they were weaned off the bottle.

Sometimes he would put calves in there that were orphaned, following the same procedure until they were big enough to put out to pasture.

When the Chief Inspector reached the closed gate, he paused to glance through. Seeing two sets of footprints in the mud on each side of the gate, where someone had opened the gate and gone into the orchard and returned, he quickly walked over to the gateway and was about to shout for his Sergeant when he heard his Sergeant ask.

"What's the matter sir?, have you found something?"

"Yes Thomas, I have, what do you think of this?"

As Sergeant Thomas arrived at the gate his Chief was bending down with his hand on the gate to support himself.

"Good grief guv. What have we here? They're better prints than those that Tom's taking casts of back there."

"I know Thomas, but what I'm thinking is how were they missed in the first place, who was supposed to have checked along here?, get Tom over here quick. Oh hell, here come Sherlock Holmes and Dr. Watson."

"I think you'd better look at these print's sir, I think they're fresher than the others." Sergeant Thomas remarked to his Chief.

"What! You think they're more recent than the others Thomas?"

"Yes sir, I do, we've had a lot of rain this last week or so, that's why Tom say's those other prints are shallow and have rounded edges, these haven't they have clean edges, but, don't ask me how long they have been here."

Commander Benfield and his Inspector arrived at the gate in time to hear the end of what the Sergeant had been saying.

"You could be right Sergeant", the Commander said giving the impression that he knew about this type of thing.

"White get that forensic chap down here quick, tell him to leave what ever he's doing and come over here, these look nice fresh prints to me, Sullivan, have you had much rain in the last twenty four hours?"

"No sir", Chief Inspector Sullivan replied.

"Could be a day or two old, what?"

"Yes sir".

"Thought so, Sullivan, still gives you something else to worry about, eh?"

Tom and DI White arrived short of breath after running across the field.

"Cor, I'm not as fit as I used to be, what have you got for me?" asked the forensic technician.

"What do you think of them Davis?" asked the Commander nodding towards the footprints.

"They're better than the others Commander, if they were made by the same boots".

"What do you mean, if they were made by the same boots, course they were."

"I don't know for sure until I've checked them, they look the same but, it might not be the same person. I won't know for sure until I get back to the lab, but, I will say this, if it will satisfy you Commander" said Tom getting annoyed. He wasn't used to being spoken in this manner, "They were made within the last twelve to eighteen hours, and that's, since you have been here."

The Commander realized he wasn't going to get any further with his investigation out here.

"Well it's stopped raining now, so you'll be able to get your casts made Davis and while you're at it get lots of photos". Then turning to his Chief Inspector, he ordered.

"Right, Sullivan, you and I have a press conference to go to."

Colonel Brown was standing by the Chief Inspector's car when they arrived back in the farmyard.

"Good afternoon gentlemen, found something interesting at my orchard gate, have we?"

"Yes Colonel" replied the Chief Inspector "Oh, may I introduce Commander Benfield from New Scotland Yard, he's now in charge of the case."

"Nice place you have here Colonel" the Commander said, shaking hands with the Colonel, "I was admiring it when we arrived earlier."

"Yes it is nice, Commander, the wife and I like it here. I was born here, that bedroom up there as a matter of fact". The Colonel pointed towards a corner bedroom window on the front of the house. "But what have you found Commander anything that I should know about?"

"Oh nothing to get alarmed about Colonel" replied the Commander as he was getting into the car.

The Chief Inspector walked back round the car to where the Colonel was stood.

"Colonel" he said, "There isn't a lot of worry about, we found some extra footprints that's all, and we're taking some plaster casts to see if we have anything on file to match them."

"I see Chief Inspector do you think that I should take extra precautions at night or something?"

"Oh I don't think so Colonel, you could leave one or two lights on in the yard and at the front, if you want to, and I'll try to get the patrol car to call round when he's in the area."

"Thanks Inspector, I may get one of my sons to come over and sleep here until this is over."

"That's a good idea Colonel, you might see about a security system, you know living out here like you are, is a bit risky anyway, Colonel; sorry sir, we must dash the Commander's got a press conference to go to" said the Chief Inspector with a nod towards Commander Benfield.

"That's alright Inspector, I understand", the Colonel gave them a wave as they drove out of the yard.

He smiled ruefully to himself as he walked into the house. He had not told the Chief Inspector that, on the advice of David Simpson, he had already made the necessary arrangements to have the most sophisticated alarm system installed and they would start installing it in the morning.

Police Superintendent Moore led Commander Benfield and Chief Inspector Sullivan into the pressroom at Stratford on Avon, Police Headquarters. The pressroom was packed to capacity with reporters from the daily newspapers, TV stations and the local evening papers. The Superintendent introduced the Commander from Scotland yard. He then informed the reporter's, that Chief Inspector Sullivan, whom they all knew, would still be ably assisting the Commander.

He then handed the press conference over to the Commander from Scotland Yard.

The Superintendent sat down, then whispered in his Inspector ear.

"Look at the little bugger" he whispered, "He's enjoying every minute of it."

"Yes" the Inspector replied "You watch, I bet I'm the one he'll drop right in it", his Superintendent did not reply.

The Commander informed the press that he was now in charge of the 'Bonfire Case', as it was now known in the papers.

He was asked to report on the progress and if there would be a prosecution shortly.

The Commander craftily replied by saying.

"That as this was his first day on the case, he did not think that he was in a position to make any statement at the moment. But he thought that Chief Inspector Sullivan who had been in charge of the case from the beginning was the right person to answer the question for them".

He sat down with a smile on his face, leaving the floor to Chief Inspector Sullivan whom he knew hated these press conferences especially when he did not have anything to report. However, Sullivan stated that he hadn't much to report at the moment, but stated that Commander Benfield had informed him that he had his own ideas on how to solve the case very quickly and he thought that the Commander may be persuaded to enlighten them on this.

He sat down looking at the Commander as he did so, the Commander had a face as black as thunder when he got up again to face the reporters, he had to think fast and the best he could do was to say.

"I will be calling another press conference in three days time that would be Christmas Eve, and, that it would be in the morning at a time to be released later".

The Commanders face was as black as thunder as he left the room.

"The Superintendent thanked the reporters for coming to the meeting stating that they would be informed of the time for the next meeting as soon as he knew anything".

Commander Benfield was late arriving in his office, the morning after the press conference. His excuse was that his car was blocked in the hotel car park and he had to wait until the hotel staff had woken the owners up to enable them to move their vehicles.

Chief Inspector Sullivan was not impressed.

The Commander was staying at ` The Mallard Hotel', one of the best hotels in Stratford-on-Avon, which was only three minutes walk away. It would have been easy to walk back to pick his car up later or send a Constable over to collect it.

After listening to his Commanders excuse for being late, Chief Inspector Sullivan told him that he was going up to Altringham to have a talk with Margaret Hodgkinson he thought that he would be able to find out from her who Jose Cordova associated with. He was under the impression that she was the only one that knew any of his movements in this country. Informing him at the sametime that he was taking D.C. Hopkins with him. Commander Benfield agreed to his Chief Inspector's suggestion, commenting that he had read his report on his last visit and hoped that it would more productive this time.

CHAPTER EIGHTEEN

After reading all the report's she had received from David Simpkins again, Brenda Armstrong sat gazing out of her office window at Courtney Transport. Recollecting her thoughts on what had happened to her since her arrival in Solihull.

Returning from her appointment with Detective Inspector Sullivan at Stratford on Avon Police Headquarters, Brenda realised that, the local Police Force did not welcome her interest in the case.

She was also under no illusion that there was any likelyhood of her getting any help from them in the future.

She had also given a lot of thought to the possibility of a partnership of some sort between Jos'e Cordova and Nigel Courtney there wasn't any working relationship as far as she could see.

The Police though, were under the impression that there was one of some kind; she would have to find out for them, having made a promise that she would, but how?

"There's only one way", Brenda muttered. "And that's head on".

She turned back to her desk and started to write, she made a list as follows:

WHERE TO START

Victim		
	1. Jean Claude	Bonfire London) Police report
	2. George Obayo	London) info only, from Simpkins Illicit diamond trade investigation
	3. Bert Pearson	Nigel Courtney den
	4. Mike Smith	Colonel Brown's farm
	5. Jose Cordova	'Chestnut Tree'

Suspects

    Nigel Courtney)
    Colonel Brown)   Positive connections 3.4.5
    Bill Selby)
    Tom Atkinson) ???
    Suspects = 1.2.

Why?   3. Caught burglar in act.
         4. Caught intruder in act.
         5. Shot intentional according to Benfield.

_____oOo_____

On a second sheet of paper she wrote:—

Jean Claude, George Obayo,	Jose Cordova, Bert Pearson
Mochamton London	B/ham. Mochamton
Connection:	According to Police,
Believe knew killer.	Wrong place. Wrong time.
Interpol.	Or could have no connection.

_____oOo_____

Check through military all info above.

_____oOo_____

Brenda typed up her request to her friends at Aldershot Military Base, and sent it immediately on her portable fax machine.

This done, she put all the papers into her briefcase then locked the briefcase in her desk drawer, and went next door to Nigel Courtney's office. He was busy on the phone as she entered his office; he waved to her to take a seat by his desk.

As he put his phone down, he smiled at Brenda and asked.

"Is this business or pleasure?"

"Strictly business I'm afraid, Nigel."

"Oh dear, this sounds ominous, what's the matter? Your friends at Stratford giving you a hard time?"

"No, it's not that, but I want to know how deeply you were involved with Jose Cordova. I want the truth this time, Nigel."

"I've told you, I'm not involved at all, cash or otherwise, I have known him for a long time mainly through the oil industry, but as regards anything else, no nothing. That joint venture thing, we're only talking, but it's cash involvement and I'm waiting for him, why?"

"Well, he's dead. He was shot last night."

"What! Where did this happen? Oh, my God, another one" he said putting his head in his hands.

"Yep, another one. He was shot outside 'The Cherry Tree' restaurant, at Shirley, I don't know the details, but I was able to clear you, by saying we were in a meeting here in your office until five thirty. So no way would any one of us, have time to go to Shirley and be there by 5 p.m. which is the time he was shot, so, do you know who he was involved with? Other than yourself."

"Oh golly, that's a tough one. I don't personally know of anybody. I know he was a frequent visitor to this country, so much so, that he had an arrangement with a garage in, I think it was, Altringham somewhere, I know it was near Manchester Airport, he had bought a car from them and they garaged and serviced it for him. He found that it was cheaper than hiring a car each time he came over, because being in the oilfield supply business he used to be going all over the place. The last time I spoke to him was about three weeks ago and he phoned me to tell me that some unsavory characters in London, he had been talking to. Were interested in buying my haulage business and also wanted my construction company to build some warehousing for them.

He advised caution when dealing with them.

Come to think of it, I had only just started to think about disposing of the company, and I had only told the Colonel about it two or three day's previous."

"A bit of a coincidence, isn't it? Worth looking into though, anything else?"

"Well, Jose' stopped at my place the weekend of the firework display in November, but you know about that, don't you? No, I don't think there's anything else, you see our business was mostly done by fax or over the phone, any cash transaction was done by 'L/C' (Letter of Credit), we didn't have any reason to meet. Take this trip for example I didn't even know he was in the country, and yet he could ring me, and we could have done a million dollars worth of business immediately, sounds stupid I know. But that's how it is in the oilfield supply business, his credit worthiness was good, as far as I was concerned, but, for knowing him personally, I didn't. I visited him once in the States, that's all."

Brenda had recorded their conversation as usual; she would listen to it later in the evening and make any notes then, she found she was able to concentrate more, when she was alone.

There was a slight pause in the conversation; both of them were deep in thought.

Brenda was the first one to speak.

"I'm rather interested in these people that Jos'e mentioned from London, as being prospective buyer's, you say that you have not heard from them."

"No, not yet."

"I wonder how they found out so quick, did you tell anyone else besides Colonel Brown?"

"No, I hadn't definitely decided to sell, I told him that I was thinking about it, because of all this hassle that it was causing."

"I haven't met the Colonel yet, so I think that now is the time to meet him and have a chat, don't you?"

"I suppose we'd better take care of that right now," said Nigel picking up the phone. "Strike while the iron's hot, as they say."

He wasn't able to get an immediate appointment with Colonel Brown the earliest time he could get was the following afternoon.

CHAPTER NINETEEN

The evening of the Carol service, the village green was a blaze of colour.

The star of the evening, a thirty foot high Christmas tree, stood proud in the centre of the green. Covered in lights of various colors', the brighter one's twinkling in the frosty moonlight night. On the top of the tree, was a large illuminated white star of Bethlehem sparkling in the frosty night air.

There were light's strung across the road surrounding the green, the shop's and the two public houses were adorned with lights, even the house's around the green had fairy light's in their window's, and holly wreath's on their door's.

The medieval street basket torches, with their red flickering light bulb's, and paper mache brown sticks, making them look like flaming basket's of fire, were brought back into service again. The Farmer's Arm's had set up their BBQ, to sell hot dogs, 'The Navigation' not to be outdone had setup their 'Hot Chestnut' stall.

The WVS, were giving out hot Bovril to anyone who wanted a hot drink to keep out the cold.

Chief Inspector Sullivan, DI. White, Sergeant Thomas and Sergeant Hopper were standing near the Christmas tree surveying the peaceful scene.

"What a beautiful peaceful scene, just what I imagined Christmas in the country was like, Christmas cards have nothing on this sir, have they?" said DI. White, breaking the silence of the peaceful scene.

"No, you're right there, Inspector, let's hope it stay's that way" replied the Chief Inspector.

"Christmas is always like this in Mochamton sir," said Sergeant Hopper, "But this year they seem to have put more effort into it, I suppose they're trying to cheer people up a bit after what's happened around here lately. I hope nothing will happen tonight, its usually very peaceful just the choir singing carols around the Christmas tree accompanied by the brass band and that's it.

It's supposed to start at half past seven. And finishes at half past eight. If a good crowd turn's out like last year it went on till nine o'clock, it was very good, we'll have to wait and see".

The Detective Inspector looked at his watch.

"Who's for a pint?" he asked.

"Good idea" said Sergeant Thomas.

"Oh you're in the chair, are you? Sergeant?", said the Chief Inspector "Good, I was wondering when it was your turn"

"As usual", Thomas muttered shrugging his shoulder's as he turned to walk across to the 'Farmers Arms'.

When the four policemen walked into the pub, they found a different scenario from the tranquillity outside. Dave Wilson and his committee of four, were busy sorting out the rolls, the smell of onions' cooking was wafting through from the kitchen.

The two Sergeants went upto the bar to get the drinks, whilst the two Officers found a quiet table in the corner of the bar.

"Hive of activity in here tonight, Joe", Sergeant Hopper said as the Landlord came over to serve them.

"Aye" he replied "Vicar told me this morning that, he'd got choir's from the other three parish's round here to join in the carol service tonight, so we thought we'd better cater for a few extra. What is it pint's of mild then?'

"I think you'd better make it 2 pints of bitter and 2pts of mild Joe. Social club should do well on the hot dog sales tonight then, if it's right what you say, that the vicar's expecting a lot of support from the other church's", enquired Sergeant Hopper, trying to pump Joe for more information on the crowd that was being expected by the vicar.

"I think the vicar's looking for support from the congregation's of the respective church's also the supporter's of Bidford and Welford Brass Band. As you know they have gathered a lot of local support since they came third in that brass band contest in Birmingham in the summer. Other than that I can't say how many are expected".

When the two Sergeants arrived back at the table with the drinks, Sergeant Hopper informed the Chief Inspector.

DI. White was most concerned about the possible increase in the number of people that could be attending, he was under the impression that it was only going to be a small village event.

"That's all we want, trust the local vicar to drop us in it, why don't these people let us know what they're doing, especially at time's like this. Right,

Inspector you'd better go and tell your boss what's happening, otherwise he'll start tearing his hair out, and we don't want him to spoil his parting do we? Thomas I think if we ask for the car's on patrol in the area to keep a close watch on the road's into the village for a couple of hours from 7:30 pm. on, I think that should do it".

As the Chief Inspector finished giving his instructions he took a hefty swig of his beer, as if giving so many instructions at one time had given him a terrible thirst. He looked across at his two Sergeants sitting opposite him, wiping his mouth on the back of his hand he asked.

"Well, what are your comments"

"Well sir", Sergeant Thomas started "I hope we don't get his boss down here", he nodded towards the back of the DI who was standing at the bar telephoning, Sergeant Thomas carried on "If we can get the car's to cover the roads as you say, I think we can cover the rest of it in here with Sergeant Hoppers men and ourselves".

The DI returned from phoning his boss looking a little perturbed.

"He's not in," he said "The receptionist at the hotel said that he went out early and she doesn't know where he went".

After getting the road patrols organized the Chief Inspector contacted his office at Stratford Police Station trying to locate his Superintendent. He was informed; the Super had invited Commander Benfield to a Christmas dinner at his Lodge in Birmingham. Also he had left instructions that no calls were to be put through to him unless they were very urgent.

All the choirs were gathered at the Church in their various colored cassocks, and because they were singing outside they were wearing black capes.

As the church clock struck the half-hour they commenced singing the well-known carol, 'While shepherds watched their flocks by night'.

Led by a young chorister carrying a lantern. They came through the lychgate in the wall surrounding the churchyard and out into the road at the far end of the green. The large gathering of people around the village green, made way for them as they proceeded towards the radiant Christmas tree. At its pinnacle, the brilliant shining star was swaying gently in the light breeze, beckoning the people towards the centre of the green.

Chief Inspector Sullivan and Sergeant Hopper were standing outside The Farmers Arms. Listening to the many voices joining the massed choirs and brass bands, singing all the Christmas carols and songs and forgetting all their problems for a while and having a good time.

Sergeant Thomas walked over to join his associates carrying a tray and four beakers. He put the tray on the wall at the side of the pub and took a half bottle of rum from his pocket. He poured a little into each cup and handed one to each of the policemen then took one for himself.

"What's this, Thomas?" asked his Chief.

"Bovril, sir with a dash of Brandy to keep the cold out"

"What do you think, Hopper, certainly warms the old socks up a bit doesn't it?" asked the Chief Inspector turning towards Sergeant Hopper who was leaning against the Pub wall.

"Certainly does hot the socks up a bit", the Sergeant agreed.

"That's it! That's what we'll call it! "Hot Socks'" enthused Sergeant Thomas "Where's Snowy? "he asked.

The Chief Inspector looked at his Sergeant

"What are you talking about, Thomas? 'Hot Socks! 'Snowy,' drink gone to your head, has it? You'll be telling us its Christmas next and we already know that".

"Well sir, a good drink like this has to have a name and when you made the remark about hot's the socks it suddenly struck me. That was a good name for the drink, as for Snowy, that's what all the lads at the nick have started calling DI White".

"Alright, alright Thomas, anyway he must be in the crowd somewhere enjoying himself. I haven't seen him for ages but I have seen the Colonel and his entourage go down to the front so we know where they are. Is there anyone else about that we should know?"

"I see that Simpkins is here, sir. His Range Rover is parked at the back of the 'Arms". Maybe Mr. Courtney came with him. I haven't seen either of them although I think I saw Mr Simpkins with Joyce Simpson and the Colonel when they went over to the Christmas tree".

The carol service eventually came to an end at nine o'clock as was expected by Sergeant Hopper and the evenings entertainment continued with the younger members of the band getting together and giving a jazz session until late in the evening. This of course kept a lot of the people together for most of the evening. Drinks were brought out from the pubs and everyone had a good time, including the Police.

Chief Inspector Sullivan was pleased to see that all his suspects were present and had drinks bought for him by the Colonel and David Simpkins when Sergeant Hopper introduced him to them.

'Yes' thought the Chief Inspector as he drove home afterwards 'a very good evening and all my clients in one place where I could keep an eye on them. Let's hope it stays like this till after Christmas".

CHAPTER TWENTY

The day after the carol service Brenda drove to see her aunt and uncle at Farnham in Surrey. He was a retired Colonel in the Grenadier Guards and they adopted Brenda after her parents had been killed in Kenya during the Mau Mau uprising in the fifties. She was only eighteen months old at the time. Her parents had gone out to Kenya on the British Government Groundnut Scheme and had only been there for twelve months when their farm was attacked at night and burned to the ground. Brenda was found in her cot in the back of an old Morris van. The Game Warden and his African helper had arrived shortly after the raid, having spotted the smoke and found her when they heard her cry. The nuns at St. Saviors Convent in Nairobi looked after her until Aunt Christine and Uncle Bert had been found in Nicosia, Cyprus. She attended boarding school in England and always spent her holidays with them. She had kept to this routine in later life whenever possible.

This Christmas was special to Aunt Christine and Uncle Bert as it was Brenda's first Christmas in 'Civvy' street. They had asked a few of her friends in to celebrate New Years Eve, but prior to that they wanted her all to themselves. Maybe they thought this a bit selfish but 'what the heck' she was the only child they had.

Uncle Bert was sitting in the lounge reading The Times and Aunt Christine was in the kitchen preparing dinner, when Brenda came down from her room.

"Usual?" he asked.

"Please" she replied.

He got up from his fireside chair and made Brenda her favourite drink, a 'Pymms' with very little ice in it.

Brenda tasted it before she sat down "MM.! That's nice," she said.

"Good. Now tell me what you have been up to".

"Not much" she replied. "I've just started on an interesting case, one or two bodies in it, the local police seem to think it could have started in London and spread to the Midlands. As a matter of fact, I've got one of my old friends checking a couple of things out for me. I'll give him a call in the morning to see what he has found".

"See what he comes up with. I've still got one or two contacts in the Metropolitan Police, that may be able to help, but lets get Christmas over first" Uncle Bert volunteered, emptying his whiskey glass.

The following morning the telephone rang three times before Brenda answered it.

"Morning Brenda" a cheerful voice said "must be nice to lie in to this time in the morning".

"Who's that? What time is it" Brenda asked.

"It's nine thirty and it's your old friend Dennis Davis otherwise known as the 'Digger' calling".

"Sorry, Dennis, I had rather a heavy night with my relations last night. How did you get this number, anyway?"

"You gave it to me some time ago and I remembered you always go home for Christmas.

However, I've got those answer's for you, but, when I received them I got a little bit curious and did a little 'digging' (hence the nickname) and I think I've come up with something for you".

"Oh good, how about a spot of lunch together" she said "Kingshead, on Farnham Road be alright for you?"

"Yes, one o'clock will suit me fine "replied Dennis.

The ' Kings Head ' was a 'free' house it had not been modernized too much and still had a bar parlor and a lounge bar as it had been in the 1930's. The father of the Landlord Ted Featherstone had converted it from a farmhouse to a public house when he inherited the farm in 1929. He eventually sold all the land after the Second World War, keeping three acres and the outbuildings.

A restaurant had been built at the side of the pub and the old barn had been converted into a play area and a snack bar for the children and coach parties in the summer months.

Dennis was sitting at the bar when Brenda arrived. He picked up the two drinks he had bought and nodded towards a table in the window. After greeting each other, Dennis gave Brenda a foolscap size brown envelope that was quite thick. A surprised look came on her face as he handed her the envelope.

"What is this?" She asked

"Ask and thou shalt receive" he answered "It's the information you requested from Interpol plus my 'digging'. I am afraid that I may have dug up a bag of worms for you. Take it home and study it then give me a call. We may have to meet again. I think it's going to be rather like old times, Major".

"You've got me a little worried now, Dennis. Can't you enlighten me a teezy wheezy bit?"

"Well, the Interpol report is as you expected, so I got in touch with Tuffy Smith, who you remember is in Arts and Treasures". Brenda nodded her head and Dennis continued.

"He's landed a soft touch to finish his time. He's attached to the European Parliament Division in Brussels. Sort of undercover policing M.I.5 stuff and briefly he tells me that there's a 'hell' of a lot of diamonds being smuggled into Europe. Also he knew Jean Claude and George Obayo quite well, he had the occasional drink with them in London when they first started their investigation. So he did some private investigating with them. They were getting on very nicely, he wasn't officially on the case, but it came under his banner, so to speak. He made a report about it to his C.O. suggesting that he should look into the military involvement because there are such a lot of troop movements from the Continent. Five days later he was posted to Brussels, 'case closed'. I checked Army records, which of course showed 'no trace'. About three weeks later Jean Claude is found at Stratford and a 'hit and run' killed George.

"There's a letter and the report from Tuffy, he sent it by mail to my home. He says in his letter to check a company in Salisbury something to do with fireworks".

"I haven't found anything about a company in Salisbury being involved in the case but that doesn't mean we won't find it later".

"Yes, it's early days for you isn't it, Brenda? I think I'll put in for some leave that's due to me because I didn't take it this Christmas. My parents are out of the country for a couple of months so I stayed on camp. Good job I did. You might need someone to watch your back for a while".

"Thank's Dennis, but that's entirely up to you. I have no one else to turn to at the moment; my two partners are busy elsewhere. I'll take the papers home and study them and I'll call you later this evening".

On her way home Brenda did a little bit of shopping in Farnham and walked around the shopping centre. As she checked round her car, she smiled and thought 'old habits die hard better be safe than sorry'. When she had satisfied herself that everything was all right she started the car and left the car park.

Her uncle was all smiles as he greeted her when she arrived home.

"I've got a pleasant surprise for you Brenda. Tomorrow we are going up to town to have lunch at the Cafe Royale with an old friend of mine. I hope you haven't made any other arrangements".

"No "she replied "But if I had I would change them, is it anyone I should know?".

"You may have heard of him, Superintendent Mayhew, he's retired from the Yard now but he thinks he may be able to pull a few strings for you".

Brenda shook her head and went to her room to read and tape Tuffy's letter and report. After she had read the report through a second time she lay back on her bed to think it over quietly. The report had told her that the 'Angola Diamonds' quality was on a par with anything that had come out of the Kimberley mines in South Africa. Also to keep control of the diamond market Consolidated Goldfield and Von Braums, the two biggest diamond-mining companies had bought out the biggest mining companies in Angola. The trouble was that the country was so rich in precious stones that people were literally picking them up out of the gravel beds of the streams and rivers. There were two main dealers in Angola who were buying the stones and they ran their own private armies so that once a person started selling their stones to the dealer's, they were under the buyer's control.

The two dealers were now shipping their stones all over the world illegally not caring how much damage they were doing to the diamond market.

The main ports of entry into Europe were Schiphol Airport, Amsterdam, Charles de Gaulle Airport, Paris and Heathrow Airport, London; also London and Antwerp and Rotterdam docks. The problem had become so serious that the Diamond Cartel in Antwerp was employing Francois de Mere Securitte Services to investigate and try to stop the smuggling. The Police forces in the respective countries had been notified of the course of action being taken by the Cartel.

The letter explained how Tuffy had met Jean Claude in the Star and Garter in Highgate, London and they had decided to go on to a nightclub known by Tuffy. A seedy place called The Blue Angel where a lot of the underworld drank and gambled.

He was known by the bar staff who classed him as one of their regular members, Jean Claude had told Tuffy he was in London on business and didn't mind losing a pound or two on the spin of the wheel. It was only ten o'clock in the evening and the Casino was already very busy when they were shown upstairs. Jean Claude did not waste any time and took the first available seat at the roulette table. Tuffy, not being interested in gambling stood and watched for a short while, then wandered over to the dice table finally trying his luck on the Blackjack table where he played for an hour. When he returned to the roulette table Jean Claude was looking shamefaced having lost all his money and he was trying to persuade the manager to let him have credit for a thousand pounds. When Tuffy approached he was asked to stand guarantor for Jean Claude until the following day. Tuffy agreed and made a mental note to find out what was going on.

By three o'clock in the morning Jean Claude had lost the thousand and also a further five hundred. Tuffy decided that he'd had enough and arranged a cab to take them to his apartment in Knightsbridge. It was nearer than Belvedere Gardens in Paddington where Jean Claude was staying.

Tuffy settled himself into a deep chesterfield armchair with a Glenlivet whiskey looked across at Jean Claude asking.

"Right Jean Claude, what's going on? you acted like a man with no arms in that Club, losing all that money at the roulette table.

Now tell me what you're up to you're a cop of some sort. I could tell that by the manner in which we've been speaking to each other this evening, but that's my training showing" then hesitating "Can I ask you, did you find anything at the Club?" he asked

"I think I've got a lead on my enquiry, but mines only pilfering N.A.A.F.I. stores. I think yours is much bigger game. Can I help? Do you want to talk about it?"

Tuffy then showed Jean Claude his warrant card disclosing that he was a member of the Royal Corp. of Military Police. In return Jean Claude disclosed his Private Investigation card issued by Parisian Police and also his Francois de Mere identity card. Having satisfied each other on their identities and Jean Claude also disclosing George Obayo's involvement they talked until daylight when they dropped off to sleep where they sat.

A further ten days had elapsed before anything of consequence happened.

Jean Claude was enjoying a cup of black coffee in his apartment at Belvedere Gardens when his phone rang. It was George Obayo telling him he was in town, and he requested a meeting immediately in a large car park at the corner of Cromwell Road and Earls Court Road. Jean Claude informed Tuffy, and they both agreed to go to the car park and meet George.

When they met him, he informed them of what was happening, and how he had taken an urgent package to Ostende, Belgium for the transport company for whom he did part time work.

A Courier met him at the ferry office in Ostende, and took delivery of the package, so he didn't have to leave the Compound. After having a meal George decided to take a walk around the compound, as he did so he noticed that the cab of a truck was tilted forward.

Curious he decided to walk over and have a chat with the driver. As he did so, the driver stepped out from under the cab and picked up a carton about the size of a shoebox, from the carrier at the back of the cab and went back under the cab again.

When he had finished, he brought the cab down and all he had in his hand was a roll of insulation tape.

This made George all the more curious, and all the more determined to make acquaintance with the driver.

Fortunately they sailed on the same ferry and George managed to get in conversation with the driver and learnt that he was going to Birmingham with a load of German wine.

George pointed to a Courtney Transport parked one parking space away from where he was parked. There was a gap now where a truck had previously been parked.

The driver of the Courtney transport truck was now having his supper in the cafe across the road.

Tuffy then instructed Jean Claude to take George back to his flat saying he would stay on watch in case anything happened.

"If it does I'll contact you on this" he said holding up his cell-phone "and you'd better come running."

Nothing did happen until six o'clock the following morning. Tuffy, from practice, had stretched himself across the backseat of his car and was sleeping with his eyes open. He used to tell people that this was his forte and had taken a lot of practice. He heard a 'clunk' and saw the cab of the Courtney Transport truck tilted forward. He immediately telephoned Jean Claude and quietly got out of the car, he then crawled alongside the truck that was parked on his left in front of his car until he reached the gap at the front of the trailer. He was just in time to see the driver give the box, which had been described by George, to another man who placed it inside a toolbox. The driver quickly closed the cab down again and they walked toward the cafe laughing as they chatted to one another. On the way to the cafe, the man with the toolbox stopped by a pale blue Transit van and deposited the box inside. They then continued to the cafe that had just opened to serve breakfast. Tuffy proceeded to make a telephone call to the nightduty room at his base giving the registration number of the van and asking them to trace the ownership.

He was walking across the car park to where Jean Claude and George were now parked when he received the reply to his enquiries. The owner of the Transit van was Mr.A.Jones, 'Hightrees' Blandford Road Salisbury.

The two private investigators and the Military Policeman were having a quiet smoke while drinking their coffee after a light breakfast, when the Courtney truck driver and his companion left the cafe.

Jean Claude using George's car followed the van to Fiesta Lighting Ltd., Amesbury Road Old Sarum Salisbury.

It was a small building, situated in a lay-by at the side of the main road between Salisbury and Amesbury. Before touch-tone telephones came into use, the building was used an automatic telephone exchange. The driver took the box into the building quickly returning to his van.

Getting more curious, Jean Claude then followed the vehicle back to Blandford Road on the outskirts of Salisbury, where the driver locked the van and went into a large semi-detached house.

Noting the address he parked in a side road where he could watch the house.

About an hour and a half later the man came out of the house wearing a smart brown suit and carrying an airline pilot's briefcase. He entered the garage and came out driving a dark blue Ford Sierra and drove back towards Salisbury.

Jean Claude followed the car around the Salisbury ring road taking the turning to Bournemouth.

As they approached Fordingbridge Jean Claude was getting very hungry and he was very pleased when the car turned into a cafe car park alongside the river. Following the driver into the cafe, he took a seat at a table near the door. The cafe was quite busy, so he was hoping he had not be seen. A waitress came over to his table and he ordered a coffee and a bacon sandwich hoping that that his suspect would give him time to eat his meal. He had noticed that his suspect had only ordered a cup of coffee. As he was taking his first sip of the welcome drink, his suspect appeared at his elbow and deposited a business card in his saucer saying.

"I think you could use this." and walked out of the cafe. Jean Claude picked up the card and read the same information that he had read on the board outside the small building plus 'Mr. A. Jones Chairman'. He was very annoyed with himself that he had been spotted and knew that he had to get back to London.

Before he left the cafe he rang his partner George and his new friend Tuffy leaving a message on George's answering machine to meet him at his apartment that evening when he would give them his full report.

Brenda then read in Tuffy's letter that he had met Jean Claude twice after that before he had been posted to Brussels. She already knew the sequence of events of the other two.

Tuffy's report had certainly given Brenda something to think about and she wondered whom she could trust. She locked the report away and went downstairs to join her Uncle and Aunt.

Superintendent Mayhew was ten minutes late for his luncheon appointment with Brenda and her relatives at the Cafe Royale. This was nothing out of the ordinary for him; being ex-Metropolitan Police it was a habit to make sure his guest's were there before him. When he saw his old friend Bert Armstrong sitting at the table with his wife and daughter, he smiled, pulled himself up to his full six foot, straightened his cravat and motioned a waiter to lead him to their table.

They were drinking their coffee before he mentioned the matter that had brought them together for luncheon.

"I believe you are now on civvy street Brenda. Why didn't you try the Met? I could have helped you there you know."

"I believe you could, Superintendent, but I didn't want to join the police force, I've had enough of the bureaucratic 'Red tape' in the forces. At least as a private investigator I can work my own way."

Gary Mayhew looked across at his old friend and said, "I can see there's a lot of her father in her, Bert".

"You knew my father? I didn't know that," said Brenda.

"Yes, we joined the army together but I left after I had done my National Service and joined the Met. Now, here I am retired at sixty-five. How can I help you?"

Before Brenda could reply he continued "If it's that serial killing that's going on in the Midlands, Benny Benfield is in charge up there. He's a high flyer and I don't want to cross swords with him"

"I know him, I've had dealings with him before. It is to do with that case, but there are two things I would like help with, if possible." Brenda replied, as she gave him the notes she had made on Jean Claude and George Obayo.

"I see that Interpol are involved not that that means much, but it does help with the background. I'll see what I can do. Might be a week before I can get back to you."

Brenda gave him her card.

"Don't worry, anytime, I've got a bleeper if you want to reach me and if not, there's an answer-phone".

"Good girl. That's enough of work," he said and they sat on for another hour chatting over old times.

CHAPTER TWENTY ONE

The morning of New Years Eve, Chief Inspector Sullivan was sitting in his office at Stratford on Avon Police Station having been told by his housekeeper. "To clear out as he was getting in her way and to leave her in peace to clean up", he had only been there half an hour when Sergeant Thomas came in.

"What's this, Thomas? Can't you rest either?"

"No sir, I know we said we'd have a rest over Christmas but I cant stop myself thinking about Cordova, the way he was shot and no clues. Very professional sir, and that waiter in the pub said that the person he saw getting in the car was a bloke but his hair was very long when he took his hat off, so could it have been a woman. Then we are saying those prints at the farm belong to a woman. Could it be the same person? Are we looking in the wrong direction? But who is it? We haven't met anyone yet who is likely to have done it".

"If you're right Thomas, old Commander Benfield isn't going to be pleased 'cos. ' I think he was lining up Nigel Courtney to be brought in next week when he got back from his Christmas break. All right for some isn't it? Call me if something breaks" he said, "I'm going home for Christmas and the New Year. You've got plenty to do he said" said the Chief Inspector trying to imitate the Commander. "Cor, I know what I'd like to do with him. He struts about here like a turkey cockbod, he thinks he owns the place".

"Anyone would think you didn't like him sir" remarked Sergeant Thomas

"Well never mind him. Lets have another look at the waiters statement".

Sergeant Thomas brought in the statement from his office.

"There sir. He clearly says the man got into his car, took off his hat and shook his head and his long hair, also he said that the car was a Citroen and it was red. Now, is that the same car that was seen at the farm? Could be couldn't it?"

"Yes Thomas. Very good, now where are the lab reports? I think we'd better check them first before we do anything. If you are right it means going back over all those statements to see if we can find anything or any reference to a woman at all.

Fancy coming up with this on New Years Eve, Thomas" the Chief Inspector grimaged and shook his head.

"Come on lets get started. I'd love to spoil old Benfield's evening for him".

They eventually found the lab report at the bottom of the 'mail in' tray on the Chief Inspectors desk having been there since before Christmas. This told them that the red paint taken off the hawthorn bush was cellular paint of continental origin also that the tyre marks were of Michelin X tyre's, footprints of half-worn shoes ladies size seven. They both looked at each other. Could it be the Citroen?

"What do you think Thomas? Could it be the same person and car? Have you any ideas Thomas?"

"Well I think we ought to go and have a pint while we think about it and before we start going through that lot".

"Good idea Sergeant. You're on the ball today," said the Chief Inspector taking his coat off the hanger and leading the way out of his office.

The following morning was New Years Day. When Chief Inspector Sullivan walked into his office at 10 o'clock, he was surprised to find Inspector Carter, D.C. Hopkins and Sergeant Thomas busy going through all the statements that had been taken.

Inspector Carter informed him that they thought they had found the names of two suspects, Margaret Hodgkinson at Altringham and Mrs. Jenkins of Garfield Transport.

"Sergeant Thomas says the Mrs. Jenkins is about five foot six and no way would she take size seven shoes, also she drives a Ford Granada so that only leaves Margaret Hodgkinson. However we are still checking the statements".

"Right carry on and don't let me stop you. Have you got the reports on those two women handy?" asked the Chief Inspector. He then went into his office with the reports to study them. He grunted a couple of times and picked up the report on Margaret Hodgkinson again reading it a second time he tried to memorize the interview that D.C. Hopkins and he had with her way back in November.

"Good Lord"' he thought, "It seems years ago since we went up to Altringham. There is a possibility she definitely knew Cordova and had access to the car. But did she know this area and Mike Smith? But, maybe someone else she knew did".

He made a few notes on his pad and sat back in deep thought. Then, as if he had suddenly made up his mind on a plan of action, he sat bolt upright in his chair and grabbing the telephone he dialed Margaret Hodgkinson at her home number, getting no reply. He then tried her office number with more success. A female voice answered, he asked if he could speak to Miss Hodgkinson hoping that it was her he was speaking to.

"I'm afraid not" the voice said "She went to Austria on a skiing holiday at Christmas and we don't expect her back for another two weeks. I'm running things here until she gets back. Can I help you?"

"I don't think so" replied the Chief Inspector "Ask her to contact me on her return. By the way, do you know what kind of car she drives?"

"She drives any of the demo cars" was the reply. "Using them helps with the advertising you know, but her own car is a souped-up Astra".

"O.K. Thank you. What did you say your name was?"

"I didn't, but it is Jenny Woods".

"Thanks Jenny, you've been most helpful. Can you remember if she ever drove a Citroen?"

"No, definitely not. We don't have any foreign cars at this establishment but her friend does. He picked her up when she left for her holiday two days before Christmas. I know it was a red car but I don't remember anything else. I don't know his name either. Margaret never discusses her friends. She is too involved with the business especially since her father was taken ill. She has put him in a convalescent home at Southport while she is away. It's a good job she took a holiday, she was killing herself running this place and looking after her father. Whenever this boy friend rang, I think he must be from Birmingham, she would drop everything and go off down there".

"Thank you Jenny. You think they've gone on this holiday together, do you?"

"Oh yes. I heard him say that they had plenty of time for a meal before they caught the plane".

"What's he like then, this boyfriend? He must be something special to make Margaret act like that. Is he good looking or what?"

"Just a minute Inspector. You're asking a lot of questions. Has she done something wrong?"

"Not as far as I know, Jenny. It is just that a friend of mine has been murdered and he had bought his car from Margaret and I wanted to have a chat with her that's all. You made me a bit curious Margaret didn't strike me as a girl who would act like that. She appeared to be very level headed".

"She certainly is, I'll give her your message when she returns, Inspector" Jenny replied ending the conversation.

Chief Inspector Sullivan looked very thoughtful 'I wonder who he is?' he thought going to the door of the office and calling his three associates to join him. Knowing that their Chief Inspector was on the telephone, they had sat in their own office wondering what he was going to come up with.

"Right. Well" started Chief Inspector Sullivan after his associates had filed into his room," I have just discovered that Margaret Hodgkinson isn't as pure as I thought she was, I've just been talking to Jenny Woods she's the person Margaret Hodgkinson left in charge of the business. While Margaret and her boy friend take a skiing holiday in Austria, incidentally her boy friend is from Birmingham and he has a red Citroen car".

"Did you get his name, sir?" asked Inspector Carter.

"No, I didn't. This Jenny I was talking to seemed to clam up when I started asking questions. But apparently, according to the new Manager, Margaret comes running every time this fella from Birmingham calls".

"That doesn't mean much does it sir? Just because this fella from Birmingham has a red Citroen, it doesn't mean to say he is involved does it?" remarked Sergeant Thomas.

"No but she knew Cordova, didn't she and I think there was more in that relationship than she was letting on".

"What can we do about it sir. When is she coming back?" asked Sergeant Thomas.

"In two weeks Thomas but I think, in the meantime, you and Carter can go up there and see if anyone else had noticed anything and see if you can get a photograph of her. There seem's to be plenty of them around the place.

"You mean so that I can show it to the barman at The Chestnut Tree, I suppose".

"You're catching on Thomas. Come on you two. There's no time like the present. Its half past eleven and if you get going you will be there by one o'clock".

Inspector Carter and Sergeant Thomas arrived at Ashwood Garage at a quarter past two, parking their car in the visitor's car park they walked over to a small office with ' Workshop Reception' in plastic letters on the glass window of the door. Entering, they asked the receptionist if they could see the Foreman.

When Ted Morcroft entered the office the two police officers showed their warrant cards, Ted grimaced.

"Oh its you lot again. I saw two oppo's of yours just before Christmas and told them that the bloke they were looking for showed up here about two weeks before Christmas and took delivery of a new blue Carlton car. I haven't seen him since".

"Can we go somewhere to talk quietly?" asked Inspector Carter. "Let's go into the showroom, the salesmen are out at the moment," Ted replied.

As they walked into the showroom they noticed many photographs around the walls showing the business dating back to the nineteen thirties when it was only a single garage with one 'Redline'

Petrol pump.

During the war it appeared that a barrage balloon company had been on the site and there were photographs of Margaret's father making parts for Lancaster bombers in the daytime and doing Home Guard duties on the anti aircraft guns at night.

A recent photograph interested Sergeant Thomas, it was not on the wall, but layed on a salesman's desk. It was a large framed photograph eight by ten inches, showing an elderly gentleman, Jose Cordova and Margaret standing beside a new blue Carlton. He looked over to where Ted and Inspector Carter were deep in conversation and slid the top drawer of the desk open. He found nothing of interest in there and opening the drawer below he found a photograph wallet. Looking over to where the other two were standing he saw that Inspector Carter had noticed what he was doing and had maneuvered Ted round so that his back was towards the Sergeant.

Quickly he took the wallet out of the drawer and found a postcard size copy of the photograph on the desk. He slid this into his pocket and replaced the wallet inside the drawer quietly closing it. He casually strolled back to the Inspector and Ted and listened to D.C. Carter carefully leading Ted into the happenings on the day that Margaret was leaving for her holiday. Ted was saying that since her father had been taken ill Margaret seldom seemed to be in the office. She was always either out shopping for her father or shooting off down to Birmingham to see her boyfriend. He said he had insisted that she asked Jenny Watson to come in full time instead of part time and then she got young Gloria Wilkins to work part time.

"So who is this boyfriend she's gone off with?" asked Carter. "My boss said she wasn't the marrying type and now you're telling me she's gone off for three weeks with him".

"Well, I don't think her dad knows about it 'cos' he's in a convalescent home in Southport and from the way she's carrying on with this bloke I think he'll be staying there. I can't tell you his name although I've spoken to him several times on his visits here 'cos' I've filled his tank for him each time and booked it out to the garage".

"Did he sign for it?" asked the Inspector excitedly.

"No. I told you I booked it to the workshop and just put the registration number down".

"You did? What kind of car was it?"

"It was a '92 Citroen, red and black".

At that moment one of salesmen and Jenny Woods came into the showroom.

Ted introduced the two Policemen saying.

"It's the Police again, Jenny".

Jenny went red in the face.

"What are you two doing here," she asked irritably," I spoke to your Chief Inspector this morning".

"Can we go into your office please Mrs Woods "asked Inspector Carter showing his warrant card. "My colleague is Sergeant Thomas".

"I am not Mrs Woods Inspector. Now if you don't mind, these men have work to do so, yes we'll go into my office and get this matter cleared up immediately".

"I agree with you madam" said the Inspector and led the way to the showroom door, holding it open for Jenny Woods to go first.

"I'm going with Ted to get the registration number, "Sergeant Thomas muttered to the Inspector as he passed.

"I'd like to go to the toilet Ted, if you could show me the way," he said mainly for Jenny's benefit.

As Sergeant Thomas entered the office on his return the Inspector jumped to his feet.

"Right Jenny" he said. "We'll leave you to get on with your work". Jenny smiled as she looked up at Inspector Carter.

"You both must think that we are thick up here". She said caustically, "I know why you are here. Your Chief didn't believe me this morning when I told him I could not help him. I was telling him the truth just as I have told you, Inspector. I don't know Margaret's boyfriend's name or his car registration number or anything else about him because she didn't tell me. I keep repeating this to you, but you may get something from Ted in the garage. I saw him filling the car up the other day and checking the oil".

"I have Jenny," said Sergeant Thomas. "Apparently he booked the petrol out to the garage and put the registration number against it for office accounting use. He gave it to me just now, as I told you it is a process of elimination, a red Citroen was seen at the scene of Cordova's murder. Margaret knew him and we wanted to cross her off the list of suspects".

They left Jenny looking a trifle worried.

On their way home, the Inspector and Sergeant Thomas made a detour and called at The Chestnut Tree restaurant.

It was five thirty and Sergeant Thomas remarked he felt hungry and fancied something to eat and a drink.

The barman on duty was Sid Watkins, who had given the statement to Sergeant Thomas after the murder. When he served them with the sandwiches they had ordered Sergeant Thomas showed him the photograph he had taken from the showroom and asked him if he recognized anyone in the picture. The barman looked very closely, shook has head and said.

"No I don't know any of them".

"What about the girl?"

"No I haven't seen her if you are thinking it is the girl I saw on the night of murder, you are wrong. The one I saw was the same height but her hair was much longer. I don't know but she looked different" said Sid hesitantly. "Don't forget I saw her in the car park flood lighting and she was in the car when she took her hat off so I couldn't see too clearly".

"What difference do you think there is between the girl in the photograph and the one you saw?" asked Inspector Carter.

"Well for one thing, the girl was much taller than the car, head and shoulders taller. She also seemed to be well built, rather butch and broad shouldered, almost like a fella but she was very nice looking. I got a good look at her face as she got into the car, it was a round face and she had beautiful red kissable lips". He shook his head and looked at the two policemen "she looked perfect to me".

Inspector Carter then surprised the barman by asking

"Could it have been a man in drag? If that person knew this place, they would know the car park was floodlit and the areas near the restaurant not being so well lit. In order to mislead people the person could have worn a wig. Do you think that's possible in this case?"

The barman looked very confused, "I suppose so" he replied.

"How's about coming down to the Stratford Police Station and we'll make an identi-kit face up for you on the computer. Sergeant Thomas will pick you up at ten o'clock tomorrow morning "asked Inspector Carter.

"Right, pick me up here, I'll be here working from eight o'clock."

It was a beautiful moonlight night as the two detectives drove back to Stratford on Avon.

"What a way to spend the first day of a new year" remarked the Inspector.

"Oh, I think it comes with the job. What do you think of our friend's statement? Bit of a change of heart don't you think?"

"No. I think it is the usual thing he has had time to think about it. I have the impression that we will get a perfect identi-kit picture tomorrow and I'm of the opinion that we are in for a surprise".

Sergeant Thomas was in the incident room at Stratford Police station checking if anything had come in while he was away at Altringham and Inspector Carter was downstairs talking to the duty officer. It was nine o'clock and they had both agreed as they drove into the car park that they would show their faces then go home.

Inspector Carter was on the point of leaving when the '999' call came in. It was from Nigel Courtney on his cellular phone from his car reporting a fire at Haydock Farm in the out buildings.

He also reported that he was following a suspicious car that he had seen leaving the farm as he approached 'Farm lane'. He described the car as a black Granada but could not read the registration number as it was covered in mud. They were driving towards Honeybourne and the car was increasing speed. His next report said that they were travelling at eighty miles per hour, which was crazy on these narrow country roads.

Inspector Carter and Sergeant Thomas went into traffic control. The shift was just changing and men were either coming on duty or leaving when Nigel's voice came over the radio informing them that he was turning west on the A46, and also asking them where the . . . . ! was the patrol car? He was informed that two were on their way but to stay with the suspect, the patrol cars were going to intercept at Willersley.

Over the radio came,

"Jesus that was close", giving the impression that the cars were travelling too fast, then came a shout. "I've lost him. The bastards turned onto that side road towards the Cliff Hotel, then came "I'm turning left going up the hill, I'm closing down. Cover your options".

Nigel continued up the steep hill climbing through the woods and round the hairpin bends of the cliff-face. As he took a sharp right hand turn on to the last half mile to the top, he saw the two red rear lights of the Granada disappear over the brow of the hill. Nigel screamed his

Porsche through third into fourth gear as he gunned the car up the hill. He flew over the brow of the hill, changing into fifth as he went. The road past the Cliff Hotel and the mile straight down towards the A424 Stow on the Wold to Broadway road was clear but he could not see a red light anywhere. Nigel stood on his brakes and swung his car into the car park of the hotel. There was only a Rover and a Jaguar in there so he turned back onto the road and began to retrace his steps. It was then that he realized that he had missed the B class road that went down into Chipping Campden. He accelerated down the hill towards Chipping Campden, as he approached the 'T' junction at the bottom, he looked to the right and spotted two rear lights disappearing through the trees that lined each side of the road. Making sure that no traffic was coming from his left, Nigel accelerated round the turn chasing after his quarry; the rear lights of the car again disappeared amongst the houses as it entered the High Street.

Dropping his speed drastically as he entered the ancient Cotswold town and driving very slowly round the bend at the beginning of the High Street. Passing the fifteenth century church on his left he stopped and looked down the street at the cars parked in front of the terraced cottages.

Not seeing his quarry amongst them, he drove slowly down the High street towards the Jacobean Market Hall. Seeing four cars parked at the end of the building he slowed down to almost a crawl. As he was passing the market hall he was looking at the cars through the archways when one of the cars started to move without lights on.

It was the Granada.

Nigel accelerated to the next turn, doing a 360-degree braking turn and with screaming of tires took off after the Granada. The noise caused by the two cars brought a lot of people out of the two pubs and faces to the windows of the houses. By the time Nigel was leaving the town and was back onto the country road, the Granada was speeding away from him. As he accelerated it disappeared into an 'S' bend taking a right hand turn off the second bend towards the village of Mickleton two miles away. The two cars charged up the hill from the junction. Both cars taking off as they went over the brow of the hill, crashing down again onto the road racing down through a railway bridge and past two cottages. Turning first left then right through another 'S' bend and into a short straight towards Mickleton. As they approached the junction on to the A46 Nigel saw a white Police car half blocking their access on to the major road, a second Police car was parked a little further along the road into the village. Blue lights were flashing and a Policeman was swinging a red light from side to side indicating to the two drivers that they had to stop. Ignoring the roadblock the Granada raced past the Policeman turning right into the village and towards Stratford-on-Avon, clipping the front of the Police Sierra as the car went through the roadblock.

Nigel stopped letting the second police car take up the chase as the Granada disappeared round a left-hand bend into the village. The Police Constable was picking himself up off the grass verge as Nigel stopped. He recognized Nigel but still made a note of his registration number. He then told Nigel to report to Chief Inspector Sullivan at Stratford Police Station.

As the police car drove away at speed to join in the chase. Nigel contacted the Chief Inspector on his cellular phone and informed him that, he was now leaving Mickleton and going to call on Colonel Brown as he had originally intended. If the Chief Inspector wanted to see him he would be at Haydock Farm'.

He then turned off the A46 towards the old Long Marston aerodrome cruising along at a nice steady fifty five miles an hour enjoying the frosty moonlight drive in contrast to the one he had just had. He switched on the cassette player and listened to the country and western music. On glancing into his rear view mirror he noticed a pair of headlights on full beam approaching at speed. 'Oh no, not again' he thought slowing down and pulling in to the side of the road to let it pass. As the car passed he looked at the muddied numberplate, then the rest of the car, sure enough it was the Granada.

Looking again in his mirror he saw nothing, not a police car in sight.

"Oh hell!" He shouted! "here we go again!"

He punched in the number on his cell phone for Stratford Police Station, reporting to the constable on duty what was happening. Accelerating away while he was giving his report, to give chase once again. The Granada was a good quarter of a mile in front of Nigel as he crested a railway bridge at the beginning of a straight piece of road. Putting his foot down harder and pushing his speed to over a hundred miles an hour he gave chase down the three-quarter mile straight into Long Marston village.

He braked heavily as he entered the village realizing that he had again lost contact and there were five roads leading off the junction at the entrance to the village. He pulled on to the car park of The Jolly Farmer pub and sat visualising which road would the driver take. He cancelled out the road past the new top security prison, it was too well lit, and then he thought of the Industrial Estate off the road through the village, you could hide up there and lay low while things quietened down. He discounted the other two roads, they led into housing estates and the third road went straight to Bidford on Avon.

Nigel took the road through the village, on reaching the Industrial Estate he turned into the main gate entrance and stopped, he thought of the cat and mouse game that would ensue and decided it was not for him and enough was enough. There was a bank of four telephone booths inside the gate. He parked his car alongside the telephone booths and contacted the police from one of the call boxes. He was informed that the Chief Inspector was on his way and that he was to leave everything to them and would he meet the Chief Inspector in the 'Coat of Arms' pub.

To say that Nigel was relieved to hear this was an understatement. He was explaining to the girl on the telephone that he intended to continue on to Colonel Browns and to inform the Chief Inspector to meet him there when he saw his car pass the telephone booth. It did not register for a few seconds as he watched it turn onto the road away from the village towards Broadway.

"Hey, that's my car", he shouted as he dropped the phone and ran out onto the road, realizing he could do nothing, he returned to the phone booth.

Within seconds the Chief Inspector and Sergeant Thomas arrived accompanied by two other cars that were dispatched to search for the Granada on the Industrial Estate.

"Now Nigel, what's this about you having your car stolen? I was told about it just as I was turning into The Coat of Arms so I thought I would save you a walk. Get in the car it's too cold to stand around here. Right Thomas back to you know, where"

"What time is it?" asked Nigel as if he was in a daze.

"Eleven thirty" answered the Sergeant.

"I was supposed to be at the Colonels at eight thirty. As I approached Haydock Farm, I saw this car coming up the drive from the farm, then I saw what I thought was flames coming from the out buildings. I reported what I had seen to your office and said I would follow it until I could hand over to you. Now look what has happened, I've lost my car!"

CHAPTER TWENTY TWO

The evening after her day in London with her adopted parents, Brenda received a call from Superintendent Mayhew asking her to meet him the following day informing her that he had some information for her. Also telling Brenda that he was staying with some friends at Petworth about twenty miles from Farnham on the road to Worthing, so they arranged to meet at The Angel Hotel in Petworth at six o'clock the following evening.

Brenda arrived at the hotel about ten minutes early and was quietly enjoying a coffee in the lounge when the Super arrived.

"Hello Uncle Gary" said Brenda reverting to the way she had been taught to address him when a child. "Have you had a good journey?"

"Yes" he replied, "we had better not stay too long, Brenda, there is going to be a sharp frost tonight. I've got three reports for you", he said dropping a large brown envelope on the table "that is all I can do for you, there are one or two reports missing according to index. I have copied all there was, it makes mighty funny reading Brenda, and by the way Benfield was on the case from the beginning but he seemed to have lost interest when that darkie was knocked over. I think it was a plain straightforward 'hit and run' but the funniest part of it is that they never traced the car. Apparently there was a red Toyota found at the City Air Terminal down at the old docks but he never bothered to investigate. At least there are no reports relating to the car. That area comes under Canning Town Station and I don't know that Division it has all changed recently".

He nodded to the waiter and ordered two coffees and two large Courvoisier brandies.

"Thanks Uncle Gary" she said opening the envelope. "I'm really grateful for your help".

Gary interrupted "Make sure you destroy those reports as soon as you have read them".

"Alright, I'll just make some notes then I'll shred them?"

"Make sure you do Brenda. I'm not supposed to have access to any reports or make any copies of them".

"Right Uncle Gary, how about a meal then I'll hit the road home". "That'll be nice" he replied.

After they had moved into the 'Cherub Restaurant' and had their meal, it was late evening before the ex Police Superintendent and the Lady Private Investigator left the Angel Hotel.

"So much for a short meeting and a frost warning" Brenda commented.

"Have a safe journey home," said the ex Superintendent leaning forward and kissing her on the cheek as she started to get into her own car. "I promise I will, and you take care, Uncle Gary. I expect we shall be meeting again shortly at Farnham".

Gary closed the door of Brenda's car and waved as she drove away. He shook his head nonchalantly as he walked over to his car and took an overnight case from the back seat.

When Brenda arrived home her uncle informed her that a George Oaksey from Birmingham had telephoned wanting to speak to her urgently, the details were on the pad by the telephone. Brenda pulled the page with the message on from the pad and read it as she proceeded upstairs wondering what on earth he wanted. She sat on the bed looking first at the telephone, then at the reports that she had taken from the envelope. After thinking for a while she decided that the reports were very important, her future actions depended on these, she could then inform George.

There were six photocopied reports and an index card in the envelope, 'Uncle Gary was right' she thought while she looked at the index card stapled to the first report. There are two reports missing if they were all on file. Not even a report on the letter from M.I.D. she quickly read through the reports, the first being dated September 20th 93 when a memo had arrived from the Met reporting assistance required by the Francois de Mere Securite Services Belgium. Their Chief Inspector Jean Claude and George Obayo were investigating a diamond smuggling ring and would contact the Police when they had something to report. Someone had written across it 'Customs and Excise'

A report dated October 11.93. From Commander Benfield stating that he and DI White had interviewed Jean Claude and George Obayo and were satisfied with their identity and had passed them to the Customs and Excise office in Dover. Brenda nodded 'not so much red tape there as there would be up here. Good thinking Benny'.

The next was a telephone message dated October 29, 93. It read: 'To Commander Benfield from Jean Claude'. Have strong lead suggest meeting with Customs and Excise and yourself soonest. Will contact tomorrow a.m. End of message'.

The remainder of the messages covered the reports from Interpol on a missing private investigator giving Jean Claude's name and description.

The next sheath of papers was the report from the West Midlands Police on the finding of a body at the bottom of a bonfire.

The last report Brenda read was on the 'hit and run' death of George Obayo in Canning Town High Street. The card index also showed two other reports that should have been there, one from Inspector Greaves, Canning Town Police Station reporting the finding of a Toyota car. The second missing report was from George Obayo to Commander Benfield.

After Brenda had finished reading the reports, she phoned George Oaksey in Birmingham, being late in the evening he answered her call immediately. He informed her of his concern, because he had not heard from her for a couple of days.

After all, people in this case seemed to be disappearing like flies.

Brenda told him not to worry, she had a couple of matters to clear up and she would return in a couple of days.

She then returned to the reports and although quite pleased with them she had a feeling that there was something not quite right. There didn't seem to be enough reports in the file it was far too thin, especially since it had been established that the corpse found in the fire was the remains of Jean Claude.

Having made a record on her tape recorder she then shredded the copies, showered and went to bed.

The following day Brenda called 'Digger Davis' having decided to take up his offer of help. He was having breakfast when he received the call at seven thirty and told Brenda that he wasn't doing anything today and was still on leave for another seven days. They arranged to meet in Aldershot at twelve o'clock midday. Having made the appointment Brenda made a note of the address of Fiesta Lighting at Amesbury Road, Salisbury and also of Mr. Jones the owner's private address as taken from Tuffy's notes. Putting these notes into her handbag she proceeded to pack her suitcase and then went down to breakfast and say her good-byes.

Digger Davis and Brenda followed each other into the car park at The Flag public house, as Digger got out of his car, Brenda wound down her window.

"Good to see you. Belated New Year greetings" he shouted.

"Same to you", Brenda replied.

After lunching together on steak and kidney pies, chips and 'mushy peas' being washed down by a nice cool glass of lager, they settled down in the corner of the lounge to discuss the case. Brenda explained to Dennis the enquiry she wished him to make for her at Salisbury and gave him the details she had already written down for him.

Later Brenda made her way to the Cumberland Hotel in Oxford Street London where she had already booked to stay the night. After parking in the underground car park at Hyde Park, she took her overnight bag from the back seat of the car and made her way through the labyrinth of tunnels. Coming to the surface alongside Marble Arch, then down into another subway to cross Oxford Street and coming to the surface again only a short distance from the entrance to the Cumberland Hotel.

While she was checking in she glanced at her watch, it was five o'clock,

"Oh good, I can grab a couple of hours 'kip' before dinner".

She mused, reverting to her Army slang.

It was seven thirty before Brenda woke up and after hurriedly taking a shower and dressing, she dashed out of her room to the elevator that was slow in coming; deciding to run down the stairs instead of waiting.

As Brenda ran out of the stair well into the Hotel Lobby, she saw the headwaiter standing at the entrance to the dining room. Walking across to him she asked what time the dining room closed. In a typically English butlers tone of voice, he looked her straight in the eyes,

"The kitchens close at eleven thirty, Madam, but we stay open all night for coffee and snacks".

"Good" she replied "I can nip down Oxford Street to the sales".

"Very good, Madam" the headwaiter replied with a look of disdain "Madam does not wish to dine now?" he asked.

"No, I'll dine later" replied Brenda and dashed back to the elevators. The door slid back as she pressed the button on entering the elevator Brenda turned and pressed the button for the third floor. As she was pressing the button the elevator door opposite opened and Commander Benfield walked out of the elevator accompanied by two Middle Eastern looking gentlemen. Brenda stepped back into the corner of lift hoping that 'Benny Benfield' had not seen her. The door closed and she seemed to be at the third floor very quickly.

Seeing Commander Benfield in London on the second of January puzzled Brenda as she walked down Oxford Street, thinking he should be up at the Police Station at Stratford-on-Avon making a lot of noise but doing very little as usual. She felt sure that she had recognized the two gentlemen with him but could not remember from where. She eventually closed her mind to them and concentrated on the job in hand, January sales shopping. She would have liked to have spent more time browsing and admiring the Christmas lights but the movement of the crowds did not allow one to stand still for long.

Despite the congestion of the sales shoppers, Brenda managed to make her way through most of the big stores finally arriving at Selfridges. It was half past eight as she walked through the door of the store and knowing that the store closed at nine o'clock, she made her way across to ladies fashions. After purchasing a few items she made her way upstairs to the gents section. As she stepped off the escalator she noticed the two gentlemen she had seen earlier in the evening with Commander Benfield at the hotel. This did not deter her from continuing her shopping spree and looking for a birthday present for her uncle. As she was looking through the shirt rack she suddenly remembered where she had seen the two men; they were two of the Marvo brothers.

Their passports showed them to be of Lebanese origin but many people in the legal profession thought otherwise. She looked over towards them as they made their way to the escalator to return downstairs. She quickly selected two shirts and a tie for her uncle and walked over to the till as the store announcer informed the customers that the store would be closing in five minutes. As Brenda faced the crowds outside the store she debated whether to return to the hotel for her meal or to visit a restaurant close by. She chose The Flamenco on Barrowgate in preference to the hassle of the crowded pavements.

Brenda awoke early the next morning and as she lay in bed making the most of her lie-in contemplating the breakfast that she had ordered from room service for nine thirty. She started thinking about the events of the previous evening, the Marvo brothers and who they were and what Benny was doing in their company. They were mobsters, not 'heavies' but sly ones who get their way with clubs, casinos and small companies by promising investment and gradually taking over without making payment.

If there were any objection people just disappeared abroad and if any relatives made any enquiries, they also disappeared.

Nothing had ever been proved against them.

It was also known that they were 'loan sharks' but they were very selective.

Again you had to have property and usually the limit on loans with cleared title was twenty per cent.

A knock at the door and a call of 'room service' broke her train of thought and after the waiter had left, Brenda thought 'even so, I can't understand why Bennie was associating with them'. When she had finished her breakfast she rang the Canning Town Police Station and made an appointment with Inspector Greaves for one thirty. Having plenty of time, she leisurely showered and dressed leaving the room at the requested time of eleven o'clock. Realizing that she was early for her appointment as she drove over the Canning Town station bridge, Brenda continued over the High Street junction and turned into the car park of the Canning Town Shopping Centre. She purchased a coffee and sat in the window of the cafe so that she could watch not only her car but also the traffic in the High Street.

She still had about a half-hour to kill. She took her notebook out of her handbag also her tape recorder, which she checked to make sure it was working. She then spoke into it giving the date and time of place before returning it to her handbag positioning it behind the material part of her handbag where it would catch any conversation.

The notebook she had decided would only be used as a blind, having made a note of some questions with which to start the interview. Hoping to get the Inspector talking, although, she was well aware of what his opinion would be of private investigators.

At 1.30pm Brenda drove into the car park of the police station and on entering the building was surprised to see it had been updated and the receptionist was no longer seated behind a window.

She approached the desk and asked to see Inspector Greaves.

"He's been out all morning, I'll see if he's returned" the duty Constable replied and spoke to someone on the telephone. When he had finished, he directed Brenda to take a seat on the opposite side of the entrance hall. Eventually a tall fair-haired young man in a dark grey pinstripe suit highly polished black shoes came down the stairs and approached the receptionist who pointed to Brenda.

He walked over, holding out his hand saying,

"I'm Inspector Greaves. Sorry to have kept you waiting. How can I help you?"

Standing up and taking his hand Brenda noticed that he had manicured nails and a strong grip; introducing herself she said.

"I'm Brenda Armstrong, I'd like to talk with you about George Obayo", choosing the direct approach.

"I see. You had better come upstairs" he replied turning to lead the way across to the stairs. Once upstairs they proceeded along a corridor lined with office doors to a door at the end.

"Sorry I can't offer you an interview room like they do on television, this is all I have".

He waved his arm around his fifteen foot by fifteen office "However, I can offer you a seat" he said offering Brenda a chair.

"Who are you and what about George Obayo? What can you tell me?" Inspector Greaves asked.

Brenda showed him her card and told him briefly about her involvement not forgetting to mention her interviews with Commander Benfield and Chief Inspector Sullivan but not disclosing everything.

"Well" he said after Brenda had finished "that was direct and to the point, but I know I can't disclose anything to you without authority from my superiors but I can inform you that we are not getting very far into the investigation of the death of George Obayo. The Yard seems to favor 'hit and run' accident but I can inform you that we think we have found the car involved.

It had been parked at the car park at the Inner City Airport at East India docks for four weeks before their security boys reported it and we only came on it by chance when I was having a drink with their Chief Security officer one night. We were talking about work when it came up in conversation and he gave me all the details the next day. I reported all this to the Yard and haven't heard anything since".

"So who's the company who own the car?" asked Brenda getting a little impatient.

"I suppose it is alright to give you that" said the Inspector walking to a filing cabinet "you're lucky, I was thinking of giving all this to our reference library, seeing as the Yard are now involved and its not active any longer". He withdrew the file and returned to his desk. "There" he said as he picked a fax out of the file and started writing the address of the hire company on a note pad.

"I see that the hire firm is Stadium Hire, Bolton and they collected the car on the 20th of December".

Brenda looked at the address on the memo then slipped it into her handbag as she got up to leave.

"Thanks Inspector, it has been most enlightening talking to you".

"Only too pleased to oblige, Miss Armstrong" said the Inspector wondering what had been so enlightening in what he had said as they shook hands at the door of the police station.

As she drove along the North Circular Road towards the A40 taking her out of London, Brenda finally decided to take Chief Inspector Sullivan into her confidence. She thought there were too many anomalies creeping into the case, she may need police help if she wanted to take a close look at the Toyota. She pulled into a transport cafe to use the telephone, not trusting the privacy of a cellular telephone any more since the disclosure of Princess Diana's private conversation on her phone. She made two calls the first to her company's office trying to contact George Oaksey. He was not there so she spoke to his partner Brian Tomlinson and asked him to make an appointment for her at Stadium Hire. Also making sure that they did not repair the damage to the Toyota as it had been involved in the 'hit and run' accident under investigation. She knew that she was skating on thin ice to ask this but she thought it might frighten them into holding on for a while, if not this is where a little help from a friend may help. That is if Chief Inspector Sullivan could be called a friend.

After speaking to Brian, Brenda then rang Stratford Police Station to speak to the Chief Inspector. Apparently she was lucky to catch him, he was just about to leave for a press conference with Commander Benfield that was much to his disgust.

"I've nothing to tell them, Brenda. It is all codology; I don't know whom he is trying to impress. It certainly isn't me".

"That's my Benny!" said Brenda.

"Yes, well you can keep him as far as I am concerned. Give me a call when you are approaching Stratford. I know a nice place as you are running into Stratford where we can meet for a pint".

Leaving the Oxford bypass and proceeding through Woodstock past the gates to Blenheim Palace, on through Chipping Norton, she contacted the Chief Inspector as she drove through Atherstone and was told that he was busy but would call her back. She was running into the outskirts of Stratford-on-Avon before her phone rang and she arranged to meet him at the Appleton Hall Hotel that she was fast approaching.

CHAPTER TWENTY THREE

After leaving the Cumberland Hotel, Commander Benfield drove back to Stratford-on-Avon arriving at his hotel at eleven o'clock. On asking for his key at reception he found three messages waiting for him requesting he contact the Station Duty Sergeant immediately. Despite this he had a quick shower and a shave before he contacted the Duty Sergeant. He was informed of the fire at Haydock Farm and the subsequent car chase ending with Nigel Courtney losing his Porsche. This made the Commander smile "Serves him right. He should leave things to the professionals" he said quietly.

The Sergeant heard the remark "yes Sir", he replied taking the phone away from his ear and looking askance at it.

"Sorry" said the Commander "I'll be right over" putting the phone down and grabbing his coat from the bed.

"Business calls looks like a late night tonight" he called to the receptionist when he tossed her his keys as he walked out of the back door to the car park at the rear of hotel. The last thing he remembered was opening the door of his car.

He regained consciousness laid along the underside of his car. It was very quiet and dark. He did not know how long he had lain there. He gradually staggered to his feet, his head throbbed, as if hundreds of tiny men were banging around inside with sledgehammers. He staggered to the back door of the hotel and found it locked. Trying to turn the door handle and banging on the door two or three times but no one opened it.

"Should be somebody there, "he grumbled as he staggered round to the front door. He found a bell button and pressed it, getting an immediate response. Mr. Hill the night porter opened the door slowly, as he did so the Commander collapsed through the door onto the night porter. Knocking the breath out of his body as he landed on the floor with the unconscious Commander on top of him.

After he had got over the shock, the night porter struggled out from underneath the unconscious Commander and ran to the phone and dialed '999'.

Inspector White arrived at the crime scene as Commander Benfield was being placed in the ambulance.

He immediately cordoned of the car park and set the four Constables who had arrived at the scene to assist him, to their various tasks. He then went to his Commanders bedroom to see if his attacker had been there and was still looking around the bedroom when Chief Inspector Sullivan and Sergeant Thomas arrived.

The hotel manager, Mr. Grimshaw met them at reception and begged them to be as quiet as possible.

"It is bad enough publicity as it is, without the guests being disturbed" he whined.

"We'll be as quiet as possible but one of our police commanders has been mugged on your property and I don't take that lightly sir" replied Chief Inspector Sullivan.

Leaving Mr. Grimshaw standing by the reception desk, wringing his hands, worrying what the press and his hotel quests would say the next morning. The Chief Inspector sent Sergeant Thomas to look at Commander Benfields car and search for any clues to show the reason for the mugging, while he went to the Commanders room to see if he could find anything there, only to find that Inspector White was doing the same thing.

Outside the Sergeant shone his torch around the Commanders Ford Scorpion. He found the car keys underneath the car and assumed the Commander had dropped them when he was attacked. He picked them up and tried the door lock to make sure they fitted, as he opened the door he found a card on the driving seat. He didn't pick up the card but shone his torch closer to read the writing. He saw a monogram which could have been a logo or a letter 'X". A short message read 'NEXT TIME COULD BE DIFFERENT'.

Sergeant Thomas slid the card into a plastic bag, took another look around the inside of the car and satisfied there was nothing else, he closed the door and slid the keys into another plastic bag. Taking another look around the car and finding nothing he then left the scene and went to report to his Chief Inspector. Chief Inspector Sullivan not satisfied that he hadn't found anything in the Commanders room. Returned downstairs to the Manager who was still standing at the reception desk talking to another man, who was introduced to the Chief Inspector as Mr. Murdoch the head hall porter who would be taking over the duty for the rest of the night. Mr. Hill was being detained in hospital. The Chief Inspector instructed Mr. Grimshaw not to allow anyone into the Commanders room or to allow anyone to touch his car. He also informed him that the police would collect the car the following day.

Inspector White had elected to sit by his Commanders bedside to take a statement when he recovered consciousness. He was still very shaken by the attack on his boss.

The Chief Inspector and Sergeant Thomas were standing by the Chief's car in the car park at the rear of the Police Station. Making arrangements to meet at the General Hospital later in the morning. There were two floodlights illuminating the car park and the rear entrance of the Police Station. The Chief was looking over Sergeant Thomas's shoulder when he stopped talking. Sergeant Thomas was standing with his back towards the fence where there were four cars parked.

The Chief Inspector pointed over his shoulder.

"Look over your there, Thomas. Is that a black Porsche?"

Get your torch," he instructed "What is Nigel Courtney's registration number?" he then asked.

"The cheeky bugger" said Thomas "He nick's it then drives it around for a short period of time then leaves it here, I wonder how long it's been parked here".

"I don't know, Thomas but I do know that when I find him he'll go down for a long stretch. Inform the Duty Sergeant. I'm going home to bed".

The following morning Sergeant Thomas arrived at the General Hospital at eight thirty only to find that only Mr. Hill was in the hospital enjoying all the attention. Commander Benfield had signed himself out at eight o'clock.

As Sergeant Thomas walked into the Police Station he found the place in an uproar Commander Benfield was ordering everybody about and when he saw Sergeant Thomas he wanted to know why Inspector Sullivan wasn't in yet. Sergeant Thomas tried to explain but the Commander wouldn't listen,

"Get him here immediately. I want action. I want this case wrapped up" he stormed as he went up to his office. Before the Sergeant had time to contact his Chief, he was called into Commander Benfield's office and asked again if he had heard from the Inspector.

"What's happening about this damned Porsche which has been dumped on us?"

Again Sergeant Thomas gave a negative reply saying that nothing was being done until the lab boys had finished with it.

"I see, so we all sit on our arses drinking tea, do we, waiting for something to happen? Tell Sullivan I want to see him when he comes in".

Inspector White and Sergeant Thomas walked out of the office together.

"What the hell is the matter with him, Snowy?" Sergeant Thomas asked.

"I don't know he's been like this ever since he woke up this morning. Says it's your entire fault. You should have cleared this up a long time ago".

"Have you been with him all night, Snowy?"

"Yes I slept in the lounge area. The sister woke me this morning when Benny woke at seven".

As the two Detectives were starting to do some work in Sergeant Thomas's office, Chief Inspector Sullivan walked into the reception area downstairs.

"Keep your head down, Guv" called the Sergeant on duty at the reception as the Chief Inspector walked passed his desk. The Chief Inspector walked back to the desk

"Got problems, have we Bob?"

"You could say that, Benfields on the warpath, sir. Signed himself out the hospital eight o'clock, been here ever since, wants to know where you are".

"Thanks Bob I'll have to find somewhere to disappear to" and he ran upstairs to his office almost colliding with his Sergeant as he opened the door.

"Good morning Thomas" he said cheerfully, "I believe we have a case of a disappearing Commander who turns up spitting fire and brimstone".

"Yes sir, sorry I couldn't stop you calling in at the hospital but he's had me in his office twice already. Blames us for everything".

"Well, I think we'll let him stew a bit longer. C'mon we've got a job to do. We're going out to Haydock Dyke Farm, I think it's a case of arson; tell Carter and Hopkins to meet us there".

As they were leaving the Chief Inspector walker over to the duty Sergeant,

"Thanks Bob. Let me know when the lab boys have finished with the Porsche. I want to be here when Courtney picks it up".

"Yes Guv. That's just what Commander Benfield said when he went out".

"Did he say where he was going? I haven't seen him, I thought I was being clever and dodging him".

"He didn't say Guv, and he didn't leave a telephone number either in case we need to contact him, "replied the desk Sergeant.

"Funny, anyway Bob he's taken his sidekick with him hasn't he?"

"No, he sent him home to catch up on his beauty sleep"

"What's he playing at Thomas?" the Chief Inspector asked as they made their way to the Sergeants car, "First he apparently blows his top at everybody for not doing their job properly then he disappears again and doesn't leave a contact number or forwarding address, what the hells he playing at"

CHAPTER TWENTY FOUR

As Sergeant Thomas and his Chief Inspector were driving over the river bridge at Bidford. They were informed by radio that the Black Granada that had been involved in the car chase the previous evening. Had been found hidden behind one of the workshops at the Long Marston aerodrome and it was now being towed to the Police Workshops for the lab boys to carry out their tests.

Five minutes later they drove into Haydock Dyke Farmyard and found that Inspector Carter and D.C. Hopkins were already on site along with the arson experts from the Fire Brigade.

"How on earth are they going to find anything in that lot?" said Sergeant Thomas as he leaned against the bonnet of his car looking at the shell of the building that had been their incident room for the last three or four weeks "What a mess!"

The roof had collapsed and the tiles were scattered all over the inside. The fire had spread along the roof trusses but it had been put out before it had reached the end of the building. The old wooden pillars that looked like tree trunks still stood intact holding up three parts of the roof. Some of the equipment had been spared but an old four-wheeled flat trailer that had been used to bring in straw bales was covered in debris. The fire officers were concentrating on what had been the office area.

"You know Thomas, these fella's can tell you exactly where the fire base was and also how it started. I should think that it was a petrol bomb through the window. I see Carter and Hopkins are looking around outside the yard. Find out what they are doing, I'm going to see the Colonel"

The Chief was into his second coffee and brandy 'Just to keep the cold out' he had said as he accepted the second one,

"I suppose Colonel, this place has a preservation order on it?"

"Yes" replied the Colonel "I'll have to rebuild the cart shed in the original style but I'll have to do some serious thinking about it first, conservationist's you know, I had a lot of trouble with the planning department when I built the old Dutch barn and milking parlor. I can't think about the people who started the fire, what type of person are they to do a thing like that?"

"Well Colonel, whoever did it was running scared. That was our incident room and they must have thought we had something important in there. I'd like to know what it was. I hope Carter and Hopkins come up with something. After all we closed this place down before Christmas".

As the Colonel and Chief Inspector walked outside into the yard Inspector Carter joined them.

"I've looked everywhere around the fire scene, sir, but neither Hopkins nor myself have come up with anything. We'll keep looking but I don't hold out much hope".

"No, I don't either, like the cars we found to be squeaky clean, very professional, but they'll slip up one day and when they do I'll be waiting for them".

"The wife and I are going down to the Falcon in the village for a ploughman's lunch, Chief Inspector. Why don't you join us?"

"Good idea, Colonel. I'll get Thomas to drive me down there".

The Falcon Inn at Bidford-on-Avon stands on the High Street and is well known for it's traditional ale served from the barrel.

The Colonel and his guest's had settled down to enjoy their 'Pub fare' when the Chief Inspectors cellular phone rang.

As he answered his face went white.

"I don't believe it, in broad daylight! O.K. we'll be right over" looking across to the Colonel he said

"Sorry about this, I'll have to postpone this lunch until a later date. We have to dash" he said picking up a bread roll, breaking it in half and spreading it with homemade chutney, then filling it with cheese and onions and wrapping it in a napkin.

"I don't know when we'll be eating again. Cheers, Colonel" he said looking out to the car park. Sergeant Thomas following his example with his roll shouted, "Wait for me" to the Chief Inspector leaving the bar.

As they drove out of the car park Sergeant Thomas asked,

"What's happened?"

"Somebody had the nerve to hijack the tow truck which was taking the Granada to Headquarters right outside Birch's Scrap-yard. Lets high-tail it to the scrap-yard where the driver of the truck is,

I bet he's all shaken up, don't you, fancy having your tow truck swiped from under your nose," the Chief Inspector remarked as he looked longingly at his cheese and onion roll, then he bit into it.

"Umm this is a good cheese roll I made Thomas, must be nearly a pound of Cheshire cheese in here. Get stuck into yours," he said with his mouth full of bread roll and trying to push strands of onion in with a finger.

They found the driver of the tow truck sitting in the security office at Birchs Ltd. scrap-yard. He was sitting wrapped in a blanket beside a radiator obviously trying to keep warm and sipping a cup of hot tea laced with brandy.

"Medicinal, of course" muttered the Chief Inspector "Now tell us what happened".

Ted Walpole the driver of the tow truck explained to the two policemen that, after picking up the Granada at the Long Marston Industrial Estate he had decided the quickest way to Police Headquarters. Was to go through to Mickleton turning left at the crossroads south of Birch's yard, over the railway bridge and through Welford.

Continueing "As I approached the crossroads I saw a car on the side of the road and a man was flagging me down. He asked me if I had any spare petrol on board and I said yes, I had a spare couple of gallons in the back. I told him that it would cost him and he offered me a tenner. As I went round to the box on the back he clobbered me on the back of the head. Look Chief Inspector, see the bump" he said turning his head and rubbing the swelling.

"I can see it Ted" said the Chief Inspector "then what happened?"

"Well, Inspector, I woke up in the ditch stripped down to me vest and pants, I felt real groggy and cold so I decided to walk up here. I was bloody freezing by the time I arrived here, I can tell you".

"Could you recognize the man if you saw him again7".

"I expect so" replied the tow truck driver.

An ambulance came screaming off the Welford road just managing to stop at the main gate, closely followed by a police patrol car with its lights flashing, and siren blaring.

"Here comes the cavalry, sir" remarked Sergeant Thomas

"Tell them to go to the scene of the crime and have a look but I don't think they will find anything. Tell them not to waste too much time on at the scene, Thomas. Everything seems too professional. See to it right away will you?" said the inspector turning from the window and speaking to the driver.

"This bloke that hit you. Did he have a local accent or did it sound like a London accent, for example?"

"No, it didn't sound local, probably London. Hoy! That hurt" the driver shouted to the paramedic who was treating the lump at the back of his head. Satisfied with the work he had done, the paramedic took the drivers arm to assist him out to the ambulance.

"Go with him Thomas" the Chief Inspector said as his Sergeant came through the office door "See if you can get anything more out of him. Quick they're closng the door"

His Sergeant ran over to the ambulance and managed to scramble into the back of the ambulance as the paramedic was closing the door.

Chief Inspector Sullivan was still standing at the door of the security office with his arms folded and pulling his lower lip when the security guard returned.

"Well Inspector, you do look deep in thought".

"Yep" replied the Chief Inspector "Had any black Granada cars for crushing here lately? Like this morning for instance?"

"You must be joking, Inspector. You're not joking are you? Do you want me to have a look?" asked the Security officer with a quizzical look on his face.

"Might as well while we are here. I'll walk across to the gate with you, it's on the way out".

Commander Benfield was sitting at his desk with his door open having eaten his salad sandwich lunch at his desk he had every intention of catching Sullivan and his Sergeant when they returned. He was not in a very good mood, but then he hadn't been all morning. Having been at the scene of the crime at the hotel and found nothing, and his Chief Inspector being out of his office and, to make matters worse, out of touch as well.

He had to make do with a strange Inspector who was not familiar with the case. Still, his new assistant had made a good job of taking statements that would possibly only duplicate the ones taken the night previous.

As Chief Inspector Sullivan and Sergeant Thomas reached the top of the stairs on the way to their respective offices, a stern voice commanded.

"In here. Both of you"

As they entered the Commanders office they saw Inspector Steele of the local C.I.D. who had been seconded on to the enquiry in place of Inspector White.

As the Sergeant closed the door, he proceeded to reprimand them for their absence from the office for the morning. He also had to inform them that they were lackadaisical in their approach to their work and that under the circumstances he had no alternative but to ask for their removal from the case.

On hearing this remark Chief Inspector Sullivan looked at his Commander and turned to his Sergeant standing by his side, not having been asked to sit down when the entered,

"You'd better leave the room, Sergeant and you Inspector. What I am going to say to the Commander is strictly between the two of us".

Inspector Steele hesitated not knowing what to do. Sergeant Thomas crossed the room and took hold of his elbow, to guide him out of the room, whispering to him as they left the room.

"I wouldn't want to hear what is going to be said in there, Bill. Come on, let's go and get a cuppa. We can bring it back here".

After they had left, Chief Inspector Sullivan, in a very quiet and controlled voice said,

"Right Commander. There's only you and me and your tape recorder".

"I have no tape recorder. You know it is against regulations".

"We all know that. I know that doesn't stop every conversation you have either in or out of this office being recorded" he walked up to the desk, picked up the desk tidy and emptied its contents on the desk. He sorted through the bits and pieces with a pencil and found what he was looking for. Stuck to the side of the pen and pencil holder was a 'bug' and opening the top drawer of the desk he found a Sony tape recorder that was working.

"I suppose this doesn't belong to you Commander".

"No, actually it belongs to Inspector White".

The Chief Inspector opened the recorder and removed the tape; he then opened the bottom draw, which was empty. Then moving to the other side of the Commander, he first opened the bottom drawer that was also empty. The Chief Inspector opened the top drawer, he removed the papers and reaching to the back of the drawer he again found what he was looking for, a pocket tape recorder which was still working with a wire attached to it; he crawled under the desk. Pushing the Commander unceremoniously out of his way he found a small microphone attached to the underside of the desk in front of the chair he was going to sit in.

"You dirty, slimey creep sir! Got any more stashed away anywhere? You talk about having me removed from the case. If I showed these to my boss" showing the commander the two tapes he had removed.

"You would be the one to be removed. Not from the case but from the force. I'll solve this case my way. You've done bugger all since you came here, leaving all the work to Snowy, Thomas and me. After finding this little lot, I'm telling you that if you get in my way, I'll run straight over you".

The Commander sat quiet for a minute or two.

"I've requested a press release for five o'clock, Chief Inspector. I would like you to attend and give a statement on the attack made on me last night. Also I would like you to report on the car chase and events leading up to it, plus your report on the attack on the tow truck driver. You know, that's quite a lot to give the press, Chiefy"

The Chief Inspector perked up a bit.

"Hmm almost as if we had a bloody war on our hands"

"I suppose it is really. I see we have about an hour on our hands. Don't you think a cup of coffee would be in order, Chiefy?"

The Chief Inspector got up to leave without answering the question.

"I know I've been a naughty boy, Chiefy, and I shouldn't have done those things but can't we forgive and forget?" He stood up and held his hand out.

The Chief Inspector ignored it and replied.

"I've got a case to solve, Benny. I'll see you downstairs at five o'clock" closing the door behind him as he left the office.

Chief Inspector Sullivan walked into Sergeant Thomas's office on his way to his own, the two officers he'd ejected from his Commander's office were still sitting there waiting for him.

"Got things sorted, have we sir?" asked Thomas.

"Shall we say that we may now have a better understanding in our work place. I think the Commander and I have come to understand one another better and Oh, Thomas, if you have to go into his office in future be careful what you say and how you say it. You as well, Steele" he said looking over to the Inspector "Incidentally, Inspector, I think he wants you to help him with his press release"

As Inspector Steele left the office, the Chief Inspector asked his Sergeant to follow him, on entering his office he closed the door firmly making sure it was shut.

"Right, Sergeant, I want you to nip down town and get a packet of each of these type of tapes. Then I want you to take a recording on each of the tapes and don't let anyone hear them"

Chief Inspector Sullivan then passed the tapes he had removed from the two recorders he had found in Commander Benfields office, to Sergeant Thomas.

"Right sir, what are they about?"

"If I knew, Thomas, I wouldn't be asking you to make a copy, would I?"

The Chief Inspector came out of the pressroom before his Commander and as he passed the Duty Sergeant he was handed a note with a telephone number on it. Underneath was written, Brenda Armstrong.

Wondering what it was all about he went straight upstairs and dialed the number.

Brenda answered immediately, making arrangements to meet later.

The Chief Inspector had just finished speaking with Brenda when Sergeant Thomas returned with the two tapes that he had managed to get recorded. The Chief Inspector asked him if he had listened to them.

"I figured that if no one else was to hear them, neither should I", replied Sergeant Thomas shaking his head.

"Alright, Thomas, don't be so goody, goody. I bet if they had been blue films you would have been at the front of the queue".

He placed the two tapes in an envelope, sealed it and taped down the flap, writing his name on the front. He then gave them to the Sergeant to place them in the safe downstairs and make sure that the deposit was recorded. He then put the two originals into another envelope, which he placed in his inside pocket, then put two more loose ones into the top draw of his desk, putting the remainder into the bottom draw, which he locked.

CHAPTER TWENTY FIVE

Appleton Hall Hotel was glowing, lit up by small white lights draped through the bare branches of the Japanese cherry trees that surrounded the hotel and the lawns.

The Elizabethan manor house is situated at the main road junction of the A46, A422 and A425 on the south side of the Clapton Bridge that carries the A46 over the River Avon to join the High Street that runs through the centre of the town. Appleton Hall had been converted into a hotel in the late thirties and had later been purchased by Trust House Forte who had extended and renovated the hall making it into one of the most luxurious Hotels in the area. It was also one of Brenda's favorite eating houses when she felt like treating herself to a luxury weekend like she had done in the past; when she was on leave from the Army after solving a difficult case.

Brenda walked into the hotel lounge and found Chief Inspector Sullivan sitting at a table in the middle of the lounge.

She ordered a gin and tonic and walked over to join him.

"Well, Brenda, this is a surprise. Is it your birthday or something that we are celebrating?"

"Well now, Inspector, I'm not saying that, but shall we say that I feel like having an intelligent conversation for a change?"

"Sounds good to me. What shall we talk about, food, wine or sport?"

"First shall we say, food and wine?" Brenda replied signaling to a waiter, "I'm starving, Inspector, aren't you?"

"Not at these prices, I'm not. My wife would have fed me for a week on what a meal costs here."

"Never mind, Inspector, the treats on me."

"Cut the Inspector, Brenda. Call me Sully, everyone else does, that is, behind my back of course. My mother christened me Vernon but don't call me that" Brenda smiled as he continued "Several kids got sore heads at school for calling me that and I never forgave my mother for it either".

"Never mind, Sully it is," replied Brenda laughing.

They were into the coffee liqueur stage before Brenda mentioned the reason for the meeting. She started to tell him what she had discovered about the case on her visit to London, not mentioning her source of information or Benny's visit to the Cumberland Hotel.

"Ooh Brenda must you talk about work. Don't spoil a delightful evening", the Chief Inspector interrupted.

Brenda apologized and said she was only bringing him up to date and that she may need his help the following day. Making it sound as if his help could be very important. 'The guile of the woman' as the Chief Inspector told his Sergeant later date.

"Well, alright, Brenda but is there somewhere a bit more private where we can discuss this" he asked looking around the restaurant.

"I suppose there is, my room. I'm staying here for the night. Coming, Sully?" Brenda answered, sweeping up her glass of liqueur as she rose to her feet and slinkily walked out of the restaurant, with the Chief Inspector following her closely, trying to remember how long it had been since he had been invited into a lady's boudoir.

Brenda led the way along the corridor on the first floor to her room at the rear of the hotel. It was in the new extension to the hotel, overlooking a large patio with a fountain in the centre and the large surrounding gardens. He noted that it was a typical hotel room, not too large, bathroom on the right as you entered, case stand on the left, double bed with bedside cabinets and bedside lights, lounge area in front of the window with two easy chairs comfortable but not too comfortable.

"Park yourself, Sully" said Brenda taking off her jacket and hanging it in the wardrobe, at the sametime kicking off her shoes into the bottom.

"Whiskey and soda?" she asked as she opened the drink cabinet.

"No thanks, Brenda, let's get on, it's getting late" replied the Chief Inspector, shuffling about in his chair as if he felt uncomfortable.

"I think I'll have one. You help yourself when you are ready" she said, taking a small miniature bottle of gin and a bottle of tonic from the cabinet, leaving the door open for the Chief Inspector to help himself.

"Right, where was I?" she asked as she settled into the chair opposite him.

"Look, Sully." she started "I think you had better have that drink that I offered because, I think you are going to need it."

"Let me be the judge of that" he interrupted.

"Let me tell you that I don't think you have been fed the right information from the beginning of the case, Sully, because I think there is diamond smuggling involved."

"My God, Brenda, what next? We've got about half a dozen bodies out there, a serial killer on the loose and we have a mugger thrown in for good measure, now you come up with diamond smuggling. I suppose you are going to tell me that the Colonel and his mates were involved."

"Yes, they are and I've got a sworn statement to prove it. See, I told you to get yourself a drink "She took a whiskey and soda from the fridge and gave it to the Chief Inspector.

"Now, do you want to listen to what I have got to say?" She went to her briefcase and took out her pocket tape recorder and placed it on the table.

"Now, Sully. I taped this for you as I drove back from London today just in case anything happened to me. I locked it in my briefcase and tagged it with your name and address" she said showing him the tag, then continued,

"Tomorrow morning you will receive a letter explaining everything and giving you the code to open this case. I want you to keep the code in a safe place."

"Good Lord, Brenda, you're making this case sound very sinister. Do you think that something could happen to you?"

"It could happen to any one of us involved in this case, Sully."

"Listen to this first and then let me know what you think," said Brenda replenishing her drink and then nestling down on the floor beside the Inspector and leaning against his legs.

It was twenty minutes before the report ended.

The Chief Inspector didn't say anything for a couple of minutes and Brenda didn't move either, waiting for him to make a move or say something.

"I can't believe this. That bastard Benfield knew all the time and never said a thing to us. I'll get him for this, Brenda. I'll get him for sure. He's been acting very strange today", he then told her briefly what had happened over the last twenty-four hours.

Brenda still didn't tell him of the Commander's visit to her hotel, thinking that she had better use a bit of discretion with this piece of information.

"So, it strikes me that you might need a bit of police support in Bolton. When do you intend to go there?"

"I'll have to get an injunction first to stop him doing anything to the car"

"I may be able to help you there, then we'll see what we can do. I think I could use another drink, how about you?"

Brenda asked for 'just a gin'. He brought her drink back first and poured it into her glass. As he handed it back to her she took the glass in one hand and reached up catching his elbow and pulling his head down giving him a long lingering kiss. After what seemed to Sully an eternity she finally let go of him. "There's a better place for this than on the floor" she said scrambling to her feet, then placed her arms around his neck as she stood up.

"I think I ought to slip into something comfy, don't you?" Brenda murmured as she covered his lips with hers, her tongue darting between his open lips as they met.

"I know what I like, when I see what I like," she murmured between each gasp for air as she surfaced between each kiss and began to remove her skirt and then undo his tie. Sully looked over her shoulder at the small mirror on the dressing table as she leaned forward to kiss him again. 'I suppose I'm not bad looking for a forty year old' he thought as his trousers fell down round his ankles and Brenda stepped out of her skirt. Not breaking contact with their lips as they feverishly removed each other's garments then lowered themselves on to the bed.

Sully rolled onto the top of Brenda, then slowly and effortlessly entered her as their passion reached fever pitch and they climaxed in each other's arms.

As Brenda lay naked in Sully's arms, she said,

"That was beautiful, Sully. I'm quite envious of your wife, you know, I took a fancy to you the first day I met you." as she ran her fingers through his greying hair.

"I'm a widower, Brenda. My wife Angie died six months ago." Sully replied, tears coming to his eyes. Brenda snuggled closer to him then, quietly and more slowly they made love again.

The following morning Brenda was up first not waking Sully until the breakfast arrived. Sully had his breakfast 'while it was still warm' sitting at the table in Brenda's bathrobe.

After Sully and Brenda had dressed ready for the day's work ahead, Sully thanked Brenda for a wonderful evening meal and the marvelous evening that followed.

"It was my pleasure to accommodate a very special guest" she replied reaching over to touch his hand.

"Ah well, back to business" said Sully as they kissed goodbye and Brenda got into her car "Where can I reach you when I get the injunction for you?" he asked.

She replied that she would be at Nigel Courtney's office because there were quite a few answers she was looking for, reference, the transport drivers and Mr. Jones.

Chief Inspector Sullivan walked into the Stratford Police Station bright and cheerful, so much so, that the Duty Sergeant when asked by the Inspector if anything had happened during the night replied by asking the Chief Inspector.

"If he was alright and did he know what time it was, because he wasn't due in for another hour?"

"Thank you Sergeant" he answered, "spring is in the air, didn't you know?" He left the Sergeant shaking his head and went upstairs taking the steps two at a time.

Another person who was surprised to find the Chief Inspector at work early was Sergeant Thomas but he treated it as normal just saying, "Good morning, Guv" as he walked past the Chief inspectors door with his paper under his arm and tea and toast in his hands.

"Morning, Thomas. Come in here, will you?" called the Chief Inspector.

"Oh good, nip down and get another cup of tea will you?" taking his Sergeants cup of tea from his hand.

"On second thoughts don't bother, Thomas this tea is cold. How much do we know about Courtney Transport, Thomas? I mean the man who owns the company and the people who run it?"

"Not much, Sir. We know Nigel Courtney but not much about his business. I've met his security chief, David Simpkins but I can't say I know much about him either."

"Yes, that's what I thought, Thomas. I think it's time that we got to know more about them, don't you? I think we'll start this morning when Courtney comes in to pick up his car. You have him in your office 'cos. I may have to go out."

"What's this all about, Guv? I thought this was a murder enquiry. Now we're checking on transport companies."

The Chief Inspector told him all that he had heard the previous evening, glancing at his notes he had made and also making up his mind that he would get a pocket recorder for himself despite what he had said to Commander Benfield yesterday.

Sergeant Thomas was just as stunned on hearing the information as his Chief Inspector had been.

"That throws a different light on to it altogether, doesn't it sir? I mean that brings in the heavy gang from Customs and Excise, doesn't it? It also explains the way Commander Benfield has been acting, I mean disappearing and not saying anything to us. Sometimes even Snowy was a bit indifferent about things. This morning they have shot off in to Birmingham early."

"Have they indeed, Thomas? I didn't know that. Let's have a look in his office, see if we can see anything."

The door to Commander Benfields office was open when they tried it. Before he opened it the Chief Inspector checked all round the edges to see if there were any traps, that if broken would have told the Commander that someone had entered his office while he was out. After making sure there were none, they entered the office and closed the door quietly behind them.

"Before you move anything, Sergeant, make sure its not rigged. You take the filing cabinet; I'll take the desk. The place may be 'bugged' so only use sign language".

"Okay" the Sergeant whispered.

After searching for about fifteen minutes and not finding anything they signaled to each other to leave the office.

Back in his office the Chief Inspector asked his Sergeant if he had found anything.

"It was rigged for sound in a file, sir, on top of the filing cabinet which was locked and also by the country scene picture behind the door."

"I found one as well, in the desk light, I removed one from the light yesterday. All the desk drawers were locked and no paper anywhere, did you notice? I mean, look at this lot" pointing to his own desk. "How can you sort this lot and put it away every day?"

The telephone rang being nearest Sergeant Thomas answered it.

"Right, I'll be down, right away, Sergeant" He put the phone down and said "That's Nigel Courtney for his car, sir."

"Blimey, he's early. I told him eleven o'clock."

"It is a quarter to, sir."

"Right, Thomas. Pop along and don't forget to go through his statement of the other night then try and get some information about his business. I still can't understand why he left his keys in his car, though, can you? It beats me!" he said shaking his head.

The Sergeant went downstairs to meet Nigel Courtney.

"Hello, Nigel" he said as they met "Come to pick up your car, have you? We'll go and have a look at it after you have signed for the keys." Having collected the keys they went out to the car park at the rear of the station.

"Apparently, there were only your prints on the keys. Whoever took the car must have wanted a lift back to Stratford. Bit of a cheek though, parking it in our car park, don't you think?"

"What's this?" asked Nigel Courtney, picking a piece of paper from under the windscreen wiper. Written in ink in capital letters it said THANKS FOR THE LIFT.

"I can't believe this, Nigel. He parks the car here and then comes back and plants this after the 'lab' boys have finished with it. Is anything missing from the inside, no stereo missing anything like that Nigel? It's getting cold out here."

Nigel checked everything inside and started the engine, and seemed satisfied that everything was all right.

"Right. Let's go back to the office and check your statement and then you can go."

On the way back to the Sergeant's office they stopped off at the Duty Sergeant's desk for Nigel to sign for his car.

Before leaving his office to go to Bolton, the Chief Inspector had received a call from Brenda to tell him that she had gone straight to Stadium Hire to stop them from commencing work on the Toyota. She had been informed that they were scheduled to start repairing it this morning. She had managed to stall them up to now by driving straight there but did not know how much longer she could hold them. He faxed her a copy of the injunction order and returned to his office to finalize things with his Sergeant before he left.

On his way out of the police station he called at the office where Inspector Carter and D.C. Hopkins were working.

"Hopkins" he called "I want you with me for the rest of the day". Then turning to Detective Inspector Carter he instructed him.

"Tie in with Sergeant Thomas, will you? When he's finished with Nigel Courtney, he'll tell you all about it. C'mon Hopkins. Chop, Chop."

Driving up to Bolton, he hardly spoke to D.C. Hopkins, which was rather unusual, but as the D.C. remarked later 'If the car had suddenly sprouted wings, the Granada would have been airborne'. The Chief Inspector contacted Brenda as they left the M6 also as they were entering Bolton for instructions to get to Stadium Garage.

It was just after two thirty when they pulled on to The Stadium Garage forecourt.

"What kept you? Chief Inspector "Brenda asked. "This is

Mr. Godfrey, the proprietor of the Garage. He is most helpful really."

"Here's the injunction which I am officially serving on you to stop you working on the car until the police no longer require it. You have already received a copy of this document by fax. As you can see the car is suspected of being used in a hit and run accident." Chief Inspector Sullivan handed the legal document to Mr. Godfrey and asked if he could have a look at the car.

After having a good look at the damaged offside headlight and wing. He looked over to D.C. Hopkins and Brenda; rubbed his chin "I think it's been through a car-wash. It looks like a strip job to me "he remarked shaking his head slowly.

After looking inside then returning to the wing he asked.

"Who hired it, Mr.Godfrey?"

"I thought you would want those details, officer, I have them all copied for you in the office"

"Right. I'll get the local lab boys to have a look, if I may use your phone" the Chief Inspector asked.

Brenda and the two policemen from Stratford-on-Avon stayed at the office until the two laboratory assistants from the Bolton Crime Division had checked over the car. They decided to have it taken down to their headquarters, which, Mr.Godfrey was only too pleased to arrange with his own tow truck.

Mr.Godfrey had informed the Chief Inspector that he had checked out the name and address on the hire documents and had been to the address, 302, Pennine Way, Bolton. Mr. James Braithwaite was no longer at the address but he added, Mrs. Watson, Braithwaite's landlady told him that he had only been there for a couple of weeks, she says that he was looking for work.

Anyway, she reckons that he told her when he moved out, that he had found a job in Burnley and had moved to 'digs nearer to his work'. "But, Inspector, he had only been there for two weeks, and in that time, he had his driving license and a full British passport made out to him at that address. Funny, wasn't it?"

"Would you recognize him again, Mr.Godfrey? What about his voice? Did he have a local accent?"

"No, I don't think I could recognize him again. I don't know about his voice either, it was a long time ago, you see.

Perhaps Mrs. Watson may be able to help you."

After obtaining Mrs. Watson's telephone number from Mr. Godfrey. Chief Inspector Sullivan contacted her and was able to make arrangements to visit her immediately.

The Chief Inspector and D.C. Hopkins arrived at the semi-detached house in Pennine Way. It was typical of the design of estate houses of the late nineteen thirties brick built with rounded bay windows to the lounge and bedroom at the front and, had been newly clad with Cotswold stone. Mrs. Watson, having been widowed two years previously, was very proud of her home and her garden, which she worked at constantly, reminding her neighbors that 'her Frank had been very fond of his garden and it had been his pride and joy'.

The two policeman walked up the garden path, admiring the newly cut lawn and the standard roses which lined the path, she opened the glass paneled front door as the Chief Inspector was about to ring the front door bell, she greeted the two Policemen with a smile,

"You must be the two policeman, I've been looking out for you."

"Chief Inspector Sullivan, ma'am," The Chief Inspector said producing his warrant card then introducing his Detective Constable.

"This is my assistant, D.C. Hopkins."

"You'd better come in, Inspector. We don't want the neighbours listening to our conversation, do we? Nosey parkers they are."

Mrs. Watson replied as she showed them into the front room and offered them a cup of tea that was accepted. As she left the room, D.C. Hopkins took the opportunity to look at the photographs that decorated all the flat surfaces available. He picked up a photograph of a workman working on the front door. It was a colour photograph showing the two houses and the contrast in the new cladding on this house and the old brickwork on the adjoining houses. He passed it to the Chief Inspector, who remarked.

"Bloody good photography and sales gimmick by the cladding company, Hopkins."

"Yes, sir, but I wonder who the man is coming out of the door."

"Oh, that's Mr. Braithwaite," said Mrs. Watson as she entered the room with the tea tray.

"Now then, Inspector, milk, one spoon or two?" she asked as she put the tray on the top of the coffee table.

"You, Constable?" she asked as she started to pour the milk into the cup. "I'm pleased you found that photograph, Constable, I was going to show it to you. He was such a nice young man, Mr.Braithwaite never thought he would steal a car."

"No, Mrs. Watson he hasn't stolen a car" replied the Chief Inspector. "We found the car in London and we think it had been involved in a 'hit and run' accident. We just want to find Mr. Braithwaite and to eliminate him from our enquiries. You see he could have been attacked and the car stolen from him we just don't know" he carried on sounding very exasperated. "You see, in circumstances like these we have to pursue every line of enquiry."

"I see, Inspector, but I don't think Mr. Braithwaite would do a thing like that. I mean he was such a nice young man, never smoked never drank, always in bed early. No, Inspector, my Mr. Braithwaite wouldn't get involved in a thing like that, he wouldn't." she said, shaking her head from side to side.

"Where did he go from here, Mrs. Watson did he leave a forwarding address?"

"No, I told Mr. Godfrey that, you know, the man from the garage. He got a job in Burnley and moved to digs nearer his work. His room was as clean as a new pin when he left. All I had to do was change the sheets on the bed. Now you will have to go. I have to get a meal ready for my two boarders. You can take that photo if you want it, but let me have it back when you have finished with it."

As he got up to leave the Chief Inspector asked

"You are sure he didn't leave a forwarding address?"

"No. I told you he didn't, there's nothing in his room either."

"No Christmas mail?" asked D.C. Hopkins.

"No, well he wouldn't have would he? He had time before Christmas to let his friends know where he was didn't he?"

"I suppose so" agreed the D.C.

"We must be going, Mrs. Watson. Thanks for the tea. By the way, we were admiring your garden as we came up the path. Who looks after it for you? They're doing a fine job "remarked the Chief Inspector.

"I do it all myself. I don't let anyone touch my Franks garden. I keep it just as he would. When I lost him two years ago, I promised him I would keep it as nice as he did. I think I have, and I know he guides my hand as I prune his roses" she said with tears in her eyes."

"You must miss him terribly".

"Yes, I do. You see, we only had one son and we lost him. He was drowned in a sailing accident ten years ago at Morecombe and we were alone together for the last eight years. Now, you must go." she said guiding the Inspector to the front door.

As they drove along Pennine Way towards the M6 motorway, Chief Inspector Sullivan called Sergeant Thomas on has cellular phone.

"Thank God you rang in, sir. He's at it again." he said, referring to Commander Benfield.

"Allright, allright Sergeant" the Inspector said repeating himself trying to calm him down. "I think we have a breakthrough. We have finally managed to find a picture of our suspect. Be in the office early in the morning and tell the photography boys to be there as well."

"But, sir. What do I tell Benfield?"

"Nothing, if he says anything tonight tell him I will speak to him when I get back. Goodnight Sergeant."

It was just turned eight o'clock in the evening when D.C. Hopkins and his Chief drove into the Stratford Police Station car park. The Chief Inspector was asleep in the back seat. When the engine stopped, he woke up.

"Thanks Hopkins, that was a nice ride back. See you in the morning."

On the way to his office, he looked into the Commander's office and found it empty. 'Good' he thought as he took the photograph from his pocket and a magnifying glass from the drawer.

After studying the photograph for a short while, he picked up the phone and dialed Brenda's number. When she answered he asked "Are you busy? Can you talk?"

"Yes to the first part. I'll call you back when I am clear."

Mystified by the reply the Chief Inspector replaced his receiver.

CHAPTER TWENTY SIX

The following morning all the detectives involved in "The Bonfire Case", were gathered in the incident room at the Stratford on Avon Police Station. At nine thirty precisely, Commander Benfield and Chief Inspector Sullivan entered the room. After a few introductory words, the Commander handed over the briefing to the Chief Inspector. Who proceeded to cover the duties of the officers present handing them a photocopy of the man coming out of Mrs. Watson's door. The photography department had improved on the enlargement and this was distributed amongst the assembled Officers before they were dismissed by the Chief Inspector.

Commander Benfield and Chief Inspector Sullivan then met in the Commander's office to decide who was to visit Courtney Transport Ltd. and Colonel Brown. The Commander chose Courtney Transport, commenting that he and Nigel understood each other.

As Sergeant Thomas and Chief Inspector Sullivan approached Mochamton, it started to rain.

"Back to normal, Thomas, Bloody weather. I bet the farmers will be moaning about this. Still, give em something to moan about, won't it?"

"I expect so, still there's one who won't be moaning to his mates, have you recognized the Range Rover in front?"

"Is it the Colonel, Thomas?"

"Aye, sir, it is that, shall I follow him?"

"I think you'd better, it may save us going out to the farm."

They followed the Colonel to Mochampton, where he parked in front of 'The Navigation' hotel.

The Colonel recognized the two policemen as they got out of their car and invited them to join him for some refreshment. As the three of them dashed into 'The Navigation Hotel', to get out of the rain, the Chief Inspector remarked,

"You're a man after my own heart, Colonel."

They walked into the lounge, shaking the rain from their coats, the Colonel asked.

"I think the sun is over the yardarm, Inspector. What's your poison, today?"

"We'll just have a couple of pints of best bitter, thanks, Colonel"

Finding the Lounge empty, they walked over to a table in the corner of the room.

"I expect it will get busy soon, Colonel" remarked Sergeant Thomas.

"Yes, it livens up a bit for lunch" he replied glancing at his watch "You'll see in about fifteen minutes they will start drifting in from the trading estates around here".

The Chief Inspector took his copy of the photograph from his pocket.

"Have you seen this man at all, Colonel?" he asked.

The Colonel shook his head,

"No, still it's not very clear, is it?"

"What about this?" asked the Chief Inspector handing the Colonel an enlarged photograph. It was taken from the same photograph, but just the head and shoulders of a man coming out of Mrs Watsons house.

"That's better, Inspector" said the Colonel looking at the enlarged photograph of the head of the man. Sergeant Thomas had carefully outlined the features in black biro before leaving the office.

"Yes, Chief Inspector, I think I have seen him over in 'The Farmers Arms' a couple of times infact, one of those times was just recently. I mean just before Christmas and I think, I'm, not sure though, but I think I saw him and Simpkins together in Stratford just the other day. I think it was the same man, but as I say, I'm not absolutely sure. If you had a clearer picture it might help".

"Thanks Colonel, that's a big help. Will you be available tomorrow if we can improve on this?"

"Anything to help Inspector. Yes, give me a call though first to make sure that I am in".

"Good, thanks Colonel. Now I think its Thomas's turn to buy a round. Isn't it Sergeant?"

"If you say so sir," said the Sergeant as he collected up the empty glasses and made his way to the bar.

They left the Colonel, talking to Bernie, the landlord about some church business, reminding the Colonel that they would contact him later, as they left.

"Come on Thomas, get a move on" urged the Chief Inspector as they got into the car. "We'll go over to 'The Farmers Arms' to see Joe, the landlord, he might recognize our friend. Don't you think?"

"Maybe, if he doesn't, someone else might recognize him. He seems to get about a bit, doesn't he?" replied Sergeant Thomas.

"That might be his undoing. After we have finished here, how's about seeing our mechanic friend?"

"I thought you gave that job to Carter and Hopkins?"

"Ooh yes, that's right Thomas" the Chief Inspector replied, remembering his morning instructions then changing the subject quickly "There's our friend Sergeant Hoppy. He's just gone into the pub", said the Chief Inspector as he got out of the car and hurried into 'The Farmers Arms,' following Sergeant Hopper.

Sergeant Thomas followed murmuring to himself, "Poor old Hoppy, he doesn't know what he has let himself in for. He should have gone straight home. This'll cost him two ploughman's as well as the beer".

As the Sergeant walked into the bar he saw Hoppy with three pints of beer and a ploughman's lunch on a tray, the Chief Inspector was picking up two more lunches.

"There you are Thomas. You're just in time. Sergeant Hopper has been kind enough to buy us lunch"

"I thought he would," muttered Sergeant Thomas then cheerily "That's nice of him, sir".

"Yes, I thought so too. Thank you for inviting us to dine with you, Sergeant" said the Chief Inspector as he sat down and before Sergeant Hopper had time to start his lunch, he flashed the two photographs at him.

"Seen him before, Sergeant. I'm, told he may have been in here a couple of times recently?"

"Is this the bloke we are looking for, Inspector?"

"Well, yes. Didn't you receive the fax that we put out to all stations?"

"I don't know, sir. It's my day off and I just came in here for what I thought would be a quiet pint"

"Sorry Sergeant. I didn't realize it was your day off. Still a policeman's never off duty is he?"

"No. I suppose not. Give them to me and I'll see if I can catch Joe's eye". Sergeant Hopper picked up the photographs and walked over to the bar. He returned to the table after having shown the photographs to the landlord.

"Joe reckons the chap has been in here a few times of late. He says he nearly always sat on his own, had a couple of drinks, then left"

"What days was he here?" asked the Chief Inspector, getting a little excited. It was then that the bar door flew open and a crowd of people came in.

"Blimey! Where did that lot come from?"

"The firm's bus brings them down. They don't have a canteen at the factory. They only drink tea or coffee or soft drinks. That's the agreement with the management of the factories, Joe, crafty beggar, canvassed two small companies. Even offered to use his mini bus to collect them and take them back. Now other factories are coming down for lunch".

"Nice one, eh! Sergeant, Come on Thomas, let's leave this lot to our faithful Sergeant here. We may see you tomorrow. Tell Joe that I'll contact him later about this".

They left 'Hoppy', to finish his lunch with all the noise instead of the peace and quiet he had expected.

It was when they had turned onto the A439 toward Stratford that Chief Inspector Sullivan took the call from Brenda Armstrong.

She apologized profusely for not contacting him before and insisted that it was urgent and necessary that they meet and suggested the place they had met before at seven o'clock that evening.

Stating,

"That she couldn't say any more but please be there".

He tried to hold her call but couldn't. He then tried calling her back but the line was dead. He looked at Sergeant Thomas and asked,

"What do you think of that, Thomas?"

"Think of what, sir," asked the sergeant.

The Chief Inspector then explained the conversation and that he had met Brenda previously, hence the trip to Bolton and again asked his opinion.

"Well, sir, for what its worth"

"Don't give me that, Thomas. You know I value your opinion"

"Alright, sir. I think you may be getting yourself into deep trouble, especially her being a private investigator, but she is helping us and we would not have obtained that photograph if she hadn't given us the lead. By the way, how is it that the Yard didn't pursue it? When the car was found in the first place, were they informed?"

"That's what I want you to find out for me, Thomas. Get off down to London on the pretext that you are visiting your friend, the lady lorry driver"

"You mean Jay-Jay? She's a transport manager not a lorry driver" the Sergeant interrupted.

"As I was saying, go down and see her pretending you want some more information on George Obayo then call in and see them in Canning Town Nick. Right?"

"Yes sir. I think you are getting the same gut feeling as I have had for a long time"

"Yes, well do it tomorrow but not a word to anyone. Understand".

The Chief Inspector went upstairs to his office, leaving his Sergeant to call on the photography department and to collect the improved blown up copy of the suspect.

In passing, he knocked on Commander Benfields door.

"Come in" the Commander called "Oh, you are in Chief Inspector" he continued sarcastically as the Chief Inspector entered.

"Yes sir. It is most urgent that I speak with you I think we have made a break through at last. How was your meeting with Nigel Courtney this morning? Did you obtain anything from him? Did you see his chief security chap? Did you ask him if he had seen the suspect?"

"I say, Inspector, hold on. I'm, in charge of the case; I'm not one of your peasants from up here that you're questioning. I'm, your superior officer".

"Yes sir. Sorry sir, I just got carried away" answered the Chief Inspector realizing that he had pressurised the Yard Commander a bit.

"Yes. Well, we didn't learn anything new from either party and, yes, I did show the photograph to both of them, Sullivan, but their answer was negative".

"That's strange, Sir. I've had two or three people say they have seen him in and around Stratford and one even went as far as stating that he had seen him and Simpkins talking to each other here in Stratford, and is prepared to make a statement to that effect. So someone's lying, sir".

"Could be a case of mistaken identity, Chief Inspector", said the Commander straightening some papers on his desk "After all, it's not a very good picture, is it?"

"Oh I don't know, sir. It seemed to be good enough for my witnesses to identify him. We don't have a name for him yet but it won't be long before we do have, Commander. Then we'll have him and his associates," the Chief Inspector said as he got out of his chair, "I wonder why David Simpkins didn't tell you that he had spoken to him. Strange that, isn't it Commander? I wonder why?" he remarked as he left the office.

Sergeant Thomas was waiting for Chief Inspector Sullivan in his office and seemed a little excited when he passed four picture's of the suspect across the desk,

"I've just got them, sir. I hope you don't mind me waiting for you in here, but I thought you ought to see these right away. The photograph people couldn't improve on the picture we had so they ran it through the computer and this is what they came up with. Good, aren't they sir?"

"Certainly are, Thomas, they certainly are. Now we'll see what Mr. David bloody Simpkins has to say about that then" the Chief Inspector said as he pointed to the print he was holding. "Our blessed Commander, bless his little heart, says that Mr. David Simpkins did not recognise the man from the previous photo. Strange that isn't it, Thomas? It's good enough for the Colonel to recognize him but not for our David".

"No sir" replied Thomas who had been trying to attract his Chief's attention to make him aware that the Commander was standing in the doorway listening to his comments on his visit to Courtney Transport that day.

"I see that you are not impressed by my visit, Chief Inspector"

"No sir, I'm not. But then again I suppose the photo you took was not as good as these are. Maybe he'll do better next time or do you want me to go, sir?" The Chief Inspector passed the few prints to the Commander.

"That's better, Sullivan" said the Commander as he compared the prints. "A lot better. As a matter of fact I just stopped by to tell you that I'm on my way out to another appointment with David Simpkins and Nigel Courtney, at six o'clock at Courtney's place. Nice place, the old Manor. Going to have dinner with them. I'm certain this will be straightened out tonight, Chief Inspector. Must dash". The Commander kept one of the new prints as he closed the door and left the Sergeant and Chief Inspector facing each other across the Chief Inspectors desk.

Sergeant Thomas looked at his watch,

"Blooming heck, sir, he's left early enough for a six o'clock appointment. It's only four o'clock".

"Yes, well, Thomas don't lets speak ill of our superiors after all, they are overworked. He'll have to go back to his hotel and soak in the bath for an hour before he gets dressed for dinner"

"Yes, sir. Shall I get some copies of these prints run off?"

"Yes Thomas, do that and pass some down to uniform branch, see if they can help. I'll want two or three. I'll take one with me tonight to show Ms Armstrong".

"Careful sir. Your slips starting to show" laughed Sergeant Thomas.

"What do you mean by that remark, Thomas?"

"Well sir, you go all gooey-eyed when you mention her name. Some people might start thinking things. I don't sir. I know you too well," the

Sergeant said hastily, holding up his hands with palms forward and fingers spread.

"I sincerely hope so Sergeant. Ring Joe Brompton at 'The Farmers Arms'. Tell him we'll be out there tomorrow with the printouts. Make it late morning. I'll contact the Colonel and ask him to be there".

Sergeant Thomas contacted 'The Farmers Arms' and left a message for the landlord.

As he was climbing the stairs to his own office the phone started to ring and he ran to answer it.

"Thomas" the man's voice said as he answered it "I just got your message Sergeant, I was wondering if I should ring you. He was in this lunchtime and now he's back again. He keeps looking at his watch as if he is expecting somebody"

"O.K Joe, don't do anything suspicious. I'll get someone over there to keep an eye on things". He dashed to the Chief Inspector's office, only to find that he was talking on the telephone.

"We've got a sighting!" he called and ran back to his own office. First of all he contacted Mochamton Police Station and spoke to Sergeant Hopper who said he would do the observation himself, providing the Chief Inspector could arrange the back up. He then went to the control room to get two police cars positioned close to 'The Farmers Arms'. As he finished making these arrangements, Chief Inspector Sullivan walked into the Sergeants office,

"What's all the panic about, Sergeant?"

"We've got a sighting of our suspect sir. He's having a drink at 'The Farmers Arms'. He must like the ale there, he was there at lunchtime as well".

"So were we Sergeant".

"We must have left before he arrived".

"Come on Thomas, don't let old Hoppy have all the fun".

"I told him sir, 'watch and observe' that's all he has to do"

"Well let's hope that is all he does".

They ran out to the Chief's Granada and as they got into the car they were informed over the radio that the suspect had taken a telephone call, then left the pub. He had got into a blue Rover car and was proceeding toward Evesham. The Chief Inspector was then asked if he wanted the car followed.

"Have we got a registration number? Yes, I do want it followed but not by a patrol car. Get a Q car onto it. Tell Sergeant Hopper to follow it in his car until you get someone over there. Get the nearest Q car onto it then let me know".

Listening to the radio conversation Sergeant Thomas looked at his Chief as he slammed the telephone down.

Changing his mind regards the chase, the Chief inspector disgruntedly looked at his Sergeant who suggested.

"I think this calls for a pint sir, don't you?"

"Yes Thomas, lets nip down to The Lamb, I'll pay".

"You sure, sir?" asked the Sergeant as he drove out of the Police station car park.

"Yes, Thomas. My treat" replied the Chief Inspector as he called control by radio to give them his whereabouts.

The low beamed ceiling bar was quiet as the two policemen entered the eighteenth century public house in the market square. Sergeant Thomas followed the Inspector over to a table near the blazing log fire.

"Mines the usual, Thomas" called the Chief Inspector over his shoulder.

"But, but, sir," started Thomas.

"Don't argue Thomas, I'm not in the mood".

"I should have guessed," muttered the Sergeant as he walked over to the bar.

"I've got a nice barrel of Old Original, Sergeant, just tapped it this morning. I know your boss likes it," said the landlord Ted Hughes an ex RAF Wing Commander.

"He needs something to sweeten him this morning, Ted" replied the Sergeant.

"I thought so. There's a poker by the fire if he wants to mull it".

"That's an idea, Ted. That will tickle his taste buds wont it?"

"There you are, sir. Old Original, straight from the wood and there's the poker to stick in it," he said as he placed the two pints on the table and pointed to the bright poker the landlord had mentioned.

"Good thinking, Thomas. A nice pint of mulled beer will go down well. It's cold enough outside for it, isn't it?"

"That's what I thought, sir," said Thomas smiling as he placed the poker in the fire.

"Inspector", called the landlord "Phone" interrupting the Chief Inspector as he sat deep in thought waiting for the poker to warm up his favorite beer.

"That's it, Thomas. They've lost our friend in Evesham. Hopper and the 'Q' car followed him into the town centre, but lost him in the rush hour traffic", commented the Chief Inspector sitting down at the table again after taking the telephone call.

"It is dark as well, sir, so one car looks like another in those conditions. Anyway traffic cops might spot him and the pokers just right for the beer so come and enjoy your pint". The Sergeant pulled the red hot poker from the fire and holding his Chief's pint slightly at an angle he plunged the glowing poker into the beer.'

It sizzled, popped and frothed for about thirty seconds, then quietened down as he removed the poker.

"Here you are, sir. Done to a tee" as he handed the beer to the Chief Inspector, he smiled as he took the mug of mulled beer. "You know how to sweeten me up, don't you, Thomas?"

"I thought I had better do something sir, if you are going to meet this Armstrong girl and, not only that, I would like a night off for a change, now that they have lost our only lead".

"Yes, well don't build your hopes too high. The night is young yet and I want you to keep an eye on things for me while I am with Ms. Armstrong".

CHAPTER TWENTY SEVEN

Brenda walked over to Chief Inspector Sullivan as he walked into the lounge bar at the Appleton Hall Hotel.

"Don't bother to order, Sully" she said taking his arm and leading him towards the stairs.

"The drinks are already in my room".

"Easy girl, I thought this was a business meeting" he replied.

"It is but I'm playing it safe. So, come on". Brenda replied tugging Sully's arm.

"Now, what's this all about, Brenda?" he asked as Brenda followed him into the room after locking the door.

"First of all, Sully" Brenda answered using the Chief Inspector's nickname "I thought we would have a drink here while I tell you what I have experienced since I last saw you at Stadium Garage. Then we'd go over to the Atherstone Hall Hotel to dine. I've booked a table for ten o'clock. Is that alright?"

He settled himself on the settee after pouring a whisky and a gin and tonic for Brenda.

"Right Brenda, what has been going on?"

"First of all. After you and D.C Hopkins left Stadium Garage I thought there was no point in waiting for you to return as I didn't know how long you would be and I had achieved what I had set out to do. That was to find the car and to put a name to the driver".

"We've done more than that. We have got a face" interrupted Sully taking the print out and the photograph from his inside pocket.

Brenda looked closely at the photograph.

"Nice house, that man looks vaguely familiar. Yes, I think I recognise him"

"Who do you think it is, Brenda?"

"He looks like one of the Marvo Brother's. Don't ask me for his name, I don't know them too well. But things are beginning to slip into place now, what do you think Sully?"

"Well, they're not slipping into place for us, we thought we had a lead then it fizzles out, like today for instance.

This afternoon he was spotted in The Farmers Arms at Mochampton where he took a call on his cell phone and left, followed by Sergeant Hopper and a back up car, they lost him in Evesham. Happens all the time"

"That figures" Brenda said thoughtfully "let me tell you what happened to me after you left. I went straight home and worked on the computer until two o'clock this morning. I woke about eight o'clock, took a shower, and made arrangements to meet Nigel Courtney at his office at eleven o'clock. Now, I arrived at Courtney Transport at five minutes to eleven and as I drove through their main gate, stopping at their security office to sign in. I noticed a red Ferrari parked across the road and that a man was in the Ferrari. As I was leaving the office I asked the officer on duty if he had seen the car before. He said he had seen it only once before, he had entered it in the logbook, as instructed by Mr. Courtney, he noted that it had been there previously. When I signed the visitor's book I noticed that Benny had arrived before me. I enquired if he was with Mr. Courtney and was informed that Benny had arrived fifteen minutes before me and that he was with Mr. Simpkins.

Mr. Courtney was not with them; he was in the warehouse the Security Officer offered to contact him for me, which I accepted. I didn't want Benny to know I was there. He gives me the 'creeps'. Nigel arrived at the security lodge just before Benny left. Now, here's the funny thing, as Benny drove through the gate, I was watching the Ferrari and the driver took a call on his cell-phone then followed Benny. Feeling a little bit uncomfortable about what I had just seen. I walked over to Nigel Courtney's office where I eventually gave him an upto date report on his return to his office, I also informed him that I thought he should be very careful on any new acquaintances.

Nigel suggested that we should go to David Simpkin's office to see what he thought about my suggestion.

The strange thing was that when we got to David Simpkin's office, his secretary informed us that he wasn't there. He had left a few minutes earlier with his visitor Commander Benfield. Nigel was annoyed about this he informed me that whenever David left the premises, he was instructed to inform Nigel. He then rang Security who informed him that Mr. Simpkins had driven straight through the gate without stopping, a thing that he had never done before.

While we were in the office David's secretary told us she was leaving for the day.

"Then" Brenda continued "Nigel took a phone call from the dispatch office and had to leave. While he was gone I took advantage of the opportunity and gave the office a once over. I found this in the bottom drawer of a desk. It is a photograph of a concert party on the back is written 'Stuttgart July 1976'. Do you recognize anyone on there?" she asked as she handed the photograph to the Chief Inspector.

"I'm not quite sure," he said. "Second girl from the left rear row. My god! Benny!" he exclaimed.

"That's what I thought" Brenda replied. "So, I returned to Nigel's office to wait for him. On his return he had called in at the canteen and had purchased our lunch, coffee and sandwiches.

I left him about one o'clock and went straight back home intending to spend the rest of the day there and have an early night. When I arrived home, I knew something was wrong. Someone had been trying to get into my computer. Fortunately I always put all my tapes and discs in a strong box. Don't worry it is well hidden, built into the floor. Then I found this card. It sent shivers up and down my spine". She handed the card to Sully it had a single 'M' on it.

"That's like the one in Benny's car the night he was 'mugged'" Sully said turning the card over.

"I can tell you that is the calling card of the Marvo Brothers. Murder and bodily harm is not their scene but greed for money is. I don't like to see that in my house" said Brenda "So I packed a small case and got out fast. That's when I called".

Brenda got up from the chair, crossed over to Sully, put her arms round his neck and kissed him.

Sully responded by picking her up in his arms and walking over to the bed. He whispered in her ear,

"I think you had better cancel that table. It's going to be a long night".

It was at varying times through the night, between their at first violent and then tender love making, that Brenda managed to tell Sully of the events that had happened to Digger Davis the previous day.

CHAPTER TWENTY EIGHT

The day after he had lunch with Brenda in Aldershot, Digger Davis drove to Salisbury. It was a beautiful bright sunny day, the frost still on the trees as he drove towards Salisbury on the A30. On arrival in the Wiltshire town, he took his time in finding the Amesbury Road to Salisbury and Fiesta Lighting.

He had visited Salisbury on military business but had never had time to wander around at his leisure. On his arrival he found a big flat-topped mound where the old Roman Fort named Old Sarum had been built. He climbed to the top and stood for a few moments looking over the rolling green hills of Salisbury Plain spread all around him, then turning to look towards the City of Salisbury with the spire of the Cathedral towering majestically over it.

Digger then turned and looked down at the layby that acted as a car park for the visitors who wanted to climb upto the castle site. His car, a red Ford Sierra was parked at the far end opposite the old telephone exchange that housed Fiesta Lighting Ltd. Although the building was small compared to other local businesses, Fiesta Lighting was a very active company, supplying pyrotechnics and lighting for military tattoos and rock concerts, marquees, chandeliers and all the fittings required for high-class weddings. It was while he was looking down at his car that he saw a dark blue Ford Granada drive into the parking lot and parked alongside the Sierra. The driver got out, then reached into the back of his car for his briefcase and walked over to the old telephone exchange, letting himself in.

Digger hurried down to his car to sit and await developments, he did not have to wait long. Frank Jones, the owner of Fiesta Lighting, came out of his small warehouse on the run, got into his car and drove out of the parking area with his wheels spinning.

Digger followed.

They drove back toward the city, turning left on to the circular road and on to the A30 driving towards London, retracing the route Digger had used earlier that morning.

Hitting the main road from Salisbury to London at 60mph Frank Jones settled down to a safe cruising speed and didn't seem to notice that a red Sierra was following him. They drove on to Guildford then Esher taking the A313 towards Waltham on Thames, turning left towards Staines. As they approached Staines, the dark blue Granada turned off the main road into the car park of a motel. Digger drove past taking the next side turning and driving round to the rear of the Motel entered the car park from the opposite end. He got out of his car and strolled into reception just in time to see the owner of Fiesta Lighting paying for a room for the night.

'Thank heaven he's stopping for the night. It's getting dark.' Digger thought as he strolled over to the reception desk and booked in for the night as well, asking for the room next to Mr. Jones, if possible. The receptionist looked questioningly at Digger.

"It's alright. We're old friends, but sometimes you wouldn't think so." Digger said answering her look.

The Excelsior Motel was a modern type of building, three floors high. L-shaped with the foot of the L built along the back of the Parking lot. The motel car park took up the rest of the site with a five-foot high hedge around giving it a bit of privacy.

Access to the car park was at the front from the A308 and the exit was at the rear on to a service road that led to a traffic light controlled junction. The ground floor was mainly taken up with the Conference rooms, Ballroom, Restaurant and offices with only a few ground floor bedrooms situated at the foot of the L. The first and second floors were hotel style with the rooms leading off a central corridor. Digger and Mr.Jones were next to each other on the first floor with windows overlooking the car park. After having a quick shower, Digger walked over to the window and stood looking out of the window, it was while he was looking at the blue Granada that he decided to call Brenda to report in.

It was a quiet night for him Mr Jones didn't go anywhere. Puzzled by the Granada not being used during the evening, Digger tried an old trick a couple of times by putting a drinking glass against the wall and listening for any sounds from the next room, but he only heard the television.

The following morning he went down for breakfast at seven o'clock, thinking it was early, only to find Mr Jones already in the dining room, reading the morning paper whilst he was eating his breakfast. Digger ordered his breakfast and collected the Daily Telegraph from the front desk. He was only halfway through his breakfast when he heard a commotion in the car park. He glanced over to where Mr Jones was still eating his breakfast and then towards the car park where he saw smoke and flames coming from his car. Digger didn't hear his registration number being called over the speaker system as he dashed through the Motel lobby. When he reached his car, the vehicles on both sides were being moved. He could hear sirens from the approaching fire engines. He could do nothing but watch the flames engulf his beautiful Red Sierra. He'd had the car from new and it was his pride and joy. He could only look into the faces of the people from the Motel, as he turned round in despair. Dawn was now breaking and he caught sight of the dark blue Granada quickly moving out of the car park along the service road at the rear of the motel.

"Bastard! You Bastard!" Digger screamed.

Two waiters took hold of him and quietly escorted him back to the motel lobby as the first two fire engines rushed into the car park. It was late afternoon by the time the police and arson investigators had left the Motel. Digger was quite exhausted by all their questions but they seemed satisfied by his answers. He had explained his professed friendship with Mr Jones by telling them that Mr Jones had been dishonorably discharged from the army and did not want to acknowledge any of his ex-colleagues. The Police and Fire Investigators accepted the explanation.

It was a very tired Digger who arrived at his home in Aldershot in a hire car. After two stiff whiskeys, consumed while lying in a steaming hot bath. He again called Brenda informing her on what had happened and that he knew that Jones had set the incendiary device. Informing her that the police were also looking for Mr Jones to help them with their enquiries. Brenda told Digger that she was at home but to keep contacting her on her cell phone because it was the most convenient way of communication, knowing that she would be moving around a lot from now on.

After the phone call, Digger poured himself another whiskey and settled in an armchair mulling over the last two days events and eventually falling asleep and letting his empty whiskey glass fall to the floor.

When Digger awoke at three a.m. from his drink-induced sleep, it was still dark. He switched on the table lamp, noted the time, stood up remarking spitefully

"Right. Time to visit Fiesta Lighting and see what that bastard is up to. If I find anything, I'll hang him"

It was a horrible wet and windy night as Digger raced across the Wiltshire Downs the clouds were scudding across the sky giving occasional patches of moonlight. The rain had stopped when he arrived outside the Old Telephone Exchange everything was in darkness as he approached it. He took a pen torch from his pocket shining it around the doorframe to see if there was a burglar alarm or trap of any kind. Digger didn't think there would be and the burglar alarm, if there were one, it would be inside. He then took out of his pocket a set of skeleton keys and took hold of the doorknob. As he did so the door opened, he then opened it sufficiently to allow him to slip through. As he slowly started to close the door behind him, he took a step into the room and discreetly shone his pen torch around the room. He was violently grabbed from behind and thrown to the ground. His arms were whipped up behind his back and he was handcuffed.

"What the hell is going on?" he shouted as he was rolled over on to his back and a torch shone into his face. It had all happened so fast that he could not retaliate and was caught completely off guard.

"You're nicked," said a voice from behind the torch. "What the hell are you doing here?"

"Hang on, hang on" replied Digger recognizing the voice, "Don't get your knickers in a twist. I might ask that of you. The door was open so I came in to see if everything was alright." Digger was beginning to feel a bit more confident now.

'If it had been Jones, I would have been dead by now' he thought.

"Anyway, what are you doing here?" he asked as he struggled to sit up and settled back against the wall. His assailant walked over to give him a hand and helped him up to lean against the wall.

"Tuffy! What the hell! Get these cuffs off quick." Tuffy removed the handcuffs while hastily giving him instructions.

"You take that side, I'll take this side. We've got to get out of here", as he quickly and expertly started going through the electronic switches in the pigeon holes around the walls and the drawers underneath the workbench which stretched the full length of the wall. They didn't find much of interest only electronic gadgets, large boxes of chandeliers and coils of heavy-duty cable. When they were about to leave, Digger flashed his torch over the shelves nearest to him. As he did so, he spotted a notebook half hidden behind a box of switches as if it had been put there previously when there must have been a few more boxes stacked on the shelf, the top box had been removed revealing the note-book and no one had noticed it. At first he was not sure whether to take it or not but, curiosity and Tuffy's urging to leave got the better of him and he slipped the book into his pocket, leaving Tuffy to make sure the door was locked.

They both got into Digger's hire car collecting his friend's car from the nearest side street that was a quarter of a mile down the road on their way back into town.

It was six o'clock in the morning by the time that Digger led Tuffy into the market square in the centre of Salisbury. People were starting to go about their daily chores and, being midweek, market stalls had been erected at one end of the market square and were being set out with vegetables and fruit from the local farmers. A large refrigerated butchers van was being parked nearby where Digger and Tuffy also parked their cars.

They crossed the road to one of the cafes and ordered breakfast. Digger couldn't wait to find out what Tuffy was doing in the U.K. and more so what he was doing in Fiesta's workshop.

Tuffy explained that he was attached to the European Agricultural Department to investigate illegal claims for grants for movement of beef from Ireland and the United Kingdom. But at the moment he was having a spot of leave and he had been talking to Brenda Armstrong, and Brenda being a friend of both of them, had told him that she had taken an interest in Fiesta. But, she had not said that you may be here as well, anyway his curiosity had been aroused, so here he was.

Tuffy, then asked the same question of Digger who also explained his involvement with Brenda, finishing with the loss of his car and assigning the blame to Mr. Jones.

The two old friends were standing beside Tuffy's new Ford Mondeo saying their good-byes and promising to meet again at the Officer's Club in Aldershot for a farewell drink, when a dark blue Granada drove onto the market square. At first, neither of them seemed to notice it until the Toby (market traders name for the market manager) in charge of the market started shouting and waving his arms telling the driver that he couldn't park there. They watched the car being parked further down the market square carring on with their conversation until they saw the driver get out of the Granada.

"Hey up. Can you see what I see?" asked Digger.

"I think, I can see what you have seen "replied Tuffy getting into his car so that he could not be seen, Digger doing the same.

They needn't have worried about keeping a low profile.

The driver of the Granada was Frank Jones and he went straight over to a greengrocer's stall, without taking any notice of the other cars parked on the square.

Tuffy got out of his car, keeping low so that he could just see but could not be seen. He watched Mr Jones give the greengrocer an envelope the greengrocer then took a carrier bag from underneath the table and handed it to Jones, who opened the bag and took out a cabbage and looked underneath. He then walked over to the butcher who seemed to know him and after a short chat served him with some meat. After paying the butcher, Jones turned to walk back to his car. The lights on the market stalls and around the market square illuminated the parked cars as Tuffy and Digger watched Jones foraging in one of the bags. He opened the rear door and placed the two carrier bags on the back seat. He then removed what looked like, to the two watchers, a white plastic bag and walking to the rear of the car he opened the trunk and placed the bag in the trunk of the car.

The two military policemen looked at each other as Jones drove from the car park turning on to the Blandford road.

"What do you think about that, Digger?"

"I think he's up to something, I don't like it. Can you spare any time today, Tuffy? I think we should follow him again today and hand it over to Brenda and her pals tonight."

"I can give you up to late afternoon but I must be at mother-in-laws tonight it's her birthday today. I'll ring her when she gets up" said Tuffy looking at his watch.

"Crumbs" exclaimed Digger "Seven thirty already and getting daylight."

"Right, Digger, you go back up the road to Fiesta and stay out of sight. I know where he lives so I'll take a quick shufty around there. I think he'll move quickly when he starts. I'll contact you on the cell phone."

"O.K. It is the only thing that I took with me into the motel."

"Good job you did. Now, get going otherwise it will be daylight and I want to take a closer look at his place."

When Digger arrived at the layby outside Fiesta, he found the small warehouse a hive of activity. There was a long wheelbase Land Rover with a hard top converting it into a van and also a short wheelbase Land Rover again with a hard top. There were three young men clad in overalls and parkas carrying the rolls of cables and the chandelier boxes he had looked at earlier out to their respective trucks and loading the vehicles. The lights were switched off in the warehouse, a man emerged with a clipboard, checked the loads, and they all climbed aboard their vehicles and left the layby travelling in the Amesbury direction.

While the men were making their final check, Digger took a call from Tuffy.

"We're on the move, where are you?"

"I'm parked in a field gateway up the road from the layby".

"I'll let you know the direction."

Three minutes later, Digger received another call from Tuffy.

"We seem to be coming in your direction."

"Right" he replied "Let me know when you hit this road, I'll tuck in behind you as you drive past."

It was getting quite daylight on another dull day as, Digger watched Mr Jones drive into the layby and let himself into the small warehouse leaving the door open. Digger followed the Granada into the layby, there being nowhere else to hide or park.

His partner seeing what was happening left his car in the field gateway and joined him in the layby.

Tuffy was settling himself in the backseat, when Digger suddenly remembered the notebook he had picked up earlier in the warehouse. He quickly glanced through the book, stopping occasionally to look at some of the pages.

"Here, Tuffy, have a quick look at this."

Tuffy flicked through the pages.

"It looks like a few names and addresses none that I know. But he's got numbers against each one then a date. Don't make sense to me. I think you should pass this to Brenda and her friends in the Midlands. Just a minute, Digger" he exclaimed as he flicked back a few more pages,

"He's got Jean Claude's name in here and it looks like the date he died, but what's these numbers? George Obayo and that date, Digger, it looks like we've got a sadist over there. This looks like a record of crimes he was involved in, definitely send it to Brenda, the sooner the better. He'd kill for this."

Tuffy closed the book and shoved it into the glove compartment then wiped his hands on his handkerchief as if he had dirtied them. They had both been dozing for about half an hour when Digger sat up with a start.

"What's the matter?" asked Tuffy, also sitting up and looking round.

"It's O.K., Tuffy. I was just nodding off and I woke up with a start."

"Hmmm. I thought we had been rumbled. Anyway he's still there but he has shut the door."

Some while later, after Tuffy had returned to his own car because the windows in Digger's car were steaming up, which may have given Mr Jones the idea that he was being watched.

Eventually Mr Jones emerged from the warehouse, got into his car and left the layby in the direction of Amesbury.

The two Military Police Investigators set off in hot pursuit following the suspect in their own cars.

"Careful, Digger. We must chop and change otherwise he'll smell a rat again." Tuffy called over the cell phone.

They followed Jones for an hour or more, watched him fill up with petrol, doing some shopping in Pewsey and Marlborough until they finally arrived on the outskirts of Swindon. As they were crossing the bridge over the M4, Tuffy who was following Jones at the time saw him pick up his car phone and replace it after having a short conversation. At the next roundabout Jones turned left into Swindon. Digger had gone ahead and stopped at a garage to fill up with petrol. As he went into the office to pay, he saw the blue Granada speed past. When he took up the chase, he saw Tuffy turn right into The Post House Hotel leaving him to follow the Granada. When they arrived at the market square in Old Town, Jones parked his car and walked across the road into The Bell Hotel, which is a sixteenth century coaching house. Digger also managed to find a place to park his car at the back of the Locarno Bingo Hall that was built in seventeen forty as a Corn Exchange.

Tuffy arrived at the same time and they walked across to The Bell Hotel together.

Entering the Hotel through the archway that covered the entrance to the courtyard where, in the old days, the horses and carriages had unloaded and loaded their passengers.

As they entered the large sun lounge built at the rear of the building, they saw Mr Jones sitting at a table with Brigadier Smythe-White. Digger selected a table that gave him a view of the courtyard and the entrance while Tuffy went up to the bar and ordered beer and sandwiches.

They had finished their lunch snack and Tuffy was about to suggest they call it a day when the waiter arrived with two more beers.

"I didn't order them" Tuffy remarked, surprised.

"No, sir. The two gentlemen in the lounge sent them over for you". Answered the waiter setting the drinks on the table and handing Tuffy a business card.

"As I thought, Bloody Mr Jones, we've been spotted, he did this to me before, at Fordingbridge."

"That's it. It's no good staying here" replied Digger "I'll post this book to Brenda and I'll ring her when I get home"

The Brigadier looked at his colleague and smiled as he saw the two Investigators leave the hotel.

"There go our friends, Jonah", he said looking across the table and using an old army nickname for anyone whose surname was Jones.

"Yes, Brigadier. I tried to scare one of them off yesterday. Even burned his car for him. I even gave his pal a friendly warning about a month ago at Fordingbridge I gave him my card when I caught him snooping around the house. I hope they will take the hint this time, Brigadier."

"I hope so" he replied not informing Jones that they were military policemen and that he had known them before while they were investigating the same kind of trade for which they were meeting today, namely 'jewelry smuggling'.

"What do you mean, you burned his car for him?"

"Yes that's right I burned his car for him, he followed me all the way from Salisbury, I thought that would stop him. I'm getting fed up with people snooping around me, Brigadier. I also have a sneaking suspicion that somebody has been in my workshop. It's hard to tell when you have staff and only a small place."

"Yes, I agree but you don't keep any of our stuff in your workshop, do you?"

"No. That's offloaded the same day, if I can. It's only when it's late like last night that I keep it overnight then I try to find a different place each time. Mind you, the wife gets funny ideas sometimes but then, she likes it when I take her up to London to see a show on the spur of the moment."

"Yes, Jonah, but that chaps car, are the police involved? We don't want any funny business with them, do we?"

"I don't know, I gave them a false address at the motel."

"I see, you were taking a few precautions then. Was all this before or after the pick-up?"

"Before, Brigadier, I left my television on all night and got a taxi to within walking distance of the pick-up. By the way, tell your friends to send only drivers who can speak English on this job. If I hadn't had his registration and my identification written in German plus my passport, I wouldn't have had those bloody things there" pointing to the Brigadier's briefcase.

The Brigadier didn't like that remark and pushed his briefcase under the table with his foot.

"Then again, Brigadier. The squarehead was all smiles when I gave him the envelope with the money in. He was all brighteyed and 'dankershun, dankershun', clicking his heels, the Jerry bastard!"

"Anyone would think you're not keen on Germans, Frank."

"Would you, sir, if they had robbed you of your parents when they bombed your home? Smashing everything and killing my mother and father and kid sister."

"Sorry, Frank, I didn't know that. I'll see to that for you and I don't think it will be very long before we have something else sorted out, so bear with it just a little bit longer. I'll have a chat with 'you know who' to see if the Police are involved in your little escapade yesterday. I do hope you don't do that too often Frank, it might be a little embarrassing for our friends."

"I hope I don't see them again and they take the hint and get off my back. By the way, what is happening up in the Midlands? Everything has gone quiet. I haven't heard any alarm bells ringing lately. You all gone to sleep or something?"

"Yes, well, everything has slowed down a bit. I think Nigel got cold feet when the Police started sniffing around after finding that P.I. chap in the bottom of the fire. Whatever made you send it there?"

"I didn't send it to the village. I sent it to a storage place at Witney and I informed your office thinking, they would arrange the disposal of it from there, anyway some one did didn't they? In no way could it have been traced back to us? I arranged it that way."

"That's all right, Frank. I'll look into it. All right? I'll be in touch, maybe tomorrow." The Brigadier left, leaving his friend finishing his drink and to pay the bill.

Mr Jones glanced at his watch as he left the hotel and hurried over to his car. He quickly checked the trunk of his car and then swiftly left the car park heading south towards the motorway. He turned left off the large Coate Water roundabout and entered the car park at the rear of The Post House motel. The red Ferrari he was looking for was parked in the centre of the car park and he parked close by. The entrance to the bar was directly in front of him and as he entered he saw Norman Marvo at the bar ordering the drinks.

"I saw you arrive, so I got an orange juice for you. I thought that after a session on the Brigadier's brandies, you would need something like that."

"Thanks" said Frank, taking a long drink from the glass "after a session with that snob of a Brigadier you need something to clean your mouth out."

"I know what you mean, Frank, but let's deal with his mate first. Have you got everything for tonight?" Frank nodded.

"Right, we have plenty of time so I'll run through the plan once again. I've got the radio in the car for you to listen in on all the wavelengths. If you're lucky you can pick up my cell-phone sometimes. So, first of all, you'll arrive at the old railway track at eight thirty, break into the yard office, set your incendiary bomb for a half hour later, then get clear and call me. I'll direct you to my place, O.K.? You're sure your device will be destroyed in the fire?"

"Yes." Frank replied with confidence. "Right. You go via Oxford. I'll go via Stow-on-the-Wold. See you later."

Frank was again left to finish his drink but he didn't have to pay the bill this time.

CHAPTER TWENTY NINE

Sergeant Thomas was saying goodbye to his wife and children when the telephone rang.

He glanced at his watch,

"Eight o'clock. Who's ringing at this time?" He remarked glancing at his wife as he picked up the telephone "Yes, Yes, I'm on my way" Putting the phone down "It seems they have found the Granada that gave us the run around the other night. It has turned up at the bottom of Birdlip Hill just outside Gloucester. I've got to pick Sully up. So I'll see you when I see you," he said kissing his wife and two children as he left.

The Chief Inspector was putting down his telephone when the Sergeant entered his office. Putting a little finger in his ear and wiggling it about a bit he remarked.

"Lor, that bloke Benfield should see a doctor, he's got verbal diarrhea."

"Yes, sir, I've heard they have discovered a treatment for that" replied his Sergeant.

"Oh yes. What's that?"

"Gobstoppers, sir. You can get them at Fletcher's on the High Street. The wife sometimes gives them to the kids when they're playing her up a bit."

"Hmm. Remind me to get some for him, Thomas. There's been a change of plan. Benny's decided to go over to Gloucester with Inspector White. I don't think they will find very much. Apparently a lorry driver found the car at first light this morning. He spotted it about half way down the slope. It looked as if it had been on fire, so he called the police who informed us when they checked what was left of the registration number."

The Chief Inspector paused then asked,

"How well did you and Inspector Greaves in Canning Town nick get on? Do you think he would fax the Obayo case reports through to you?

Instead of you going down there again I'm sorry to spoil your fun with, what do they call her? Jaw Face?"

"Jay, Jay, sir. I'll bet you are! I didn't spoil your fun last night, did I?" replied the Sergeant sulkily.

"Well, have a chat with Greavesy, there's a good chap. I've got one or two things to tidy up here. I'd like to have a chat with Nigel Courtney and his security chap, David Simpkins."

After speaking with Inspector Greaves, Sergeant Thomas thought he would have a chat with Jay-Jay. Her secretary apologized for her not being available, but said she would pass on his phone number to her as soon as she came into the office. He was reading through the reports, Inspector Greaves had faxed to him when she called.

"Thank goodness you called, Sergeant. Hey, what's your Christian name? I can't keep calling you by your rank, can I?"

"Nobody calls me by my Christian name but I'll make an exception to the rule in your case, Jay-Jay. My name is John."

Jay Jay burst out laughing.

"I know, I know but I only let my special friends call me Jack. Anyway how are thing's down there?"

"Well" she hesitated "I think I've got somebody snooping around George Obayo's flat."

"What makes you think that?"

"You know I have left my husband so when the solicitors informed me that George had left everything to me, I moved into his flat. That was when I received a phone call from a, Mr.Jones asking me if I wanted to sell the flat. I told him 'No' and that I was living there. About a week afterwards when I got home from the office I had a feeling that someone had been there and looked around but I wasn't sure. I felt that some things had been moved however, as I say, I wasn't sure. The next day, Mr. Jones came to the office and offered me a ridiculous amount of money but I turned him down again. All the same, he left his card asking me to contact him if I changed my mind."

"Did you see his car?" asked Sergeant Thomas.

"Yes. It was a dark blue Ford Granada and I got the registration number for you." anticipated Jay-Jay "but that's not the end of it. About three nights later, I had the same feeling when I returned to the flat and I was certain I could smell cigar smoke. But this time someone had been into the flat and left a card with a single 'M' on it. What do you make of it, Jack? I called the police and they said to change the locks, which I have done. I've had Chubb locks fitted. The police asked if anything was missing. I told them 'no' and they said there was nothing they could do."

"Well, Jay-Jay, it looks as though you have done all the right things that can be done but it also looks as if someone is trying to frighten you into selling. I'll have a chat with Inspector Greaves. I'll see what I can do. Oh, fax me a copy of Jones card, will you?"

He gave his fax number then rang off. He sat for a few minutes after the conversation and then proceeded to his Chief's office.

"What make of car, did you say that was that they found this morning, sir?"

"They found more than a car, Thomas. The car had landed on its wheels and they found a body slumped across the front seats."

"Yes, but what was the make and colour, sir?"

"I thought I told you, Thomas. It was a Ford Granada and they think it was dark blue. Why? What have you got?"

"Well, sir. I think that is him" replied Thomas handing the Chief the faxed copy of the business card with the registration number and make of the car, which he had written across the card.

"My God, you could be right, Sergeant. I'll get in touch with Gloucester Police and I'll let them have this. Good work, Thomas." said the Chief Inspector smiling at his Sergeant and feeling very pleased with himself that they had solved one of the mysteries that were cropping up in the Midlands.

"Would you like a coffee, sir?"

"Yes, Thomas, but not from here. I think you deserve a better one than you can get here for solving this case, don't you?"

"That's very kind of you, sir but I thought we were going out?"

"Yes, well" his Chief replied, pulling his right ear, then rubbing his chin,

"I've got to wait for a phone call first, Thomas, before I can go to Courtney Transport."

"Well, sir, we could arrange to meet Simpkins at Courtney's place this evening, couldn't we?"

"I suppose so", replied a worried looking Chief Inspector.

"Come on, let's go and get a strong cup of coffee" he added cheering up a bit and leading the way out of the office.

They were sat at a corner table in the Stratford Licensed Tearooms and Restaurant, sipping their brandy laced coffee, when the Chief Inspector received his telephone call. He didn't disclose the message to his Sergeant but he was a lot more cheerful.

"You know, Thomas, I don't think it'll be long before we wind this case up for good and all, and I think what you discovered this morning was the start of it."

"I hope so, sir, but what baffles me sir is this Jones fellow from Fiesta Lighting at Salisbury. I mean he was only involved with the fireworks display at the Bonfire and Firework display and he gave a very negative report to the Salisbury police. As I remember, that's why we never bothered with him. Now it looks like he set fire to the Colonel's place, gave us the run around and what have you, and now, it looks as if someone's given him the chop, doesn't it?"

"Yes, well, Commander Benfields at the crime scene. He'll sort it out for us. We have an errand to run ourselves. That was Brenda Armstrong on the phone."

"I thought as much. What does she want? Some information on whom we may suspect?"

"No. She's not like that, Thomas. She's on our side. Brenda is passing me more info than I'm giving her."

Sergeant Thomas interrupted again,

"So what else are you giving her? She's not doing anything for nothing. Women aren't like that, are they?"

The Chief Inspector was getting a little annoyed by this time. "Look Sergeant, I'm not asking for your opinion on women. I'm telling you that Brenda Armstrong, whose friendship I value very much at this moment is helping us an awful lot with our enquiries at the present time. Plus the fact that she has just phoned from her home in Bromsgrove to tell me that she had not had another visitor. I had asked her to call me as soon as she arrived home, to let me know that everything was all right, after what had happened to her last time. Now she informs me that she has received a letter and a small book that had belonged to the recently deceased Mr. Jones. An old army friend whom she had persuaded to investigate Fiesta Lighting for her sent it to her. Apparently he had accidentally slipped it into his pocket whilst he was visiting the premises in the early hours of the morning one day last week. He also informed her, that he had followed Mr. Jones to Swindon where he met Brigadier Smythe White. She says the book is written in some sort of code. Her friends think it is a record of his illegal activities. She also told me that, she was waiting for the police to come and inspect her house, and for the Chubb burglar alarm company to come and investigate why her alarm didn't work. I want that book, Sergeant, so I think we'll head in that direction and pick it up."

"I'm sorry, sir. I didn't realize she was on the danger list.

I think we'd better make a move", replied the Sergeant, picking up the bill and moving to the counter.

"Oh, thanks Sergeant that's very decent of you I seem to be out of change for the moment" quipped the Chief Inspector as he walked past Sergeant Thomas who was paying the bill.

The Sergeant was instructed to stop, as they were passing the police station to enable his Chief to pick up the photograph of the army concert party that Brenda had given him the previous evening. Chief Inspector Sullivan thought they could then visit The Chestnut Tree restaurant at Shirley and show it to the barman, Sid Watson, who would not be on duty until one o'clock.

The Cherry Tree Restaurant was on their way to Brenda Armstrong's home in Solihull.

Sergeant Thomas was looking at the photograph and thinking that he could recognize Commander Benfield, while the Chief Inspector answered his phone.

"I'll be there right away, have you phoned forensic on this one? Good, I'll let you know after I get there."

He replaced the phone.

"Come on, Thomas, you can forget that. They've found a car in the river at Herbert's Boatyard, it seems there's a woman in it."

The boatyard was located on the north bank of the river alongside Clopton Bridge. They hired out punts and rowing boats to holidaymakers and to young couples when the young man wanted to show his skill with either punting pole or oars. In the early postwar years, they had built and hired out motor cruisers, and in recent times were hiring out the long steel constructed Canal Boats. Starting October, as soon as the holiday period is finished, at least a third of the fleet is refurbished. The boats are floated onto stocks, and then, hauled up the slipway at the end of the forty-foot channel into the boat shed where the work is done. It was when one of these boats had been slipped back into the water and was being maneuvered out of the channel back into the river that it struck the car. According to Charlie Wilson, the yard foreman, the level of the water had dropped over the last couple of weeks so that was maybe the reason that the boat had struck the car. Also, the boatyard had been closed for January so there was no knowing when or how the car got into the river. All this Charlie had told the Constables who had been first on the scene.

All that could be seen of the car was the red roof against the bow of the canal boat.

The Chief Inspector walked over to the edge of the riverside wharf. He looked down at the car roof,

"You say there is a body in there?" he asked one of the Constables.

"Yes, sir. Charlie Wilson says there is. Martin Herbert put his wet suit on to have a look when the boat got stuck. They were going to haul it out with that crane." he said pointing to a crane standing near the waters edge "but they changed their minds when he told them that he thought that there was a body in the car. That's when they called us in". The Constable replied.

"Good, Good. I'll leave you to it then" said the Chief Inspector as he left the Constable on the wharfe and made his way to the office to see Martin Herbert.

When he entered the office it was so nice and warm he decided he was going to stay in the warm until the police frogmen had recovered the car.

Eventually, the car was slowly lifted clear of the water and swung round onto the riverbank. After the slings were removed the Chief Inspector stepped forward and opened the passenger door at the front. Water gushed out and soaked his feet as he did so. There, laid across the front seats, not wearing her safety belt was Margaret Hodgkinson.

"I thought I recognized the car, Sergeant, now we know where she disappeared to. It looks as if she's been in the water a long time."

"Yes, sir. I wonder why we haven't heard from her office? She was suppose to have gone on holiday for a fortnight."

One of the laboratory technicians stepped in front of the Chief Inspector.

"That's alright, Chief Inspector. We'll take over from here," he said as he bent over to have a look in the car.

"Right you are, Gordon. Thanks" he replied recognizing the technician. "I'll get some of our lads to rig up some screens for you."

"Too late. It's already been taken care of" the technician replied, as two policemen approached down the dockside carrying white plastic sheeting and yards of yellow tape were being used to cordon off the area where the body of Margaret Hodgkinson lay in the car.

After establishing that the two boats that were being put back in the river had in fact been in the boat shed since November. Also the channel had been empty of boats as a safety precaution against flooding over the Christmas period. The Chief Inspector and his Sergeant returned to the office of Martin Herbert to question him on the security arrangements of the boats and the boatyard whilst everyone was on holiday. Martin informed the Policemen, that Group 4 security patrolled the premises night and day over that period. This year, however, his two engineers had returned from their holidays a week earlier to rebuild the engines for the two boats to enable them to get them back in the water on time, keeping to a schedule was essential when maintaining a fleet of holiday boats.

Access to the boatyard was across a tarmac road at the rear of a very large Stratford Corporation car park. A six-foot high wooden fence separated the boat yard from the car park. The entrance gate was the same height and comprised of two ten-foot wide gates and a wicket gate at the side for the staff to enter. To get Margaret's red and black Citroen into the yard, the murderer had to pick the lock on each gate and then close them after entry. As they walked round the yard the Chief Inspector observed to his Sergeant,

"You know, this killer is a professional at his job. He seems to be able to pick any lock he comes up against and he picks his crime scenes very carefully. But most important, Thomas, assuming this is the same man. He knows all about security systems, he has broken into three places with systems installed."

"Yes, but with some of these systems you don't have to be a 'Rocket Scientist' to break in, do you?" Sergeant Thomas indulgently replied.

They had wandered through the gate and across the car park to the adjoining road bridge, where a small crowd had gathered, using the bridge as their observation platform to watch the activities of the Police.

Sergeant Thomas nudged his Chief Inspector and motioned towards the Centre of the bridge with his hand. When the Chief Inspector stopped on the edge of the crowd, Thomas whispered in his ear,

"We'll see more over there, sir." Moving to the Centre of the bridge "That's better, sir" he remarked leaning on the parapet of the bridge.

"Can't see much though; they've got it well screened off."

"Yes, Sergeant, they have but it's not the kind of day to stand around on a bridge either" the Chief Inspector replied rubbing his hands together and stamping his feet.

"I bet it's like the black hole of Calcutta down there at night." said the Sergeant ignoring his Chief and still leaning on the parapet of the bridge gazing down into the boatyard.

"Yes, well, Thomas, let them get on with their job and we'll get on with ours. We're going back to the office down there to set up an incident room."

After arranging with Martin Herbert for the use of an office for two or three days, he joined his Sergeant on the riverside dock where two mortuary attendants had just loaded the body into their van and were preparing to leave the dock. The pathologist, Dr. Watkins was informing Sergeant Thomas that in his opinion the body had been in the water for a few weeks and he would give them more details later. When he had finished, the Chief Inspector asked Dr. Watkins if he had any idea of the cause of death.

"No, but as I said, the body has been in the water for more than a week possibly a month" he replied as he picked up his bag and slapped the Chief Inspector on the back.

"My God, Inspector, you are keeping me busy these days and such a variation. Still, you are keeping my staff on their toes. Be in touch later".

He left them staring at the car and wondering what else they were going to find.

"Anything else in the car?" asked the Chief Inspector noticing that Inspector Carter was holding a plastic bag containing a handbag.

"Yes, sir, there was one large suitcase. I've sent it to the laboratory." replied the Inspector.

"Nothing else, like a vanity case or something?" asked Sergeant Thomas.

Inspector Carter seemed taken aback by the abruptness of Sergeant Thomas.

Who noticing the Inspector's reaction quickly replied,

"Sorry, sir, I mean a woman usually carries a toiletry bag with all her cosmetics in, doesn't she?"

"I suppose so, Sergeant", answered Inspector Carter more amicably.

The Chief Inspector returned after having a good look at the car. "It looks as if everyone has finished here, Inspector, so you can let the recovery truck take the car back into the workshop and let them have a look at it. What are you going to do with that?" he said nodding to the plastic bag "Framing it?"

"No, sir. I meant to give it to the doctor before he left."

"Give it to Sergeant Thomas and we'll drop it off as we go past."

As Chief Inspector Sullivan and his Sergeant left, leaving Carter and some men to clear up, the Chief was still puzzling how the murderer had got into the boatyard without triggering the alarm and this was still bothering him when they arrived back at the station. When he entered his office, Inspector White was waiting for him.

"Hello, Snowy, enjoy your trip to the country? Where's your mate? Having a rest after a tiring journey?"

"No, sir, he's gone out; said he wouldn't be long. But he's shook up a bit, sir, never seen him like this before, here's a photograph of the body, turned a bit white he did, when he saw it."

Inspector White passed the photograph he had been holding to the Chief Inspector.

"Do you know him as well, sir?" he asked noting the reaction of the Chief Inspector.

"I certainly do, White, I certainly do."

As he reached into one of his desk drawers, he looked across at his Sergeant.

"You were wrong, Thomas, it wasn't our friend, Mr. Jones. It was our other guest, the one we chased the other night, remember,

Mr. Braithwaite."

The Chief Inspector pronounced the name in a broad Lancashire accent.

The Sergeant smiled when he heard the name and repeated it in the same dialect,

"Mr. Braithwaite, sir? What were he doing in Mr. Jones' car?"

"Alright, Thomas, less of the theatrics, you'll have Snowy here thinking we're not taking this as serious as his Commander is. Any ideas on where he has gone?" the Chief Inspector asked.

"None, sir."

"Right, Inspector. Get in touch with Salisbury Police tell them we want Jones picked up in connection with a suspicious death. I don't suppose we know cause of death, do we?"

Inspector White shook his head." No idea, sir", he replied.

"I see, so have we any extras on the photograph, Snowy?" asked the Chief Inspector patiently," If so, I'll keep this."

Inspector White didn't reply to Chief Inspector Sullivan's question but turned and left the office.

"Queer fellow, isn't he Sergeant? He's lost without his Commander. I'll leave you to contact Hodgkins garage at Altringham. I've got a lot of work to do on this Jones character".

CHAPTER THIRTY

It was late afternoon when Commander Benfield returned to his office. He was as nervous as a kitten as he took a bottle of Grouse whiskey and a glass from the third drawer of his filing cabinet and poured himself two fingers of whiskey. He emptied the glass in one swallow then poured himself another drink.

"That never touched the sides, Commander. I bet you needed that. Yes, I will have one with you, thank you."

Chief Inspector Sullivan remarked quietly as he slowly closed the door.

Commander Benfield had the look of a schoolboy who had been caught raiding the larder, as he reluctantly took a second glass from the filing cabinet and poured the same measure for his Chief Inspector.

"Oh, it's just a livener, Chief Inspector. I've had a very busy day."

"Yes, Inspector White told me that the body in your car wasn't who we expected it to be. Is that why you left in a hurry, Commander, when you got back from Gloucester?"

"I had to go to my hotel to change and have a bath, Chief Inspector, it was awful" the Commander replied with a shudder.

"He was killed with a garrote the doctor said. Whoever did it did an amateurish job of setting fire to the car, almost as if he wanted us to find the body intact."

"Maybe he does, Commander, have you seen the deceased before?" asked the Chief Inspector, watching the Commander closely as he fidgeted a bit then closed the filing cabinet drawer and walking slowly over to his desk, as if he was trying to think up an answer to the question.

He sat down and motioned the Chief Inspector to sit.

"I can't say that I do know him, Chief Inspector, in fact, no, I have never seen him before."

"I think you have seen him before, Commander. In fact he has been around here a lot just recently."

The Chief Inspector flicked the enlarged prints across the desk to the Commander.

"It's Mr.Braithwaite, Commander, and he's been around the Stratford district a lot just recently and, I think you may know him a bit more than you say you do." the Chief inspector finished with menace in his voice.

"Chief Inspector, I don't like the tone of your voice and I don't like you insinuating that I am a liar. I suggest you leave my office until you have cooled down. Then and only then will I accept your apology, I also want a full report on this other incident, that you have been involved in today."

The Commander jumped to his feet as he finished.

Chief Inspector Sullivan realizing that he may have overstepped the mark a weeny bit quietly left the office.

When he had gone, the Commander picked up his telephone and rang Brigadier Smythe White. When the Brigadier answered he spoke to him in clipped tones.

"One of your very close friends is dead, she was drowned. There was also one other body found in a burnt out car. He was killed with a cheese wire. I think we had better meet right now. Your place I'll be there in an hour."

The Chief Inspector had left the Commanders' office with a satisfied smile on his face and as he entered his own office Sergeant Thomas remarked.

"You are looking pleased with yourself, sir, have you frightened our friend to death?"

"Nearly, Thomas, I think he'll have to change his underwear again. I accused him of knowing Braithwaite and he ordered me from his office to cool down and to apologize to him."

"Are you?"

"Am I what, Thomas?"

"Going to apologize, sir."

"I am not, he's as guilty as hell, Thomas, and he knows, that I know. Trouble is, I have to prove it especially with him being a Senior Police Officer."

"Yes, it is nasty proving he is 'bent'."

"In more ways than one, Sergeant, but let's not go into that. What have you got there something good I hope?"

"It's the report of the contents of Margaret's handbag, the bag is downstairs if you want to have a look at it but before we do that, sir, I took a call from Brenda Armstrong for you, she said everything is fixed at her place and would phone you. I'm afraid I took it on myself to tell her to pack enough clothes for a week and to get herself over here, because it isn't safe for her to be on her own. She's agreed to do that." Thomas said passing the list to the Chief Inspector.

Glancing down at the list, the Chief said.

"Good thinking, Thomas, there's a receipt for The Bridge Hotel. Come on, Sergeant, let's have a look at these contents."

He was a little disappointed as he viewed the contents, which had been placed in plastic bags. The receipt was a crumpled piece of paper and was a credit card receipt drawn on The Bridge Hotel, High Street Stratford-on-Avon.

The Chief Inspector and his Sergeant introduced themselves to the Manager of the hotel, explaining the reason for their visit, also producing a copy of the credit card receipt. The Manager checked his computer records and confirmed that Margaret had indeed stayed at the hotel for one night on December 23rd. The Manager also read off the computer that Margaret had left a small case behind in her room. The case had not been collected so it had been registered as lost property and placed in the lost property cupboard. The Manager asked the two Policemen to accompany him downstairs as the cupboard was in the basement of the hotel.

Realizing there was no point in checking the room as it was five weeks since Margaret had stayed there, the Chief Inspector interviewed the chamber maid who cleaned the room's on the floor that Margaret had been booked into.

Apologizing she said.

"She was sorry she could not be of much help but could remember that the bed had not been slept in and the vanity case had been left on the dressing table. Nothing in the room had been used and if it had not been for the case being found on the dressing table, she would have said that the room had not been used at all".

After making arrangements to interview the night porter when he came on duty later, the two left the hotel and returned to the police station where Sergeant Thomas visited the Property Dept. and obtained the keys that had been found in Margaret's handbag and found two of them fitted the vanity case. He opened the case slowly not knowing what to expect and found a new Instamatic camera loaded with a film that showed twelve photographs had been taken.

"I think we'll have these developed, Tom," said the property Sergeant as he listed the contents of the case.

"Ah, this may be interesting" he said as he picked up a note book in a maroon leather cover from the bottom of the case and handed it over to Sergeant Thomas who flicked through the pages

"It's her personal telephone directory, Joe. I'll take it with me also that film. The Chief Inspector is bound to ask for it to be developed. I'll just sign for these two for now."

On his return to the Chief's office, he reported what had been found in Margaret's case and that he was having the film developed.

"Good, Good" responded the Chief Inspector "I hope what is on that film and this photograph will tell us a lot more about this case. I want you and Snowy to go over to The Chestnut Tree with this photograph of the army concert party and show it to the barman."

CHAPTER THIRTY ONE

It was a beautiful spring morning as Nigel Courtney stood at his office window looking at the crocuses and snowdrops in full bloom in the flowerbeds surrounding the parked cars. He was thinking that at last the awful winter was over when a red Ferrari pulled up at the security lodge at the main gate. As it continued to the visitor's car park, he made a mental note of the registration number and thought he recognized the man who got out of the car and approached the main office. Contacting the gate security they informed him that the visitor was a Mr. Taylor from Cobham Security Systems, Salisbury who had an appointment with Mr. Simpkins. Nigel still had the conviction that he knew the man but not as Mr Taylor. About half an hour later he suddenly remembered the man's name as Mr Jones and thought he recognized the car parked in the visitor's car park. He told his Security Officer to inform Chief Inspector Sullivan that Mr. Jones was here and he hurried to his Security Chief's office, Mr. Jones came out calling 'Good afternoon, Mr. Simpkins' as he closed the door.

Nigel knew immediately that something was wrong as David, like himself, always showed his visitors off the property. Mr. Jones realizing that he had been recognized pulled a small revolver from a shoulder holster pointing it at Nigel.

"It's alright, Mr. Courtney. Nobody's going to hurt you; you are just going to take a ride with me in your car. I prefer it to the Ferrari that's too conspicuous. Besides, the Porsche is more comfortable."

He smirked at Nigel as he turned him around and walked him to the door and over to the Porsche. They got into the car and drove out quickly through the main gate without slowing down. Nigel did this on purpose because it was one of the company rules that all vehicles slow down at the gate enabling the security officer to check the driver, then book the driver and vehicle out. The Security officer immediately knew that something was wrong and quickly dialed Chief Inspector Sullivan's number but received no reply. He phoned David Simpkin's secretary who on entering her boss's office found him lying unconscious on the floor and his safe door wide open. She immediately returned to her office and dialed '999' for the Police and ambulance. It seemed no time at all when a Police car came screaming into the car park closely followed by the ambulance. The security officer escorted the police and Paramedics to David's office where he was still lying unconscious on the floor covered with a blanket that his secretary had thoughtfully placed over him.

Shortly after leaving Courtney Transport Services, Nigel was given instructions by Mr. Jones to turn off the Solihull High Street, down a side street amongst some derelict factories and warehouses and ordered to stop. He was told to get out of the car, instead of being shot, which he expected, he was given a pair of pliers and a screwdriver and instructed to remove the number plates and fit replacement plates. He was then told to get back into the driver's seat and still being threatened by a wave of the gun, was made to take a circuitous route and not to exceed fifty miles an hour. As they were approaching Redditch, a Police patrol car came up very fast from the rear. It followed them for a short while to enable the driver to read the numberplate then it flashed past them. When the Police car was out of sight, Nigel was instructed to increase his speed and take a turn for Studley. They had driven through Studley and were nearing Alcester when another patrol car drove past them going in the opposite direction. Mr. Jones watching the patrol car in his rearview mirror saw the brake lights of the police car come on as the driver applied his brakes, he instructed Nigel to take a turning coming up on their right. With a screaming of tires and roaring of the three-litre engine, they headed down towards the village of Inkberrow at great speed. As they approached another road junction, Mr. Jones gave instructions to turn for Broom and to 'step on it' as they were running late. Nigel carried out the instructions to the letter hoping that he may scare his passenger, but Mr Jones just sat there with his revolver pressed into Nigel's side and appeared to be enjoying the ride. It was starting to get dark as Nigel drove the Porsche over Bidford Bridge towards Honeybourne. On reaching Bidford Flying Club, he was instructed to turn in and switch off his lights.

The flying club is small having six privately owned single engine aircraft and six gliders with one tug aircraft. The grass landing strip stretches down the field behind the clubhouse that is a converted nissen hut. Four more nissen huts acting as hangers for the aircraft were built alongside each other beginning behind the clubhouse and along the northern side of the field.

One or two of the aircraft were picketed outside and it was towards one of these that Nigel drove the Porche.

As they approached the first of the two picketed aircraft two men could be seen untying the picketing ropes. The clamps had already been removed from the ailerons and rudder. The removal of the picketing ropes being completed, one of the men walked towards the car.

"You. Courtney, out of the car and no funny business." Mr. Jones ordered snatching the ignition key from the ignition switch as he got out, he then ran round to the driver's side and slammed the driver's door shut behind Nigel as he got out, he then pushed him towards the dark outline of the man that was approaching them.

"You ought to be more careful," said Jones "I could have been the police."

"With a Porsche!" the man laughed then stopped "What the hell, Jones, you must be mad."

In the gathering darkness Nigel thought he recognized the voice as the man stopped, still some distance away in the half-light. Puzzled by it all Nigel recognized the tall dark figure and was positive it was Brigadier Smythe White. He had only met him once at a brotherhood meeting at the Birmingham Lodge but had been with him and the Colonel most of the evening.

"Have you got the Money?" he asked.

"It's in the back of the car" Jones replied.

The Brigadier pulled his ex-army revolver from his duffel coat pocket.

"You shouldn't have brought him along, Jones."

The Brigadier said pointing his gun at Mr. Jones who was standing holding Nigel's right arm, and fired, knocking him back over the bonnet of the Porsche.

He fired a second time hitting Nigel in the stomach.

"That'll stop you being nosy, Courtney", the Brigadier snarled.

Nigel felt a numbing feeling in the pit of his stomach as the bullet hit him. Sinking to the ground in front of his car, he didn't lose consciousness immediately.

The Brigadier collected the briefcase containing the money, which had been stolen from the safe in David Simpkin's office; Nigel then heard footsteps close by and the very familiar voice of Tom Atkinson.

"What the hell do you think you're doing? I told you no more killings. Come on. Let's get out of here otherwise we shall be late in France, are they both done for?

"Yes, I don't think we'll have any more problems with these two" the Brigadier replied as they both returned to the aircraft.

Tom Atkinson was an ex-R.A.F. pilot and to keep his pilot's license he had to do two hundred flying hours a year. When he first left the air force, he joined the Staverton Flying Club near Gloucester, then, as his accountancy business improved, some of his farmer customers who owned aircraft let him use them to accumulate his flying hours, to enable him to keep his pilot's license.

That was, until he started financing, Brigadier Smythe White's ventures, who was a good organizer but needed Tom's services in his successful jewelry business. The Brigadier could not resist temptation and when he was offered a supply of illicit diamonds again who better to arrange his finance than his accountant. Tom, forever the cautious accountant, offered the finance but wanted insurance cover and this was how, at his suggestion, the Brigadier brought in his old friend, Colonel Brown who was not aware of the accountant's involvement.

It was at this time that the accountant bought his first aircraft, a small Cessna.

Nigel was in agony as he heard the aircraft taxiing down the grass airstrip. He managed to crawl round to where Mr. Jones had rolled off the bonnet of his car, and recovered his gun.

The aircraft had reached the bottom of the field, turning the aircraft ready for take off Tom started to run up the engine. When it was almost on peak revs, he released the brake and the aircraft shot forward on its take off run. As it passed over where Nigel lay close to the Porsche he fired two shots. One struck the engine but only did minor damage, nicking a fuel pipe but not immediately causing a fuel leak. The other shot missed completely and Tom and the Brigadier happily flew on towards Arramanche in France. The aircraft they were using had been stolen from one of Tom's oldest clients, Francis Pike.

The accountants own aircraft, a twin engined Cessna was awaiting their arrival at the Arramanche Airport.

As the aircraft disappeared into the distance, Nigel started to crawl towards the road before he passed out.

Danny Myers was returning to his farmhouse after milking his dairy herd of Friesians when he heard two small explosions. At first he thought it was a car backfiring and stood still for a few moments looking towards the flying club that was approximately three quarters of a mile along the road towards Bidford. As he continued his walk towards the house, he heard the aircraft engine startup, now he knew something was wrong. Being a member of the Club, he knew there was no night flying. He ran indoors quickly and told his wife to contact the Mochamton Police and inform them that he was taking the Land Rover and going to have a look. As Danny drove out of the farmyard, his lights caught the plane as it took off over the road, then as he approached the Club; the headlights of the Landrover showed Nigel lying unconscious in front of the clubhouse. Having checked that Nigel was still alive he ran back to the Land Rover and contacted his wife on his car telephone to call an ambulance. He returned to the victim who was dressed only in thin slacks and a shirt, and covered him with his own heavy waterproof parka.

Nigel recovered consciousness and muttered,

"Jones is over there, beside my car." He then lapsed into unconsciousness again.

Sergeant Hopper drove into the club car park and leapt from his car almost before it had stopped. He followed Danny as he ran towards Nigel's Porsche, both arriving together shining their torches on Mr. Jones as he lay on the ground.

"What's going on, Danny?" Sergeant Hopper asked.

"I don't know but this blokes in a bad way" Danny replied as he checked Mr. Jones' pulse.

"He's very weak, Sergeant."

Mr. Jones moaned and opened his eyes

"Smythe White did this to us" he muttered. "Simpkins did the rest." He looked at Sergeant Hopper and tried to raise himself onto his elbows.

Staring at the Sergeant he said, "Your bloke knows the toff" he muttered and sighed as his head fell back on the ground.

"He's gone," said Danny "What was he talking about, Sergeant?"

"I don't know but I think I know someone who does, we can't do any more here, Danny, let's go back to the other one."

Nigel was moaning quite a bit now, and sirens were wailing in the distance as they tried to make Nigel as comfortable as possible and assured him that his colleague had told them who shot them.

The ambulance arrived accompanied by police cars, all with their sirens wailing and lights flashing, making a cacophony of sound and light.

Chief Inspector Sullivan was in the first car and ran to where the paramedics were working on Nigel, shouting to them to get him to the hospital as quickly as possible and telling Sergeant Thomas to go with them and not to leave him.

He walked over to where Mr. Jones was laid and Sergeant Hopper quickly informed him of what the victim had told them before he died.

"You know who he's talking about, Sergeant, not a word to anyone mind, that's dangerous talk."

"Yes, sir, but I'm not dumb, either, I've been noticing things as well."

"Never mind, Sergeant, mum's the word, tell your friend as well, tell him nobody spoke a word. Understand?"

Chief Inspector Sullivan and Sergeant Hopper were sitting in the kitchen at Danny Myers farmhouse to where they had retired to take the farmer's statement and were enjoying a coffee with a brandy chaser.

On being asked if he knew anything about the Flying Club Danny gave the two policemen details of the farmers who were club members and owned their own aircraft. He also gave details of the members who kept their aircraft on their own farms. He then mentioned that Francis Pike would shortly be collecting his aircraft to take it back to his farm he had been storing it at the airfield while he had some work done on his own landing strip. But he allowed Tom Atkinson to use it to make up his flying hours they must have had an arrangement on costs.

"Come to think of it, Inspector, Tom was here this afternoon doing an engine run, he left as I arrived at the club. The club secretary was just about to leave as well. I told him that Tom Atkinson had been doing an engine run on Mr. Pikes Cessna and he remarked, 'that he didn't know why Tom was doing this on Francis Pike's plane, because he had his own aircraft and he was pretty well up on his flying hours.' I thought nothing of it till now. I wonder if it was him flying it."

"Did you phone Francis Pike, Sergeant?"

"Yes, sir, I told you I only got the answer-phone."

"Oh, yes" replied the Chief Inspector "Check if Atkinson's at home now then."

Using Danny's phone, Sergeant Hopper rang Tom Atkinson's home and again he got the answer-phone. The Chief Inspector thanked Danny for their drinks, as they left the farmhouse. Danny watched them drive out of his yard.

Peace and tranquillity reigned once more.

As they got into their cars, the Chief Inspector instructed Sergeant Hopper to follow him and he led the way to the nearest public house which was The Farmer Arms at Mochamton. He ordered two pints of Old and Mild and left Sergeant Hopper to pay while he went to the far end of the bar to make some telephone calls.

When he returned, he half emptied the glass at one go.

"I needed that, Sergeant" smacking his lips "I'm only having this one pint, then I'm going back to Stratford, I've got several things to sort out. In the meantime, I'd like you to go back to Danny Myers and see if you can find out any more on that plane that took off tonight. I want destination and who filed the flight plan. If Danny can't help you, see if he can get the club secretary to help."

Realizing he wasn't going to get another pint of beer, he left the bar.

"Yes, sir, very good sir, three bags full, sir." muttered Sergeant Hopper staring at the back of the retreating Chief Inspector.

The first place that the Chief Inspector visited on his return to Stratford-on-Avon was the hospital. The report from Sergeant Thomas was that Nigel Courtney was still unconscious but stable. The doctor didn't expect any improvement until they had operated to remove the bullet. He was very weak and it couldn't be removed in his present condition.

There was a Police Constable standing outside the door of the private ward where Nigel Courtney had been taken for protection, feeling satisfied with the arrangements Chief Inspector Sullivan gave further instructions to his Sergeant.

"Right, Thomas, leave things to the Constable, tell him to let us know when Nigel regains consciousness, and Oh, get someone to cover for you, then meet me down in the path. Lab."

When the Chief Inspector entered the Pathology Department, he found Dr. Walker's assistant hosing down the pathology table.

"Oh good. Just finished, Joyce?" he asked.

"I think so" Joyce replied "but the report isn't written up yet. I've got to say, Chief Inspector, you keep coming up with some different ones, don't you?"

"Why, what have you found?"

"Well, the killer knew his job, she didn't feel much, if anything" said Joyce dragging the information out a little, making the Chief Inspector agitated, "We think a long hatpin or something like it, between the ribs and straight into the heart. He knew his job, Inspector", said Joyce demonstrating the thrust of the weapon and shaking her head.

"When was she killed?" he asked.

"Here's Dr. Walker, ask him. About five weeks, we think, don't we doctor?"

"Yes, Chief Inspector, before Christmas I would say five weeks definitely", answered Dr. Walker. "Neatest piece of work I've seen for a long time" he continued "no mess, Chief Inspector, not a lot of paperwork for me either."

"I suppose next you're going to tell me where, when and what they were doing?"

"Well, if you're going to be like that, Chief Inspector, I will. I would say they had a meal just prior and I would say she was in the back seat of the car, maybe cuddling each other because the hole in the skin is in direct line with the hole in the heart. We found the puncture in the heart fairly easy, but we had to find what caused it. When we carefully inspected the skin over the left breast we found a minute speck of congealed blood at the puncture wound. We then confirmed this as the entry wound by using a magnifying glass. No mess at all, Inspector.

As regards how long has she been dead, I would say by the condition of the body it has been immersed in the water for about five weeks. Give a day or two 'cos. the temperature of the water can mess things up a bit but I still say about five weeks, Inspector, yes, five weeks" the doctor reported pursing his lips and nodding his head as he turned and walked back to his office.

"You'll have my report in the morning, Chief Inspector." he called over his shoulder.

Chief Inspector Sullivan was returning to the main floor of the hospital via the stairs when he met Sergeant Thomas coming down to join him.

"Ah, Thomas, fixed things, have you?"

"Yes, sir, D.C. Hopkins is up there until midnight, then uniform branch will take over until the morning, both officers will be inside the room. We don't want to take any chances, do we?"

The Chief Inspector told his Sergeant the result of the post mortem as they walked out of the hospital to the car.

CHAPTER THIRTY TWO

It was getting late in the evening when Chief Inspector Sullivan joined Brenda Armstrong for dinner at the Appleton Hall Hotel. After the meal they went up to her room as they had done on previous occasions to discuss the developments of the case. It was almost midnight, when sitting up in bed naked and savoring a large brandy each, Brenda began to tell Sully of the results of the Police visit to her home and the improvements to the alarm system. But the most important thing was the book and the letter she had received from her ex Army colleague Dennis Davis the previous day. She put down the brandy glass on the bedside table and reached across Sully for her handbag on the table beside him. Returning to her side of the bed after a passionate ten minutes, she took the notebook from her bag and flicked through it.

"It's got the murdered victims names in it plus dates and numbers alongside the name, I assumed a code of some sort, Sully" she said as she passed the book across to him,

"I solved it easily, each letter of the alphabet is numbered. The figure's 419 appear frequently and those letters, according to the code are D.S. Now then Sully whose initials are D.S.? she asked kissing him on the cheek.

"My God, you could be right, Brenda. It fits, it's the simplest of codes but it works; but what do all these other numbers mean?"

"Well, darling" cooed Brenda "I think our friend Mr Jones was into something with the Marvo Brothers, like our other friend, Benny."

Brenda was getting passionate again rolling on to the top of Sully whose resistance being low, gave in to her advances.

The following morning Chief Inspector Sullivan phoned Sergeant Thomas asking him to get in touch with the Solihull General Hospital where David Simpkins was, to find out his condition and to ask how many police were on duty at his bedside, if any and to do it now. He then phoned Stratford Police Station front desk and asked if Commander Benfield was in yet. He was informed that his assistant Inspector White was in but the Commander was not. Inspector White had checked his hotel and had been informed that the Commander had left very early and had informed the night porter that he was going to London. He put the phone down quickly and rushed to the bathroom were Brenda was having her shower, which usually lasted anything up to thirty minutes, fifteen minutes if she was in a hurry, he tried the bathroom door and found it locked. "Brenda, Brenda" he called trying the door again. She got out of the shower when he called a second time and opened the door with only a towel around her wondering what all the noise was about.

"Benny's on the loose he's not at the station and he's left word at the hotel that he has gone to London, I don't believe it. He knows darn well that his bubble has burst, and that it's only a matter of time before he's picked up unless he does something about it."

"Okay, Okay Sully let's slow down a bit shall we? Have a shower while I get dressed and for heavens sake calm down you'll have a heart attack." Brenda replied.

He did as he was told and while he was getting dressed, room service arrived with some packed sandwiches that Brenda had ordered.

She was sitting calmly having a cup of tea, when the Chief Inspector suddenly stated,

"I'm not leaving you here, Brenda, you're coming with me. We're going to Solihull to have a word with David Simpkins. I wouldn't be surprised if that's where Benny is heading now, would you?"

"I wouldn't be surprised at anything that happens now. I think Simpkins is the danger-man, he's not the one at the top but I think he knows too much about Benny's involvement for his comfort." She hesitated for a minute "Yes, I think that's where he's headed. But, is it really necessary for me to come with you?" she asked.

"No" Chief Inspector Sullivan agreed "but I'm only thinking of your safety, my dear, besides where can you go around here where you'll be safe while Benny's on the loose?" he asked.

Brenda assured her lover that she would be allright and that she could look after herself, kissing him lightly on the cheek as they parted each getting into their own cars at the front of the Hotel.

Chief Inspector Sullivan drove straight to his office in Stratford Police Station and after briefing his staff on their duties for the day he left with Sergeant Thomas for Solihull General Hospital to try to interview David Simpkins. Mr Jones had missed the lethal spot on the head when he had hit Simpkins with the butt of his revolver but had left the security officer suffering from severe concussion.

CHAPTER THIRTY THREE

Commander Benfield was in a state of panic as he came downstairs from his hotel room. He surprised the night porter who was just starting to prepare the breakfast trays for the guest's who had booked early morning calls, he glanced at his watch as he walked through from the kitchen, hearing the familiar noise of a key being dropped on his desk.

It was five forty five am looking across the reception desk he saw Commander Benfield standing nearby looking at a hotel brochure.

"Morning, Commander, you're not on my list for early morning breakfast."

"Sorry about that, I had a late night call from London." Commander Benfield replied dropping the brochure.

"Have to go down there early, thought I'd better drive. More convenient." he added slowly as if he were thinking of something else as he was speaking.

"I'd better unlock the door for you then, Commander."

The night porter came from behind the desk and removed the door keys from his pocket, which were attached on a long chain from his belt. He relocked the doors after the Commander had left and made a note in his night porter's logbook.

Swearing vengeance on three people, Chief Inspector Sullivan, David Simpkins and Brenda Armstrong for the position he was in, the Commander drove out of the hotel car park. Not thinking where he was going, he suddenly realized he was heading for the Police Station driving past his office he continued on towards Evesham. Then on to Bromsgrove having made up his mind he was going to deal with Brenda first. Not being a naturally violent man, he hadn't made up his mind what he was going to do to her when he arrived outside her house.

Dawn was breaking as he pushed the front door bell.

No one answered, so he tried again and again.

In his frustration Benny kicked the door twice.

Still there was no answer.

The big toe on his right foot started to hurt from kicking the door as he retraced his footsteps down the garden path. Feeling very angry, he looked down at his foot in the gathering daylight of the February morning. As he stared at his foot he noticed some bricks standing on end at an angle of forty-five degrees along the edge of the concrete path. They had been put there to stop the soil from spilling on to the path.

With a sudden urge he picked up one of the bricks not noticing that it had broken in two and threw the portion in his hand at the window, breaking it and setting off the burglar alarm.

The alarm scared him, when it started to wail.

Scared and angry, he ran to his car and was speeding away from the scene of his crime as the bedroom lights in the adjoining houses came on one by one, as Brenda's neighbours were woken by the noise.

Not having had much success in his first venture of vengeance, Benny headed towards Solihull General Hospital. On his arrival, he found the place was a hive of activity. The casualty department was busy as usual and the wards were busy serving breakfasts to the patients. The exception was the private ward where David Simpkins lay unconscious. One uniformed policeman was sitting on duty outside the ward, Benny walking briskly up to him, flashed his identity card. The Constable hastily jumped to his feet, straightened his crumpled uniform and exclaimed.

"Sorry sir, I didn't know you were coming in early".

"That's alright, lad," said Benny, using his charm "I thought I'd have an early morning look at Simpkins. He's a very important customer, Constable, mind if I take a look?"

"I suppose it's alright, sir, the nurses have not been in yet, last time they looked in was five o'clock, sir."

"I see." replied Benny "I'll just take a peek, I won't be long," he said as he pushed open the door and walked into the room.

The Commander walked over to the bed and stood looking down at David sleeping peacefully amidst drip tubes and wires connected to the E.C.G. equipment.

"Bastard! You talked me into this, Dave, and you're going to pay for it as well." Benny picked up a pillow from a chair alongside the bed putting it over David's face holding it down hard.

The Constable, being curious as to why a Commander from Scotland Yard was visiting so early in the morning, had put a call in to his control and they had told him to keep a watch on him while they made enquiries. Looking through the window in the door he saw the Commander pick up the pillow and knew what he intended to do with it.

Realizing at the same time Commander Benfields intentions and that he would need assistance to stop him.

Very quickly, he ran to the last ward on the wing; he had seen a male nurse enter the room and hoped he was still there.

As the Constable burst into the room, the male nurse straightened up from what he was doing and the female patient quickly adjusted the front of her nightgown.

"Quick nurse. I need help." the Constable called as he dashed into the room, and grabbing the male nurse by the arm he started to pull him out of the room and down the corridor.

"There's a murder being committed and I need some help to stop it" he shouted as they arrived at the door to David's ward and pushed the nurse in front of him into the room.

Benny was kneeling on the side of the bed pressing down on the pillow. David was struggling weakly as they burst into the room and grabbed the Commander pulling him off his victim taking him completely by surprise, for he was so intent on what he was doing.

The Constable quickly threw Benny to the floor and handcuffed him then radioed for assistance.

The nurse pressed the emergency bell and was giving David oxygen when the doctor arrived.

While the medical staff was examining David, a very subdued Benny asked his captor if he could go to the toilet. Seeing no harm in that, the Constable accompanied him to the single toilet down the corridor. Benny asked for the cuffs to be removed and the policeman being extra cautious attached one of the cuffs to the chrome hand rail on the toilet wall put there for the use of physically disabled patients.

His Inspector arrived with a Sergeant as he was closing the toilet door giving Benny a bit of privacy.

While the Constable was giving his Inspector his report, the Sergeant being curious at the length of time Commander Benfield had spent in the toilet, opened the door and took a look inside. Suddenly he flung the door open knocking the Constable who was standing with his back to the door, sideways. As the Sergeant jumped into the toilet there was a small crack and Benny sank to the floor. He had shot himself in the mouth with a small revolver fitted with a silencer that he had taped on the inside of his crotch.

Chief Inspector Tomlinson and Superintendent Thorpe of Solihull Division of the West Midland Police Force arrived at the scene meeting Chief Inspector Sullivan and Sergeant Thomas who had arrived shortly after Benny had committed suicide.

A doctor and nurse had confirmed the death and were supervising the removal of Benny's body.

After discussing the problem caused by Benny's suicide, they went across to the ward where David Simpkins was being treated.

The crisis appeared to be over and things were quietening down as Sergeant Thomas knocked on the door and pushed it open and attempted to walk into the ward. The Doctor left the nursing sister he was talking to and ushered the Policemen back out of the ward.

"Not now, gentlemen, don't you think you have caused enough excitement for one day?"

After discussing the details of David's injury and accepting an extra policeman on duty outside the ward, the Doctor returned to his duties in the ward.

Chief Inspector Sullivan was very peeved at losing Commander Benfield. He had really wanted to nail him to the wall as an example to all police forces for what he had actually been, a bent cop. He was even more peeved that he couldn't interview David Simpkins, another man in a position of trust and was annoyed by the whole situation.

These two men were in positions of trust and hiding behind security badges.

As they were leaving the hospital car park, he vented his feelings on his Sergeant.

While they were waiting for the traffic to clear at the exit gate

Sergeant Thomas took an envelope out of his inside pocket and dropped it into the Chief's lap.

"I should have given these to you before, but you were in such a hurry to get over here, sir."

The Chief Inspector picked it up and started to take the photographs out of the envelope.

Sergeant Thomas then added,

"They are the photographs out of Margaret's camera. I think you will find one or two very interesting especially the dates."

"See what you mean, Thomas, this first one of the group proves that Benny was involved before he came up here. It looks as if he was one of the main players."

The photograph was of David Simpkins, The Marvo Brother's, (alias Braithwaite) Jose Cordova and Benny and appeared to have been taken in a restaurant.

"The date's interesting, Thomas. November 30th. That's before he came up here on the case."

"Aye, but he was on the case in London, wasn't he?"

"Yes, but we don't have to think about that, do we?"

"I suppose not, sir, still the photograph should help you with the Super, shouldn't it?"

Thomas was busy negotiating the heavy traffic as they were approaching the busy suburb of Shirley the Chief Inspector was also very quiet as he studied a close up head and shoulders photograph of David Simpkins. At the bottom of the photograph, there appeared to be the red roof of a car. The date was the twenty third of December.

"Thomas, that photograph of Simpkins and Benny in 'drag', where is it?"

"Either Snowy or Hopkins have it, sir, they've gone over to The Chestnut Tree to show it to the barman."

"I wonder "replied the Chief Inspector. "I wonder if Simpkins did it? Step on it, Thomas, we could call at The Chestnut Tree and we may catch Snowy and Hopkins before they leave."

The Chief Inspector then called control on the radio and asked them to contact Inspector White to stay at The Chestnut Tree until he arrived. Control passed him a message to contact Superintendent Moore as soon as he returned to the office.

Inspector White and Detective Constable Hopkins were sitting facing the door as the Chief Inspector walked into the bar, closely followed by Sergeant Thomas.

"They have Old Tom here, Thomas, mine's a pint."

"Aye, aye, sir." replied Thomas nonchalantly "So is mine" he continued as he walked over to the bar and ordered the drinks.

As the Chief Inspector sat down he asked for the photograph that they had brought with them and watched Inspector White as he placed the photograph on the table.

"I'm sorry about your Commander, Inspector," he said softly.

"Why? What has happened, Chief?" Snowy asked with surprise.

"Oh. You haven't heard then?" and feeling not quite sure of what to say, the Chief continued,

"Well, Inspector, he committed suicide at Solihull General this morning. He did it just before we arrived there, I'm sorry but I thought that someone may have informed you."

"No, sir, I suppose I had better report back to the Yard, hadn't I?"

"Yes, well, you can come back with us when we go, no need to hurry. Had any results with this?" the Chief Inspector asked.

"The barman thinks it was David Simpkins sir "replied D.C. Hopkins.

"Good, bring him over, let's try him with this one, Hopkins" said the Chief Inspector pulling the photograph of David Simpkins from the envelope.

Hopkins brought the barman over to the table after the Chief Inspector had put the two photographs together.

"You're being very helpful, Sid, D.C. Hopkins tells me that you recognized one of these two on this photograph. Can you point that one out to me please?"

Sid pointed to David Simpkins and picking up the new photograph, the Chief Inspector asked,

"Would you say that this man is the same as the one you picked out on the other photograph?"

The Chief Inspector looked over to his Sergeant, who was taking notes of the interview, as he asked.

"Is it the same person? If you are certain, beyond reasonable doubt, that it is, please look at my Sergeant as you say so."

Sid looked closely at the photographs for a while then picked them both up. After a short pause, he looked over at Sergeant Thomas and nodded his head.

"Yes, I am certain that is the same person as the one I saw on the night of the murder. He was wearing the same blonde wig, as he is in this photograph". Sid said holding up the photograph of the chorus girls.

The Chief Inspector took a small magnifying glass from his pocket and handed it to Sid, who, using it to take another look at the photograph said,

"Yes. I'm absolutely certain that is the person I saw the night of the murder, the only difference is that the person was dressed in a sports jacket and trousers and was wearing a trilby hat." He returned the photograph and the magnifying glass to the Chief Inspector with a satisfied look on his face.

"Will that be all, gents?" he asked glancing over his shoulder to the bar.

"No. I'll have another pint I don't know what these other two want. He's paying," said the Chief Inspector nodding towards Inspector White.

Sergeant Thomas smiled as he heard the remark,

"I'll have half I'm driving, I'll have to come back and take a proper statement, sir."

"Yes, Thomas, get photography to take a copy of Simpkins off this photograph and blow it up a bit then we'll get an artist to dress it up the same as Sid here described as well."

When the barman brought over their drinks, arrangements were made for the Sergeant to return to take his statement the following day.

CHAPTER THIRTY FOUR

It was late afternoon when Chief Inspector Sullivan finally came out of his Superintendent's office having been grilled intensively about Commander Benfield's suicide. He was also instructed that under no circumstances must he so much as taint the character of Commander Benfield. If he did, he would be blackening the name of the British Police Force. He was then dismissed and told to have his full report of the incident on the Super's desk the following morning.

Sergeant Thomas heard his Chief's door slam, as he closed it violently when he returned to his office.

He smiled to himself thinking "I bet he's had a rough time and I bet he's been asked for a full report by the morning".

He picked up the barman's statement, which he had just typed and went to see his boss.

He was waved to a chair as he entered; the Chief Inspector as usual was talking on the telephone to someone he knew at Scotland Yard. He was giving them full details of Benny's workload since his arrival at Stratford Police Station looking suddenly over to his Sergeant with a startled expression on his face.

"You want me to put all that in the report you must be joking. My Super wouldn't accept that, the good name of the police force and all that, you know."

As he put the phone down he said,

"That was one of my old oppo's, he's a commissioner down at the Yard and apparently they've had a suspicion of leaked information etceteras for some time and have been watching Benny because of his lifestyle. Anyway, contrary to what the Super says I have to give the plain untarnished truth in my report."

The Chief Inspector slapped his hands down on his desk and made a move as if to get up but didn't.

"Now, what have you got for me, Thomas?"

"I've typed out that statement, sir, it was a pretty conclusive identification, wasn't it? So all I'll have to do is get Sid to sign it, I've made arrangements to pick up that photograph of Simpkins in half an hour, sir."

The phone rang again.

"Yes, Brenda" he said as he looked over at his Sergeant and smiled. Sergeant Thomas politely left the room.

Brenda said she had been informed of Benny's death and told him of Benny's visit to her house at first light this morning.

Her neighbour had telephoned her and the police. She had apparently caught sight of Benny as he ran to the car when the burglar alarms had gone off.

A W.P.C. then entered the Chief's office and handed him a fax from the West Midlands Police Headquarters, on which they had forwarded information received from Arramanche Surete in France.

It read 'A British light aircraft crashed on the beach at Arramanche at 04:30 hrs this morning. One of the occupants was killed in the crash. The name of the pilot was Mr. Thomas Atkinson, address 42, Avonview Road, Mochampton, Warwickshire the passenger was Brigadier Smythe Whyte, address Manor Park Farm, Broom, Warwickshire. The pilot suffered only minor injuries, has since flown on to final destination Marbella, Spain, in own aircraft.'

After reading the fax a some-what surprised Chief Inspector renewed his conversation,

"Hello, hello, Brenda all our suspects are falling like ninepins on this case. The Brigadier and Tom Atkinson crashed on the French coast at half past four this morning. French Authorities say that Tom Atkinson flew on to Marbella.

What next? Good job David Simpkins is in hospital at least we can keep our eyes on him."

"That figures," said Brenda interrupting an irate Chief Inspector. "I suppose you've got to do a report for your Super."

"Yes, by morning" the Chief Inspector replied.

"Thought so, I'll be at your place at seven o'clock this evening; and type it for you I'll also fill in some blank spaces on the case because I have a feeling you may require them. I had a very interesting conversation with Tom Atkinson junior this morning. Don't be late, Sully".

The line went dead, as the Chief Inspector put down his phone he shouted for his Sergeant.

"Thomas! Get in here, Quick!".

Thomas ran in to the office, it was most unlike his boss to shout for him.

"Look at this fax, Thomas, I thought that Hoppy checked their flight plan before they left."

"He did, sir and he had a copy faxed over from Kidlington. It's on your desk, sir."

Chief Inspector Sullivan rummaged around on his rather untidy desk and found it.

The plan was made out to Plymouth, departure at seventeen thirty hours. E.T.A. Plymouth, twenty hundred hours.

"Have you checked this out with Plymouth?"

"No, sir, but according to this, they didn't arrive."

"Right let's check it now shall we?"

It was approximately five minutes before they were connected to Plymouth Flight Control and after introducing himself to the Traffic Clerk, enquired if the Cessna registration number Alpha Charlie Echo Mike had arrived at Plymouth airport during the previous evening. The Traffic Clerk at Plymouth airport informed him that he was the third person to enquire including the owner.

"No, it had not arrived, the pilot had rung in from Waylands Farm, Blandford reporting he had put down there with engine trouble. We've heard nothing since."

The Chief Inspector enquired the time of the message and was told nineteen hundred hours, the pilot had also reported no damage and everything was under control.

"There you are, Thomas. Pre-arranged fuel stop on the way to France. I wouldn't be surprised if the farm is either derelict or non-existent. In fact, I think there's another person involved here if not two."

"Yes sir, it does appear to be a well planned getaway. I think I'll contact the Wiltshire Police at Blandford to see if they know the farm."

As Sergeant Thomas got up to leave the office, the Chief Inspector asked.

"On your way out ask Snowy to pop in for a few minutes will you?"

On his return to the office, Sergeant Thomas reported,

"Blandford say the farm's a derelict, sir. Oh sorry sir" seeing Snowy sitting there.

"That's alright Thomas, we've finished, but both of you look at this flight plan".

Turning the plan so they both could see it, he said,

"See, Kidlington, Lyneham, Taunton, Plymouth. Direct route, only problem is, look where Blandford is? way down here, way off the route."

Hesitating he looked at his assistants, and continued.

"Right. I want you Snowy, along with D.C. Hopkins to go over to Arramanche tomorrow. Your job will be to find out how many were on the plane when it crashed and how many were on the second aircraft when it took off for Marbella. I'll arrange for you to see the aircraft. I hope it crashed above the high water mark and they haven't moved it. If they have it will no doubt be in a warehouse somewhere in town. It's only a small airport but can take small commercial aircraft, so I've been informed."

He then turned to Sergeant Thomas. "You, Thomas and Inspector Carter, can go down to the Waylands Farm and have a look at that. I think you're going to find that interesting. I think there was someone on the ground with the lights and the fuel we'll see."

He stood up, ending the briefing and picking up the flight plan and some papers he left the office and walked down the corridor to the Superintendent's office.

CHAPTER THIRTY FIVE

Having given his main support team their instructions for the following day. Also realizing that he didn't have to worry about the rest of the Investigation team until the briefing at eight thirty the following morning. Chief Inspector Sullivan feeling very pleased about the way things were going, gave himself an early night and was looking forward to an enjoyable evening with Brenda Armstrong whom he would be seeing very shortly.

His house was one of eight, pre-war built, detached houses each standing on half an acre of ground. Access was only from the front being served by a service road that ran parallel to the A4023 Stratford on Avon, Henley in Arden road. The houses stood well back from the road, each with it's own style of driveway, some were straight concrete drives, some curved with a gravel surface.

One young couple who had recently purchased number eight had a stylish white shingle drive going up one side of the lawn and down the other side with a small parking area across the front of the house with a double garage at the side.

It looked a picture when the landscaping company finished it. Then one day the wife was leaving in her car, her husband was returning from his game of squash and they met head-on.

Now they have two separate gates marked enter and exit.

The Chief Inspectors house was very symmetrical in layout having previously been owned by a retired Major of the British Army.

It had square lawns front and rear.

The bottom half of the garden at rear of the house was laid out as a kitchen garden, a part of it had a small orchard with fruit trees set out with the smallest at the front tallest at the rear. All outside paintwork was white just like the barrack square. The only good thing the Chief Inspector thought the Major had done was to install marker lights down each side of the drive.

Chief Inspector Sullivan had purchased the house four years previously, following his promotion. His wife had loved the house and they had planned many alterations and were looking forward to working on it together when tragedy struck and she lost her life.

Brenda arrived at the house shortly after Sully.

When he opened the door he found her loaded with three plastic bags of groceries and a briefcase. After welcoming embraces they proceeded to the kitchen where the coffee was already percolating and Brenda immediately set about preparing the meal she had promised.

It was nine-o clock before they retired to the lounge having stacked all the dirty dishes in the dishwasher.

As Brenda sank into one of the deep armchairs, she noticed that the room although clean but tidy lacked a woman's touch.

"Not me" she thought "Oh no, not me."

The Chief Inspector sat opposite Brenda in the other armchair on the opposite side of the fireplace.

"Nice place, Sully" started Brenda "Who keeps it tidy for you?"

"I have a woman that comes in, three times a week. She's had an easy time lately" he replied looking across at Brenda over his wine glass, "But you're not here to talk about my house are you?"

What have you been up to today?"

Brenda had a couple of sips of her wine as if she was gathering her thoughts before answering.

She started hesitantly by retracing over the incidents that had happened to her, especially the two in London. At this point asking Sully if he had looked at the book and studied it.

Sully replied that he had quickly gone through it but had passed it on to Thomas to try and make something of it.

Brenda was a little disappointed at this but continued with her presumption of how the case had developed and the involvement of Jones from Salisbury, It was at the inclusion of Jones into the conversation that Brenda started to unfold the developments of her day.

She informed Sully that after he had left her at the hotel that morning. She thought that as a Private Investigator acting on behalf of the Colonel and Associates she should visit Tom Atkinson's Office to see if she could learn anything further of his involvement in the case.

Brenda found everything was quiet and working smoothly but she was shocked when, on asking at the reception desk for Mr. Tom Atkinson she was shown to his son's office. Where she discovered that she had been completely mislead by Tom Atkinson Senior. Learning that he had not had an active part in the company for six months; and although he still kept an office there. He only used it three or four times a month for a few hours only, to service a few accounts of his original clients. When asked about his fathers flying habits, Tom, Junior told her to her surprise, that his stepmother was also a pilot and like his father was licensed to fly multi-engined aircraft. This was the reason that they had purchased a twin-engine Cessna when he retired to enable them to fly to their villa in Marbella.

Tom explained that his father had met his present wife while he was away at the London School of Economics studying but didn't say any more on the subject. He seemed as if he didn't want to talk about his stepmother.

When asked about the Brigadier, Tom said that he had been one of the Company's biggest accounts but wouldn't say anything further due to client's privacy. However she did learn from him that Mr. Jones was well acquainted with his father, and had been coming to his father's office with the Brigadier on and off for about twelve months. She had shown him the artist's impression of Marvo and asked him if he had seen him at all but Tom had clamped up then and had ended the meeting.

"But, I think that Tom, senior was the brains behind the whole operation and the Brigadier was the Field Commander. We know," she said leaning towards Sully to refill her glass "that Jones was the link-man between London and Birmingham on diamonds.

Also he was the one that Jean Claude struck up an acquaintance with in The Blue Angel. That club, I found out is owned by the Marvo Brothers. I also know that Benny was an associate of theirs. I nearly ran into them as I came out of a lift at The Cumberland at Christmas, come to think of it"

She carried on after taking another sip of wine.

"I wonder if he did see me, I tried to hide as soon as I spotted them when the doors opened".

"We'll never know, Brenda," said Sully shaking his head.

"However" continued Brenda "We have now established two links with the Marvo Brothers who, as I've already told you Sully, are well organized and have contacts all over the Continent as well as in the U.K. Inside sources say that the Mafioso and the Marvo Brothers respect each other. When Jean Claude was introduced to The Blue Angel by Tuffy and started his enquiries at the Club with our friend Jones, he was the one who started the series of killings. The Brigadier then panicked and contacted Simpkins, who was in charge of security at Courtney Transport, asking for his assistance. Now according to Jones little black book, Simpkins then attended to Jean Claude who, with the help of the Marvo organization was shipped to Witney. To be collected by either Simpkins or Jones and delivered to Mochamton bonfire site. Then the truck was either disposed of or driven back to London and repainted and number plates changed.

Organization Sully; Marvo organization.

The same type of setup dealt with Obayo.

They found out that he worked with Jean Claude so the 'hit and run' was set up. But at the same time they were getting interested in the Brigadier's jewelry company and also Nigel's little smuggling operations. This is where they started to use Benny and call in the favors he owed them."

"Do you think then that Benny was in that deep with them?"

"I don't know "she answered honestly. "But I wouldn't be surprised if he was. You don't live Benny's lifestyle in London without a bit extra from somewhere. However to continue, again according to the book, Jones himself was involved in the 'hit and run' but I think the following break in at George Obayo's, was done by the organization to see if they could find anything connected to their enquiry's into the smuggling ring. Apparently there was nothing there, he must have passed the information to his office and Customs and Excise just before he was 'topped'.

About this time Jose Cordova was frequenting The Blue Angel and playing the tables. He became very friendly with the Marvo Brothers and by keeping quiet and listening to their conversation, he learnt where they were to strike next in their take over operations. Courtney Transport was to be the next one, then the Brigadier. He managed to warn Nigel, who consequently stopped the smuggling except for the last batch of stones that he brought over himself. Simpkins, being in Nigel's confidence was told where he had obtained the information, and he, of course, informed the Brigadier and Benny who passed it on to the Marvo organization. They in their turn gave instructions on the action to be taken. The rest is history, Sully, Simpkins was the hit man from the beginning and Jones the strong arm man."

Brenda sat back looking relieved at having got it all off her chest.

"Very good Brenda, how long did it take you to work that out? And what about Braithwaite or Marvo in the car? Who did that? Who hit Benny over the head at the hotel?"

"As regards Benny, I think that was Marvo; it was their kind of work. Just a frightener to make him toe the line, now Marvo I think his name was Norman I'm not sure. Either Simpkins or Benny could have murdered him. Both were involved, I think, after all, where were they that night? I don't know. Do you?"

"No I don't Brenda, but I do know that Simpkins wasn't supposed to survive the attack from Jones in his office. Nigel overheard him say to the Brigadier that he wouldn't survive what he had done to him."

"Well those are my thoughts, Sully. Now, what do you want in your report about Benny? It's for your Super, isn't it?"

"You know, Brenda you should have joined the police force, your thinking on the case is exactly like mine but of course you've had more freedom in your investigations than I have."

Brenda didn't reply as she walked over to the typewriter on the table in the window and fed some paper into it.

Sully pulled a chair up alongside Brenda and started to give his version of the report on Benny.

It was gone midnight when they finished the report.

"Thank heavens for that Brenda, I would have been struggling for another hour. Would you like to stop the night? If so, how about a nightcap?"

"No thank you, Sully, I'm not stopping, I've got an early start in the morning. You see, Sully, as you have just remarked, we are two of a kind and we think on the same wavelength. We are both dam good at our job and we're both good at making love. I want it to stay that way. I think we'll spoil it if it gets any more serious so I'm not going to spend the night here. Also, I have to tell you that I have resigned my job with the Oaksey, Tomlinson P.I. I've got a position with Courtney Transport. I have taken over David's job as Group Security Officer. The Company Secretary offered it to me this afternoon when I called in. They're in such a mess down there without Nigel. I can see I'll have my hands full for a while sorting things out."

Brenda took a long brown envelope from her handbag and gave it to the Chief Inspector.

"My report on the case, I've sent the same report to an associate of mine at the Yard. It always pays to keep in with them doesn't it?"

Brenda made her way to the front door and as Sully held the door open for her, she kissed him on the cheek saying.

"It's goodnight not goodbye Sully."

A very disappointed Chief Inspector closed the door and climbed the stairs to bed and a lonely nights sleep.

CHAPTER THIRTY SIX

After the debriefing meeting the following morning Chief Inspector Sullivan accompanied by another Police Sergeant visited Nigel who was still in Stratford Hospital. They found him sitting up in bed and very cheery, leaving the Sergeant and the Constable who was on guard duty to take a statement. He went back to his office and rang the Solihull General Hospital, asking to speak to the doctor in charge of David Simpkins. The Doctor eventually answered after what seemed to the Chief Inspector an eternity. His reply to the Inspector's request to take a statement from David was.

"No! Definitely Not the patient cannot remember anything not even his name."

"I cannot accept that doctor, I want to charge him with murder."

"I can't help that, Chief Inspector, you may be able to charge him but he won't remember what for. We're carrying out a few tests on him and I will let you know what we find. By the way, his wife visits him every evening and he doesn't even know who she is."

It was late afternoon before the Chief received a call from Inspector Carter at Blandford. Who with Sergeant Thomas and the help of the local Police had found a derelict farmhouse, also a burned out van and some empty jerrycans plus twelve torches left in the ground, that were being checked for fingerprints before they returned.

Asked if there were any footprints around the van, Carter replied 'yes' and they had taken plaster casts to be studied upon their return.

The following morning Sully received a fax from Detective Inspector White. It read "Four seat Piper Cub aircraft: Alpha Charlie Echo Mike: crash-landed Arramanche beach. Removed by French authorities to hanger at local flying club; cause of crash lack of fuel caused by punctured fuel line. Three persons on flight: Pilot T. Atkinson, passengers Mrs. F. Atkinson, Brigadier Smythe White. Mr.and Mrs. Atkinson continuing flight to Spain after check up at local hospital. Brigadier died of heart failure; pressing for post mortem on Brigadier. Only luggage here Brigadiers case; French police say nothing suspicious about crash. Own aircraft used for flight to Spain, twin-engine Cessna. Aircraft had been here for a week having a thousand-hour service.

Chief Inspector reread the fax, looked up at Sergeant Thomas and Inspector Carter with a look of disdain on his face, "Well, that's it lads" he said "End of story we've got a murderer in hospital and the Doctors won't let us charge because of loss of memory. One of the ringleaders who died of a heart attack and the other one who is going to live in luxury for the rest of his life."

He picked up an internal memo.

"Send this fax to Snowy, the number is on here".

He gave the fax he had received to Sergeant Thomas.

He then wrote.

"Come on home boys. The birds have flown".

THE END.

CPSIA information can be obtained at www.ICGtesting.com
Printed in the USA
LVOW042007270911

248122LV00001B/3/P